THE DEAD HOUSE LIVES.

There, above me in the clearing, stood a large, two-story chalet, reaching like some dark sentinel through the low-lying, milky fog. There was no way, at least on this earth, that it could be there. Yet I was awake and sane, and it towered over me. I could even see the pale reflections of the night sky from its dark windows.

Unable to stop myself, I started back up the hill. It must have been to try to verify my sanity. Maybe, God forbid, those tormented souls I had sensed were trying to show me their place in time.

I had not gone five paces before the house started to disintegrate before my eyes, dissolving into vague dark masses that coalesced and became groups of shadowy trees. The glinting from the windows was no more than the gaps between treetops that allowed a glimpse of the night sky.

I stopped at the edge of the cleared area. There was no need to go farther. All that remained were the ruins of a dream home savaged by whatever evil possessed this wretched island . . .

NOW I LAY ME DOWN TO SLEEP...

Also by Frank Lambirth

Behind the Door

Published by
POPULAR LIBRARY

NOW I LAY ME DOWN TO SLEEP...

FRANK LAMBIRTH

POPULAR LIBRARY

An Imprint of Warner Books, Inc.

A Warner Communications Company

POPULAR LIBRARY EDITION

Popular Library® and the fanciful P design are registered trademarks
of Warner Books, Inc.

Cover illustration by Mark & Stephanie Gerber

Popular Library books are published by
Warner Books, Inc.
666 Fifth Avenue
New York, N.Y. 10103

 A Warner Communications Company

Printed in the United States of America

First Printing: July, 1989

10 9 8 7 6 5 4 3 2 1

NOW I LAY ME DOWN TO SLEEP...

FRANK LAMBIRTH

POPULAR LIBRARY

An Imprint of Warner Books, Inc.

A Warner Communications Company

POPULAR LIBRARY EDITION

Copyright © 1989 by Frank Lambirth
All rights reserved.

Popular Library® and the fanciful P design are registered trademarks
of Warner Books, Inc.

Cover illustration by Mark & Stephanie Gerber

Popular Library books are published by
Warner Books, Inc.
666 Fifth Avenue
New York, N.Y. 10103

 A Warner Communications Company

Printed in the United States of America

First Printing: July, 1989

10 9 8 7 6 5 4 3 2 1

Chapter *ONE*

They sit before me, a cautious encouragement mirrored in their faces. My liberty, perhaps my life, depends on their accepting that I speak the truth. I came to this island, isolated in the Great North Woods of Canada, joined later by a family of four. They are all dead—murdered—yet there was no living soul except myself within two hundred miles of the tiny island. I have lived the past eight terrifying days in a minute universe stalked by the same horror that struck them down. Even now, surrounded by policemen, I cannot shake the premonition that I will never leave this hellish place. I start to talk, hesitantly at first, then with more assurance.

It started ten days ago on a bright Tuesday morning in Seattle when Alan Mayfield handed me the open book, his pale blue eyes appraising me as he did. We were in the muted opulence of the boardroom of Mayfield's company, Puget Enterprises. I had the strangest feeling that my reaction to the volume in my hand would go a long way in determining whether I would be offered the job.

I flipped the book shut over my thumb. It was old and much read, with a worn blue cover. Eroded gold lettering on the front and spine proclaimed *Mysteries of the Great North Woods*. The polished way in which he had introduced it into the conversation told me that it was a volume Mayfield proudly exhibited to many visitors.

Reopening it to where my thumb rested, I began to read.

STONE WARRIOR ISLAND

Unique among the countless tales of dark deeds and strange occurrences told about Canada's North Country is the horror-laden history of otherwise insignificant Stone Warrior Island.

The island is located in a small dot of blue water much like countless others scattered over the Canadian Shield country between Lake Cree and Lake Wollaston in the northern part of Saskatchewan Province. The lake's dimensions are seven miles by four, with a single wooded island of twenty-four acres interrupting its aqueous surface. The sole distinction that this body of water enjoys, besides the bloodthirsty tales told about it, is its splendid lake trout population, one of the best in northern Saskatchewan.

Thanks to a questionable land deal arranged in 1906 among the Canadian-Pacific Railroad, the Canadian government, and an early western land baron, Laird Brobham, the island at Stone Warrior has been in private hands for years. The area enjoys a reserve status that prohibits any other private ownership of land within twenty miles of the lake.

Stone Warrior came early to its macabre reputation. It is first mentioned in an old Cree Indian legend dating from 1600. According to this tale, a renegade band raided a Cree camp located near Lake Wollaston, burned what they couldn't steal, and made off with several Cree women. When the Cree warriors returned from an extended hunting trip to find the camp devastated, the chase was on. They cornered the abductors at what is now Stone Warrior Lake. The renegades prepared to make a last stand on the island.

While the Crees worked into the night constructing rafts, the cornered band cavorted around campfires in a frenzied war dance, preparing for the final conflict. At this point Stone Warrior's bizarre phenomenon manifested itself for the first time.

The Crees reported that during the night a large loon settled on the lake and started emitting the ear-splitting screams for which it is renowned. It was an unsettling experience for superstitious warriors facing death in the morning, especially since loons did not frequent the area.

Even today, the common loon is not listed among the species observed at Stone Warrior Lake by Canadian waterfowl experts. Loons seek boggy areas for their nesting habitat. Stone Warrior and the other lakes in the immediate geographic area lie in granite cups, with abrupt, rocky shorelines lacking marshy fringes.

On that fateful day, with the morning mist shielding the lake's surface, the Crees landed on the island. Bewildered by the lack of opposition, they advanced cautiously through a heavy stand of timber. Reaching the island's crest, they were stunned by what they found.

Their prey lay dead, scattered about a large granite slab, the only open ground on the island. Incredibly, the bodies bore no marks of violence. The dead were frozen in unyielding postures like stone statues. The Crees were so amazed by the rigidity of their late enemies that the lake, thereafter, was known as the Lake of the Stone Warriors and was avoided as a place of great evil.

Historians explain the stonelike corpses as being the result of rigor mortis. The Crees of the period always fled the sites of their battles, for they believed that the souls of the slain could transfer to living bodies. Probably, that morning at Stone Warrior marked the first time they had seen the dead in a state of rigor mortis. Yet the question remains, in the light of subsequent events, of how the renegades died without apparent cause.

If there were other grotesque events at the lake during the next two hundred years, their accounting is irretrievably lost. The next time the lake's

name was inscribed in Canadian folklore was in
1820.

In the early 1800s, competition developed between the Northwest Company of Montreal and the
Hudson's Bay Company, with both striving to gain a
monopoly over the Western fur trade. The struggle
was so intense that at times it flared into bloodshed.
Stone Warrior Lake played host to one incident in
the violent conflict.

In the early spring of 1820, an outlaw group of
Northwest Company trappers, accompanied by two
squaws, ambushed a fur-laden band of Hudson's Bay
men near Stone Warrior Lake. Their plans for a
quick escape with the stolen furs were thwarted by
an unexpected spring thaw, which turned the surrounding land into a quagmire. Converging bands
of furious Hudson's Bay vigilantes brought the
slow-moving bandits to bay at Stone Warrior.

A still existing journal recounts the fate of the
gang. After a two-day siege the Hudson's Bay group
made a dawn assault on the island. To their relief,
there was no resistance.

After landing, they discovered the bodies of the
thieves and the two squaws. The trappers were puzzled about what caused the deaths of the eight victims since no wounds were discovered on them. The
old journal reports that on the night preceding the
attack, a loon settled onto the dark waters and kept
the men awake with its piercing cries.

The next chapter in the saga of this desolate, for-
bidding sheet of water grew out of Louis Riel's revo-
lution against the Canadian government in 1885.
When the uprising collapsed, hundreds of Métis,
half-breed inhabitants of the region, escaped into
the wilderness.

Nine of the rebels, fleeing toward Lake Wollaston,
encountered an unarmed party of eleven adults.
They killed all but three women of English stock,
whom they forced to accompany them. After a long
chase, Canadian troops cornered them at Stone

Warrior Island. Since the Métis immediately
dragged their captives into view and cut their
throats, the decision was made to starve them out.
Battling with men who had nothing to lose would
have extracted a heavy loss of lives.

On the third night of the siege, the troops were
disturbed by the midnight cries of a large loon, first
spotted along the lake shore about dusk. The coming of morning revealed no further activity among
the Métis. Three days later, the troops landed on the
island under cover of darkness.

They found the Métis dead. The military doctor
dryly noted that there were no wounds on the
bodies and suggested that the "savages" must have
found some herb that furnished the means for mass
suicide. The army medic, apparently not an easily
impressed man, concluded his report by commenting that the corpses still displayed rigor mortis
some ninety-six hours after their deaths on the
night the loon visited Stone Warrior's haunted
waters.

Stone Warrior's grim story gained another
chapter in 1928 when Angus Brobham, the son of
the original owner, was building a hunting lodge on
the island. By midsummer a construction party was
nearing completion of the spacious chalet. On the
evening of July 11, the workers crossed to the
mainland to fell the last logs needed to finish the
job. Three men remained on the island, two late-ar-
riving ne'er-do-wells, who had done little but cause
trouble, and the architect, who also functioned as
paymaster. The shore party was awakened at midnight by yelling from the island. Soon after, flames
flared in the windows of the lodge. The building
burned past dawn, leaving only the foundation,
chimney, and a mass of charred timbers.

The shore party returned at dawn to discover the
architect, his throat cut. He had been tortured, his
hands and feet slashed to ribbons, in the belief that
he was concealing a large sum of money.

The crew started a perfunctory search, not expecting to find the hoodlums. However, their bodies were discovered a short distance from the charred shell of the chalet. The police report noted that the bodies of the suspects were unmarked and that no cause of death could be determined. The three men were buried on the island, as all the past dead had been. The locations of the graves are unknown today.

The police report supplied the now-familiar chilling motif, commenting that the sudden appearance of a large loon, with its hideous cries, had masked the agonized screams of the tortured man.

It is a relief to report that since 1928, Stone Warrior Lake's spectral loon has not returned to claim still more victims.

I lowered the book to find myself under Mayfield's silent scrutiny. He nodded abruptly, and I suspected that I had passed some sort of test. Mayfield expected the story of his island to be treated with reverence.

Chapter
TWO

His words confirmed his pride in Stone Warrior's deadly history. "It may seem like a silly spook story, but let me tell you something, young man. I've spent some dark nights alone on Stone Warrior when it was damned easy to recall these tales. Nothing happened, mind you. It's just that a man gets some of the damnedest, weirdest feelings.

"Well, at least you didn't laugh at me. I suppose I'd better shut up. This isn't the way to talk a potential employee into spending time by himself in the back end of nowhere."

He took the book from me with a reverence more appropriate to an edition of the Gutenberg Bible and returned it to the wall safe. The suddenly somber mood was broken when Mayfield smiled, pointing toward the massive conference table.

"Let me show you the island on the map."

A large, tightly coiled chart lay across the table. He unrolled it on the flat surface, anchoring it with heavy glass ashtrays. It was a detailed map of Saskatchewan Province.

Rubbing his hands in satisfaction, he started pointing at blotches of blue ink on the expanse of paper. "Wilhite, look right here. You see Reindeer Lake? It's this big body of water above my finger. To the northwest is Wollaston. Here, due west from Wollaston, is Pasfield Lake. Do you see it?"

He glanced up, forcing me to nod at the unnecessary question.

Mayfield trailed his hand across the map's surface, his face taut with concentration. Stopping, he tapped the chart with his finger. "See the small lake there? That's mine. That's Stone Warrior."

His finger was camped by a small speck of blue near the top of the chart. The name Stone Warrior had been carefully lettered in. I studied the immediate environs of the lake and then searched the map's surface in ever wider sweeps, seeking some symbol of civilization. Mayfield had not exaggerated about its being a wilderness lake.

Finally, I spotted a tiny settlement up near Lake Athabasca, an outpost called Fond du Lac. It was at least two hundred miles from Stone Warrior Lake.

I grinned at my host. "When I said I wanted to find a place in the boondocks, I must have had your place in mind—no worry about the neighbors."

Mayfield chuckled, pleased by the remark. With smug satisfaction he guided the chart as it coiled itself into a loose roll and motioned me back into the big, sun-filled office with its glass walls overlooking Puget Sound.

Settling into the leather chair behind his desk, he slid an ornate box toward me. I declined the cigar and watched while

he chose and lit one. Turning back to me, he let the hail-fel-
low-well-met look fade from his face. Alan Mayfield was
ready to talk business.

He was a small man with the kind of tan one picks up
piloting a fancy yacht around Puget Sound. Despite his fifty
years, he could have left me behind in a mile run. He was the
type of fellow who could be gracious in relaxation and hard as
nails the moment business talk started.

Mayfield wasn't selling me now; he was telling me. "Wilhite, I bought the island because I need to get away from
business once in a while and I like to fish. I'm here to tell you
that Stone Warrior has lake trout that would scare a man. It is
a damned good place for me to take clients and combine a
little business with pleasure.

"When I bought the island, I still had the three kids at
home. They enjoyed spending the summer there." He frowned
at the reminiscence. "To tell you the truth, though, when they
became teenagers they started finding excuses not to go. Well,
everybody changes. Nowadays we use it mainly to entertain
business clients and their families.

"My daughter was the one who saw your newspaper ad
about wanting a caretaker-maintenance job in the boonies and
told me about it. It's hard to find a reliable fellow willing to
spend a summer in the wilds. I like the idea of somebody with
your background being up there. It just won't do to hire another bum who steals from my guests and flirts with their
wives. Christ, the stories I could tell you about the creep I
hired last year. Why—"

He put the cigar down and stared at me. It was the sort of
look I'd always dreaded getting from my father. His voice
was hard.

"Son, you ought to know that I checked up on you after we
talked on the phone. I found out that you had a little trouble
—a few personal problems—and I—"

He stopped, seeing the frown on my face. I had good refer-
ences, and I'm a hard worker. I couldn't see that the problems
I had growing up were any of his business.

I tried to change the frown to a vacuous smile, but he was
too shrewd for that.

"I had to find out about you, young man. I won't make the

same mistake I did last summer. I can't risk my investment, my business associates, and my family around a stranger without checking his background.

"I'm surprised that more of you young people haven't had trouble, with the world as screwed up as it is. I think that I'm getting a damned good worker, a dependable man, and I bet you're going to find this summer a great experience. There's something about the North Country—the quiet and the fresh air—that braces a man. What I'm saying, Mr. Wilhite, is that the job is yours, if you want it."

Mayfield was right. He was taking a big chance with anybody he hired to work at an isolated spot like Stone Warrior Island.

My smile was genuine. "It's a deal, sir. I'll do my best to justify your faith in me."

My new boss relit his cigar and began to go over the arrangements for flying into Stone Warrior. When we talked on the phone, he had asked me if I could leave within twenty-four hours if I got the job. I had promised him that I could. The only thing I had to do was drive back to my brother's house in Sequim, Washington, and pack my gear.

Mayfield said his secretary would call me when the travel arrangements were complete. I would be flying on commercial airlines to Saskatoon and the rest of the way in a pontoon-equipped bush plane.

I lost track of what he was saying, feeling the excitement building within me. It was something I had wanted to do ever since I was a kid—fly to some far-off lake with a grizzled old bush pilot.

He brought me back to reality by sliding a sheet of paper across the desk. It was a typewritten list of tasks necessary to get the island ready for his arrival. Most of the jobs were what one would expect. The surprise came with the last item—activating the satellite television antenna. I looked up to catch Mayfield smiling.

"That's right, Wilhite, a damned satellite antenna. Listen, the women are bored within a week unless they can watch those god-awful soap operas, and the kiddies aren't much better. There's nothing to getting the TV system operating, though. Just remove the canvas covers and plug in the cable.

"Oh, there is one other thing. At the end of last summer, I purchased a small safe, which Chambord flew in on the last flight. You will have to uncrate it, but it shouldn't be difficult."

Ostentatiously, he glanced at his Rolex. It was a cue for the new caretaker to be on his way. But there was still one thing that puzzled me.

"I don't understand about opening the other house. Do you want me to have it ready for the owner, too?"

"No, no, no. It belongs to Gene Bengston, my business partner. As a matter of fact, the key ring has keys for both buildings on it. The houses are near twins so you better be sure that you remember mine is the one on the left. They sit side by side—and, for God's sake, don't lose those keys. The only other set that will open my place stays here with me in Seattle.

"Bengston is lending his home for a month to a cousin from New York—a Peter Delvecchio. This Delvecchio seems to have his head screwed on right. Gene wouldn't agree to let him use the place until the guy flew out here to meet me. When strangers are cooped up on a small island in the middle of nowhere, they had better be able to get along. This Delvecchio fellow is a real family man—typical old-school Italian.

"He had some trouble with his kids, at least with the older girl, and he wants to get them away from all the damned teenage hassles for a while. He hopes that the change of scene will help his youngsters get their act together.

"You won't much more than get there before they arrive. They're scheduled to land a day or two after you. Get the generator going and prime the water pump right away. Maybe whoever flies you in will give you a hand with the generator. Get the antenna into operation. Easterners like the Delvecchios will probably need some assurance that civilization is still out there after their first night.

"Otherwise, play it by ear. I told Gene's cousin my man would be willing to help them settle in, but I let him understand that you work for me, not Bengston. Just try to keep them out of trouble."

Mayfield sprang to his feet, anxious to get on with the affairs of Puget Enterprises. "When you get to Saskatoon, call the boys who handle our flights into Stone Warrior. Those small flying operations are nonscheduled.

"The head of the outfit, a real nice guy, is a Frenchman named Mustard Chambord. He will know to expect you. Good luck, Wilhite! I've got a feeling we're going to hit it off this summer."

He came around the desk and gripped my hand with a paw that, despite his small stature, was twice the size of my slender one. "Just remember one thing. Don't listen to any loons calling while you're up there—okay? See you in about two weeks."

My last view was of him chuckling at his little joke.

Chapter
THREE

It was close to eleven o'clock when the elevator reached the lobby of the Northwest Gateways building, and I followed my fellow passengers out into the streets of downtown Seattle. The excitement had been building in me since Mayfield's secretary handed me the ring of keys that would unlock long-closed doors over two thousand miles away.

It was early afternoon when I reached Sequim, a small town lying near the mouth of Puget Sound. Turning north on First Street, I headed for my brother Rod's home. For the past year I have been living with him and my sister-in-law Evie, at least on the days off from my job at a pack station in the Olympic National Forest.

I pulled into the driveway of the sprawling gray ranch house, eager to tell Evie the news. She must have been awaiting my return. As I entered the house, she called from somewhere in the rear.

"Is that you, Linc?"

"No, ma-am, it's a stranger—Nanook of the Far North."

Evie, small, auburn haired, and in her early thirties, rushed into the living room, arms wide apart wearing that ready grin of hers. She skidded to a stop, yelping, "You got it, Linc! You got it! I told you not to worry. I said you were a cinch to land the job."

Ignoring my protests, she pulled me down onto the sofa and demanded the details. I tried to give her a thumbnail sketch of my interview, but, as always, Evie wanted to know every particular. I finally quieted her long enough to make her understand that I had to call old man Fairbaugh at the pack station.

Fairbaugh had reached the age where he was little more than a picturesque figurehead for his business, loafing around the corral in his western gear. I would have to drive out there to make up the trip confirmations and place grain and hay orders for the rest of the summer.

While I talked with the old man, Evie had time to think. She was sitting upright on the sofa, her eyes deep pools of concern, when I returned to the living room.

"Linc, do you really think this going off into the wilds is the best thing for you? I mean—you need to be around people who care for you. You know—your own family. A good-looking twenty-five-year-old guy—when you're ready to socialize again, people will swarm around you—especially the girls."

I dropped onto the sofa and took her hands in mine. "Listen, worry-wart. You and Rod have been wonderful to me. For the first time in my life, I understand what family means —what living in a home surrounded by love is like."

Evie squeezed my hands. "We want you to—"

"Evie, it's been two years now. I can't go on grieving forever. I have to get out and make a life for myself. I've had more than my share of hard luck, but the world goes on. It's time for me to try my wings again.

"If I can cope with the hassles of opening Mayfield's lodge and catering to the whims of a bunch of spoiled rich people for the rest of the summer, I'll be ready to rejoin the human race. I owe it to Laurie."

Evie's freckle-spattered face remained solemn a few seconds longer while she digested what I had said. Suddenly that serious little visage unfolded into an infectious grin.

"Come on, tell me about it, Linc. What's this northern outpost like?"

She listened, enthralled, to the story of Stone Warrior Island. However, I was wasting time when I should be on my way to the pack station. Quickly I finished the tale and headed for the door with Evie following, still talking. She stopped in midword.

"Gosh, I was so excited I almost forgot. Talk about coincidences—Rod was fueling the boat this morning, and he mentioned your interview to the fuel dock operator. This guy told Rod about a young fellow here who worked as caretaker for Mayfield at Stone Warrior Island."

"You're kidding. Who is it?"

"He didn't know the guy's name, but his father is Charlie Klugg. Rod said he's a preacher in some little offbeat church. This Charlie also has worked part-time as a hand on the fishing boats. He has a tackle shop at Two Mile Lake."

The minute she mentioned the lake, I remembered the place. It's a dingy little store with an old-fashioned gas pump out front.

Evie's eyes widened. "Oh, there was another thing. Rod said the dock operator heard there was something peculiar going on between the father and son. But, anyhow, the son was at Stone Warrior Island last year."

Startled, I almost mentioned Mayfield's innuendo that there had been trouble last summer, but caught myself in time. It was no occasion to start her worrying about something else.

She was escorting me out to my pickup, still chattering gaily, when I remembered about taking my specimen case. It would be a once-in-a-lifetime chance to secure an insect collection from one of the few ecologically balanced areas still existent.

I stopped, intending to run back to my room and set the case out so I wouldn't forget, but then I remembered that I was out of the stuff I use as a lethal agent. It is used in a jar to ensure that captured insects are killed without external damage. It's a necessity for a collector. It wasn't possible to make the trip to Fairbaugh's and back and have time to buy any. My only chance was to borrow some from Dr. Levinson, a retired entomologist who lives on the next block. Evie would have to contact him.

Goodhearted as always, she agreed to see Levinson while I was at the pack station. I repeated my instructions a second time because Evie is a little flighty.

"Remember, take the smallest vial you can find in my specimen case. Tell him that I need a lethal agent for my killing jar. An oldtimer like him is sure to have something I can use."

"But, Linc, what do these jar things look like?"

"Look, a killing jar is just—Evie, I haven't got time to explain. Just see Dr. Levinson."

I backed the battered pickup out of the driveway, knowing that if Evie were given enough time she would find a new batch of worries.

The engine worked hard as the old truck laboriously mounted the flanks of the Olympic Mountains. The sense of being rushed was growing stronger. The sun was positioning itself for its long dive into the Pacific Ocean. The steady climb had brought me into taller and thicker groves of trees rising from a fern-choked forest floor. The narrow asphalt road, twisting and looping as it climbed, was heavily shaded and empty in the gloomy twilight of the dense woods.

It seemed that I had driven for miles, and I was wondering if I had taken a wrong turn when the gutted ruins of a large chalet, destroyed by fire several years ago, came into view ahead. A few yards beyond the ruined building the road curved sharply, topping a small rise. There below me, still bathed in the golden light of the afternoon sun, was the jewel-like blue of Two Mile Lake.

The road ended in a gravel cul-de-sac. Immediately in front of me a path wound down a steep bank to a small floating dock where several rental boats bobbed gently in the afternoon breeze. A new coat of paint had been applied to the sign reading KLUGG'S, stretching across the building above the porch, but otherwise, it was as I remembered from the fall before when I had fished there. The peeled log walls were bleached to a silver gray and bowed out precariously. The aging fishing lures displayed in the dingy windows, coated with a thousand days' dust, hung lifelessly on their yellowing cards. The porch was flanked on the right by an ancient gaso-line pump with modern prices and on the left by a newish glass and steel telephone booth.

A boy of seventeen, clad in a white T-shirt and faded jeans, was stretched atop a bench on the porch. A portable radio rested on the seat beside him, with a set of bright blue head-phones clamped over his ears. His vacant eyes never moved, even when the truck door slammed.

Only when I stood a few feet from him did he free his head of the earphones' embrace and push himself upright. His ex-pressionless eyes looked at me from a thin, pinched face overburdened with heavy black brows. His voice was disinter-ested, uneducated, and impolite.

"Yeah, mister. What can I do for you? You lost? Most peo-ple that come back here nowadays are lost."

I tried smiling. "I don't think I'm lost if that sign means what it says. I'm looking for Mr. Klugg's son."

"You're looking at him. I'm Calvin. But I sure don't know you."

We had onlookers to the conversation. Somewhere in the near-darkness of the store, behind the grimy plate-glass win-dow, there was movement. At the same time a curtain stirred in a second floor window of the ramshackle house that clung in lopsided desperation to the hill above the store.

The atmosphere was distasteful with an air of decay about the place. The covert watchers and the boy's surliness added to my discomfort.

"I don't think you're the fellow I'm looking for. Do you, by any chance, have an older brother?"

"You mean Marvin? Marvin don't get to talk with people. What business you got with him?"

"If he's the right one, I want to talk to him about Stone Warrior Island. I understand—"

That was as far as I got. The screen door crashed open, and a tall, incredibly thin man of middle age charged out. He had long, black, unkempt hair and a heavy five-o'clock shadow. His bony wrists jutted out of the sleeves of his faded gray work shirt, and suspenders held up pants that were much too short for his pipestem legs. His voice, deep, resonant, and loud, was a striking contrast to his inadequate body.

"Mister, did I hear you mention my boy Marvin? What do you want with Marvin?"

"Mr. Klugg? My name is Linc Wilhite."

I extended my hand to shake, but his arms remained at his sides while his eyes, huge in their deep sockets, regarded me balefully. He slowly brought up both arms, hooked his hands inside his suspenders, and worried the material with his thumbs. The strange, gaunt figure was struggling to control himself.

"Mister, I'd be obliged for an answer to my question."

"Mr. Klugg, I work as the wrangler at Fairbaugh's Pack Station. My brother is Rod Wilhite. I understand that you worked for him on his boat a couple of times."

There was a slight nod. He was waiting for more.

"My brother heard that your son worked for Alan Mayfield, the man who's employing me this summer. I would like to talk with your son if you don't mind."

The boy Calvin was off the bench, his face flushed. "Pa, he asked me about Marvin and Stone Warrior Island."

The scarecrow of a man balled his hands into fists. He stepped to the edge of the porch, within arm's length, towering above me.

"You better give me a straight answer. Who put you up to this?"

Trying not to show my uneasiness, I held my ground. "I told you, sir. I've been offered a job as caretaker on Stone Warrior Island by Alan Mayfield. When I heard your boy had worked there, I wanted to hear about his experiences. I certainly didn't mean to cause you or him any trouble."

The boy joined his father at the edge of the porch, and the hostility of their frustration struck at me in hot waves of emotion. There was a trembling in Klugg's resonant voice when he answered.

"Mr. Wilhite, my Marvin was a wonder. He wasn't like me or Calvin here." He squeezed his son's thin shoulder. "This here's a fine boy, but him and me—we ain't bright like Marvin. Marvin was a good son, and he loved the Lord. He did good in high school and got a chance to go to the seminary."

He stopped abruptly and dug a knuckle into his eye. Tears stood in the corners of Charlie Klugg's eyes.

"He loved being a servant of the Lord, and he was gonna be a regular educated preacher, but the boy had to work summers to stay in school. Then, last summer, God have mercy on his soul, he fell into the snares of the Anti-Christ."

Tears were coursing down his worn cheeks now, and the boy was looking at his father with genuine concern, awkwardly patting his arm. The man took a deep, shuddering breath.

"My smart, good-looking, God-fearing boy went to that hellhole, mister. They sent him home seven weeks later, and I didn't recognize him. He came back possessed by Lucifer."

I stared at the grieving man in bewilderment, not knowing what to say.

"Mr. Klugg, I'm sorry. I don't understand—maybe he's just changed, sir, and—"

"Changed?" He laughed, a bizarre, unnatural cackling that echoed in the clearing before the store. "Oh, my, yes, he's changed. He surely has."

Abruptly he came off the porch and, seizing my elbow in an amazingly powerful grip for one so slender, turned me toward my truck.

"Mister, you're wasting your time. Marvin's not gonna talk to you or anybody—ever—about Stone Warrior Island. I don't want to ever hear that name again. I want you to leave —now."

He released my elbow, and I retreated toward the truck. Halfway there, I turned around. The two of them had held their positions, watching me steadily.

"Mr. Klugg, I don't understand what you're talking about. If there is something wrong with working for Mayfield, I hope you will reconsider and call me. Just look up Rod Wilhite in the phone book. It's a number in Sequim."

He took a couple of steps toward me. There was a change in his demeanor. His voice had grown solemn, mournful. "Sonny, do you still intend to go to Stone Warrior Island?"

"Yes, sir."

He shook his head. I recognized the change in his face. He

wore an expression of anguish. His words were barely audible.

"May God have mercy on your soul."

I stood by my truck and watched the two of them file into the store. Neither looked again in my direction.

Chapter FOUR

Fairbaugh followed me around like a puppy as I toiled. The old man's emotions bounced between exhilaration that I was off the payroll and depression when he contemplated trying to keep the business going.

By the time I arrived home, the sun had long since sunk into the dense sea fog that clung tightly to the tide-roughened waters of the Strait of Juan de Fuca, leaving the houses of Sequim barely visible in the gloaming. Pulling into the driveway, I felt a twinge of guilt because the lights were still on in the dining room. Rod and Evie had waited dinner for me.

When I entered the brightly lit dining room, my brother bounded across the room, his hand extended.

Rod is out of the same mold as our father, a big-boned, medium-height man with a quiet air of confidence. I take more after our mother, being taller than my brother and father, with her thick black hair and small bones.

He pumped my hand with his work-callused paw. "Congratulations, you son-of-a-gun. Evie says you got the job. I told you you were on a roll."

Evie stood in the doorway to the kitchen, saying nothing, watching us with a warm smile. She turned to get back to her dinner, but stopped in midstride. "By the way, Linc, you had the strangest phone call about five minutes ago. Somebody asked for you, and when I said you weren't here, he said he would call back later—that it was desperately important he talk to you. At least I'm pretty sure it was a he. He talked in a whisper."

She grinned. "Hey—you couldn't be getting phone calls from the ghosts on Stone Warrior Island, could you?"

She laughed gaily and disappeared through the doorway.

Rod snapped his fingers. "Incidentally, Linc, Dr. Levinson wasn't home when Evie went over, so after I cleaned up I ran your errand. I had him fill one of the small vials from your specimen case. I labeled it and left it on your bed."

It was a great evening—lots of laughs and no syrupy sentimentality. Evie had prepared my favorite dish, prime rib. For the first time since Laurie went away, I felt really good—felt that I belonged. A few minutes past ten we were startled by the ringing of the phone.

Evie glanced at me. "You had better answer it, Linc. It must be your mysterious friend. I don't think anyone would be calling us this late."

The pleasant evening had caused me to forget about the earlier call. My hello produced nothing but bursts of static. The whisper, when it came, was without substance.

"May I speak to Linc Wilhite?"

"I'm Linc Wilhite. Who is this?"

"This is Marvin—Marvin Klugg."

"Great! I wanted to talk to you. I wanted to ask—"

"Shut up!"

For long moments there was only the humming and static, and I thought something had frightened my cautious caller away. The whisper came back on the line, no longer so ethereal.

"Listen to me. Meet me at the ruins of the old chalet at eleven o'clock. Park your car on the road two hundred yards below the place and walk the rest of the way. Be on time."

There was an edge in his voice. "If my father discovers that I am out, it will go hard with me."

His words startled me. This was more than I had bargained for. I had the feeling I was plumbing depths that were beyond me.

"Listen, Marvin. It looks as if I'll be leaving early in the morning. I need to get some sleep and—"

"Be there at eleven. I must see you about Stone Warrior Lake."

He broke the connection.

It wasn't hard to visualize a stealthy figure slipping soundlessly out of the booth beside the Klugg store and gliding up the slope until it merged into the darkness surrounding the house.

Rod and Evie stared at me, their curiosity unconcealed, when I returned to the table.

"I have to go out for a while. It was that Klugg fellow. I think the whole clan must be nuts, but he does have my interest aroused. Something Mayfield said makes me want to meet this guy."

"Linc, you need your sleep if you are going to be traveling tomorrow," Evie protested. "Can't it wait until—"

"Evie, he's a grown man," Rod interrupted, "if you haven't noticed."

He rose from the table. "It's my bedtime. I guess I won't be seeing you in the morning. The prediction is for building seas by noon, so I want to clear the fishing grounds early. Remember—I'm rooting for you, buddy."

He stuck out his hand, and I shook it. For a moment it seemed he was about to embrace me, then thought better of it. Blushing at displaying his emotions so nakedly, he walked briskly past me into the unlighted hall.

Five minutes later I was on my way to see Marvin Klugg.

I pulled the truck over onto the skimpy shoulder for a second time, cut the lights, and slid out. It was pitch dark along the narrow road, snaking its way through the towering trees. High overhead, a slender thread of star-pricked night sky traced the same sinuous course as the pavement, providing the only relief from the blackness of the forest floor. The darkness was filled with the soft sibilance of restless treetops, stirring in the cool air flowing down the flanks of the mountains to the sea.

Even before stopping the first time to reconnoiter along the lonely route, I knew I had made a miscalculation. At night and on an unfamiliar road it was impossible to estimate within two miles the distance to the Klugg store, much less locate a spot two hundred yards from the chalet ruins. It was so dark under the trees that it would be easy for anyone unfamiliar with the area to walk right past the fire-gutted shell without seeing it.

Clutching the flashlight, I trudged slowly up the ever-climbing strip of asphalt. Fatigue from the excitement of the day accentuated my regret at accepting the strange invitation.

Sure that I had walked far more than two hundred yards, I paused, trying to decide whether to give up and go home to bed. Standing alone in that ancient forest, listening to the mournful play of the wind through the tall spires overhead, it took little consideration for me to decide to return to Sequim.

I was turning to retrace my steps when a tiny patch of night sky came into view ahead and not far above ground level. It was the crest where the road topped the rise and ran downhill to the cul-de-sac at Klugg's.

Shrugging off my apprehensions, I started forward again, aware that the woods were thinning. Seconds later, the burned-out chalet appeared in silhouette, off to the left on higher ground. Neither sound nor light came from its charred remains.

Crossing a shallow depression running along the side of the road, I climbed a gentle slope littered with decaying forest debris. A waist-high barrier of quarried stone and charred timbers was all that remained of the collapsed facade of the building. To the left was one of the two remaining standing walls, its solid blackness pierced by ragged rectangles of night sky that once had been windows.

Once inside the shell, balanced precariously atop the tangles of fallen beams from the collapsed roof, I stared up, suddenly afraid, at the unsupported remains that seemed ready to tumble down any moment. Each puff of wind elicited ominous creaks from that fire-weakened stone deathtrap. That was the only sound around the bones of the fire-ravaged structure.

"Marvin?" I called softly.

The ruins, still steeped in the smell of burned wood after all that time, soaked up the words. A second call, softly still, and then a third went unheeded. There was an eeriness about the place that would not allow me to raise my voice.

I remained a few moments more before my courage vanished, and I turned to flee from that fearsome site. Stumbling often on the unseen detritus beneath my feet, I had reached the mound of debris that marked the front boundary of the chalet when the sharp edge of a piercing voice pinioned me in my tracks.

"Stop where you are and turn around very slowly. Do you understand? Very slowly."

The precise voice, its enunciation perfect, not a Klugg voice at all, startled me. I obeyed, suddenly afraid of having been lured into a trap. The gutted chalet was a perfect place for robbery and, afterwards, murder. Had my stupidity placed me in the clutches of a family that enticed its victims to graves that might never be found under the fern-crowded floor of the forest?

The voice sounded as if it had come from some distance away. There was no sense of anyone nearby, but as I started to relax, a hand gripped my shoulder, pulling me around. The beam from a small flashlight splashed across my face for a split second.

"Wilhite, it's about time you got here. It must be twenty past eleven. Give me your hand, and I will lead you. Be careful—you could bring the whole place down on us."

He didn't wait for any remonstrance on my part. A large, oddly soft hand gripped mine and urged me forward into the heart of the collapsed building.

Despite his caution, I almost fell several times. Just when it seemed we were moving without purpose, a faint glow appeared ahead at ground level. When we reached the sliver of light, he stopped and, releasing my hand, pulled aside a heavy tarpaulin.

There was some sort of room below ground level, clearly revealed in the harsh light of a gas lantern. Marvin's breath was warm against my ear.

"Quick—down there! Slide down that timber. It's safe enough."

His struggle with the tarp, trying to secure it across the narrow opening through which we had descended, granted me time to survey my surroundings. Apparently a cellar had underlain the entire structure, but the floors and walls had fallen into most of it, leaving only the one corner where we were. The air, warmed by the gas lantern, was rancid with the smell of soiled bedding and human sweat.

"It's my little home away from home, Wilhite. What do you think of it?"

Luckily, Klugg didn't seem to expect an answer. Besides the lantern, the hideaway contained only a couple of chairs without backs and an old mattress on the floor, atop which rested an oil-darkened pillow and two filthy blankets.

His voice continued to fascinate me. There was none of the Klugg twang in it. The diction, the pronunciations, and the modulation were those of an educated man with a trained voice. But I had no doubts about whom I was talking to.

Marvin was a close image of his father, with the same unkempt mop of long black hair plus a full beard. However, he had a much broader face. No doubt, if he groomed himself properly, he would be considered handsome by some people.

He motioned me toward one of the broken chairs and settled on the other. For long moments he stared at me, and the lantern revealed a hot, smoky blackness in those motionless eyes. His gaze pierced the core of me like a cruel lance. I could neither move nor turn away.

He laughed, and the spell was broken. "You are puzzled by the way I speak, I see. You didn't expect a Klugg to speak like a civilized human being, did you? Well, I owe my vocal proficiency to my dear father. The only pleasure he allows me is a radio. To preserve my sanity, I started trying to mimic the announcers on the college stations. Now I have come to see a profitable reward in my hobby. So, my man, you are no longer sure you are dealing with the bumpkin you envisioned —right?"

I started to deny any such thoughts, but he hurried on to another topic before I could open my mouth.

"I have to be cautious, Wilhite. My father does not allow me to have visitors. I'm not even permitted to talk to the occasional fishermen who frequent the lake. Sissy and I sometimes come up here at night. My father has a nasty habit of locking me in after dark when they are sleeping. It took me six months to figure a way, with my sister's help, of sneaking in and out during the night. Dear father and Calvin keep me under close surveillance the rest of the time. Luckily, both Sissy and I find certain satisfactions in escaping at night."

I had relaxed a bit when Marvin led me into his underground sanctuary, but now the uneasiness was returning. This was a situation that I neither understood nor wanted to become involved in. I tried to collar my racing thoughts—to find something to say that would allow me a graceful exit and a fast trip back to Sequim. My curiosity had vanished in the presence of the strange Marvin Klugg.

"Marvin, I feel badly about this. I didn't understand what your situation was. I had no intention of causing you any trouble. I wouldn't think of asking you to talk under the circumstances, but thanks, anyway."

Before I could rise, he was on his feet and standing between me and the exit from the caved-in basement.

"Don't get up, friend. It's okay. We are safe enough for the moment. Believe me. I wouldn't take any unnecessary chances for a stranger. So relax."

Even as he talked the tall scarecrow of a man was sliding his chair over to where he could sit between me and the opening out of the cellar.

"I want to talk to you, too, Wilhite," he said. "Another of my little vices is eavesdropping, so I overheard your conversation this afternoon. You said that you are going to Stone Warrior. I find that very interesting. It is as if the members of a very exclusive club are suddenly being brought together. As you know, I was last summer's inductee, though it seems a lifetime ago now.

"I couldn't resist meeting you. Question: do we have the same qualifications to be so chosen? I must know."

He was completely mad. No wonder they keep him locked up! I dared not move. He was resting lightly on the edge of the chair, his body tense. Marvin Klugg was like a great cat ready to spring.

"Pay attention to me, friend. I know you think you're

trapped in some desolate, godforsaken place with a raving
maniac who may attack you without the slightest provocation.
You are sitting there, sweating, afraid, cursing yourself that
you came, wondering if I will let you leave here alive. Isn't
that true?"

Chapter FIVE

Under his intense scrutiny, I nodded before I could stop
myself. An ugly parody of a smile creased his intense face for
a split second. My involuntary reaction had pleased him.

"This time last year, I affected the same All-American look
you wear as a badge of respectability—clean shaven, my hair
cut. I was enrolled in a seminary, the joy of my father's life,
studying to be what the good people call a man of God. Unfortunately, God doesn't pay tuition at seminaries, so I took
the summer job at Stone Warrior Island. Well, Wilhite, I came
home without the All-American look, and I seem to have lost
the man of God label somewhere along the way."

I was determined to remain silent, not to encourage him.
Yet I blurted out, "But what in heaven's name happened? Is
there something wrong with Mayfield—with that partner of
his? Tell me."

Marvin appeared not to hear me.

"When I saw Mayfield's ad, I jumped at the chance. No
other summer job interested me after I saw it in the paper."

He paused for a moment, then he began to snicker. The odd
note of merriment continued for some thirty seconds before he
spoke again.

"You see, my fellow Warriorite, poor Marvin was a bit
troubled in his soul. He wanted time by himself to wrestle
with old Lucifer. The poor man of God who lived at the

Klugg manor on beautiful Two Mile Lake felt more than a little envious every time a tourist drove up in a fancy car, dressed in all his Eddie Bauer and Pendleton finery, with a wife wearing her designer clothes, tight as a second skin. Not the way a man of the cloth should feel—right? And, oh, yes, on occasion poor Marvin would look beyond those straining fabrics to the soft flesh they encased and wonder what earthly delights that pampered flesh might offer. Alas, there were lonely nights when the poor fellow would succumb to the sin of—shall we say—abusing himself, and then he would spend a perfect month in hell, praying for the absolution of his transgressions.

"I saw the utter isolation of Stone Warrior as a Godly temple in which I could purge myself of lust and envy."

He paused again and grinned at me. "Well, I found the place, and I surely did purge myself—in a manner of speaking."

He dropped his head, running his hands through the long, tangled mane of hair. His head still bowed, he started to speak again. From time to time his voice would break, and he would laugh for a moment or maybe cry—I couldn't tell which.

"I went into the wilderness—a modern Moses, I fancied— to let the icy-cold light of God's purity reach into my heart and scour the sin from it. Seek and ye shall find. Well, I found, all right. I found I had been enslaved all these years by the senseless mumbo-jumbo my father drummed into me. I was saved, Wilhite, saved! I found my salvation. I warmed myself . . . in the brimstone pits of the Devil. Listen to me, man! Stone Warrior Island is a gateway to Hell."

Whatever monstrosities of the mind tormented Marvin Klugg, they were far more than I wanted to hear. I thought again about bolting from the cellar, but it was as if he could read my thoughts. He leaped to his feet and crouched between me and the fallen beam leading out of the basement.

"No! You stay there! You wanted to know, and by hell, you are going to.

"Mayfield told me I would be on the island by myself for a week, opening the place before he and his guests arrived. But something went wrong with his plans. The week went by, and no plane arrived. By the tenth day I was getting panicky, wondering if I would be stranded there for weeks. It was nine-teen days before they finally showed up. Mayfield never even bothered to explain why they were late—just said something about he bet I was glad to see them.

"That first week alone on the island was everything I had envisioned. I truly felt I was a modern Moses ascending the mount. I would do my work each day and then, after dark, would sit on the dock and stare up at the night sky, as pristine as the first day man walked on this earth. I thought I was as near to God as man can be.

"What a fool I was! I looked away from earthly wisdom into the emptiness of a night sky."

He stepped nearer, and his voice became so soft it was difficult to hear over the hiss of the lantern.

"But after the first week, as the days of uncertainty grew, the island became a disquieting place at night. I could no longer pray. At first it bewildered me, but soon I began to sense their presence. I realized I was not alone on Stone War-rior."

I stared at him, unsure if I had understood him correctly. "Not alone! Do you mean there were people trespassing on the property?"

That odd snickering erupted again. He leaned forward to where his face was a bare foot from mine. Behind Marvin's stooped body, the lantern etched his shadow like a distorted question mark against the wall.

"Trespassers? Well, they certainly don't belong on the is-land—or on this earth, for that matter. They belong in hell. You don't yet understand, little man. Stone Warrior Island is the end of earth—the beginning of the Kingdom of Satan. His emissaries are there, awaiting those who will embrace him.

"But I digress from my little history. Each night after I finished the evening chores, I continued in the same manner, meditating through the long northern twilight and into dark-ness. It must have been on the ninth or tenth night that I became aware I was being watched. It was a gradually accel-erating awareness, a discomfiting feeling at first, then I began to see shadows where they had no right to be—shadows that grew denser and changed locations when I wasn't watching. I could sense a sort of restlessness that permeated the air—a restlessness that soon became audible, yet indescribable.

"I thought perhaps it was the Lord testing me. The next night I had to force myself to walk down to that dock. The moon was just coming up when I dropped to my knees to pray for strength. Almost immediately I sensed them around me. I tried not to look, but I heard the sounds rising, complex and unintelligible at first. But gradually they became recognizable. The night was filled with screams, laughter, shrieks, and chants. When I turned around, the shore behind me was filled with menacing, moving shades. Terrified, I ran for the house.

"That was the last time I went out after dark, but it no longer mattered. Within a couple of days I could sense them at the windows and the doors . . . all the time, day and night . . . pressing to gain entrance. I was a prisoner within the building. Day by day, I sensed their presence growing stronger, probing the walls, reaching for me, seeking to embrace me.

"Finally on the eighteenth night of my imprisonment on Stone Warrior, the very foundations of the house began to buckle under the forces that groped for me. In my terror, I screamed, 'Please, don't. I yield. Take me and do whatever you will.'

"Wilhite, it was a miracle. Even as I surrendered myself an incredible feeling of relief swept over me. As the minutes swept by, I realized I was changing, radically. I felt powerful —sure of myself—as I had never before felt. There was still a presence around me, but it was dark and warm and thrilling. The quintessential spirit of evil had drawn me into its embrace. I recognized it as an inexpressible ecstasy that I had unknowingly longed for all my life.

"The next morning the planes bearing Mayfield and his guests arrived. I ran down to greet them as a shark swims toward its prey. I had become a predator determined to take, not give."

Marvin was on his knees before me, grasping my hands in his. I tried to free myself, but he was far too strong for me. Holding my arms imprisoned as effortlessly as if I were a child, he searched my face, his own eyes hidden in the great dark pools of shadow that filled his eye sockets.

"Why were you chosen to go, man? Do you lust, unknowingly, for the ultimate ectasy, to plunge into absolute degradation?"

When I didn't answer he tilted his head up, and the harsh lantern light was full on it. I was scared out of my wits by what I saw. His face bore a malevolence beyond description. His eyes fixed me with a hypnotic compulsion that I could not resist. I heard myself answering the question.

"I . . . I've had problems, a tragedy. I want to leave the past behind—to start over."

An electrical surge passed from his hand into mine. His gaze never left my face, and he grinned—a grin that was knowing and conspiratorial and . . . infectious. It was all I could do to resist returning the grin, but suddenly I felt filthy. It was as if we had shared, for an instant, some ultimate obscenity.

He started to speak again, and his tones were richer, deeper. There was a seductive quality to his words, and it commanded my absolute concentration. I was aware of nothing in that cellar but the warmth engendered by the mesmerizing velvet of his voice.

"The moment those people stepped ashore I knew what I had come to Stone Warrior Island for. Mayfield and the other men were strutting around in their expensive outdoor clothing, wearing their wealth like banners, shouting at one another in the loud, assertive voices they use to convince themselves of their importance. Their bored, silly wives and daughters wiggled in front of them, half naked, the wives flaunting themselves before each other's husbands and the daughters tempting them all—even their own fathers—with their forbidden bodies.

"I began to take what I wanted. It was so damned easy. They had so much they never missed what I stole—the money, the jewelry, the silver. It amused me to hear them complaining about missing a ring or a bracelet and deciding that it must not have been packed.

"By the time they had been penned up for three weeks, some of the women were ready for anything. Late one night, one of them trailed me through the woods to the far side of the island, where I often swam late at night. I didn't know she was there until I turned to swim back to shore and saw her waiting there, nude, muttering something about not having skinny-dipped since college days.

"She couldn't keep her conquest to herself, the stupid pig! She had to brag about it, and soon I had a second enticing concubine in my harem. But I made a mistake, Wilhite. I did make a mistake.

"I began to lust after the Bengston girl, all blonde and tan and luscious. Damn, how I wanted her!

"One night I became careless, and they caught me peeping in at her window. It was the bitch's fault. She would come out of the shower and stand, buck naked, before the open window to finish drying herself.

"After they caught me watching her, they put two and two together. Before long they were compiling a list of the stuff I stole and questioning me about it. The next morning Mayfield organized a search and, by noon, they had found my little treasure trove under a rock near the antenna. The pilot, that Chambord, arrived the next day with a planeload of supplies, and Mayfield decided to send me back with him. After I handed out a few fat lips and black eyes, the fat slobs thought better of the idea. They had to send for the Mounties to get rid of me.

"But are they really free of Marvin Klugg? Those poor, simple fools—rid of Marvin Klugg? I've only had a sample so far of what I want—just an hors d'oeuvre."

He chuckled, and it broke the spell of his voice. He released my hand and tilted his head back in a paroxysm of near-hysterical laughter. It went on and on. Only when he was gasping for breath did he subside.

"My fellow acolyte, I am going to return to Stone Warrior. I steal a dime here, a quarter there. Any time the old man is careless, it costs him. It's slow, but it adds up. It may take a year—it may take two—but one day Mayfield and his friends will look up to see me coming ashore, and it will be too late. He and his friends will have only a few moments to prepare to pass through that gateway to hell. Then I will pleasure myself with the flesh of their women until I am satiated. In time, I will tire of them, and they will follow their men to perdition. I will use their wealth to find another Stone Warrior.

"I warn you, Wilhite, take care. Whatever dark pleasure you seek at Stone Warrior, do not take what is mine—or I will kill you."

He leaped to his feet at the sudden noise above us. In a reflex action I came off the chair and found myself in the corner, my back pressed to the cold concrete, determined to sell my life as dearly as I could.

A small figure, clad in blue jeans and a heavy plaid shirt, popped into view at the opening and scrambled down the sloping timber. I blinked in surprise. It was a young girl, not over sixteen, with the same jet black hair that all the Kluggs possessed. She squinted in the bright light, trying to get a good look at me. She tugged at her brother's sleeve.

"Marvin, we gotta get back. We've been out about two hours now, and you know Papa always gets up in the middle of the night to take a leak."

Marvin pulled her tight against his side. "Just relax, Sissy. It can't be much after twelve. The parental bladder never requires tapping before one-thirty. We must not be inhospitable to our honored guest."

He pulled her forward, and I sensed an uncontrollable glee in him. "Mr. Wilhite, this is my sister Sissy—the only one the Klugg household comes furnished with, worst luck."

Before my astonished eyes he began slowly, even tantalizingly, to unbutton the heavy workshirt she wore, his gaze full on me. I could feel the energy exploding from him as he drew the shirt open and slid his hand over one of his sister's exposed breasts to tease the rising nipple of the other. She leaned against him, shivering, and, as I watched, unable to turn aside, the soft teenage face tightened, and her lips, drawing back over her teeth, gave her the look of a predator.

"Marvin, you sure we got time?"

He ignored her question, still watching me with those glittering eyes. His voice held that insinuating, hypnotic quality.

"Won't you join me, Mr. Wilhite . . . begin to wallow in sin, so to speak? I assure you there is enough here for both you and me. Sissy would love it . . . and so would I."

She threw her head back, moaning. Abruptly they were locked in an embrace, and he was pulling her toward the mattress on the floor, his stentorian breathing filling the small cellar.

I have no idea how I found my way out of the ruins without breaking my neck or bringing the fragile walls crashing down on me. Reaching the road, I fled down its dark surface, my feet jarring hard against the unseen pavement.

Once within the truck, I sat, trying to calm myself enough to drive those winding miles back to Rod's. I have seen my share of obscenity before but nothing like the utter degradation—the evil—in the basement of the burned chalet. I understood clearly now the hostility of old man Klugg and his younger son, striving to hide from the world the shame of that monster.

By the time my pulse rate had steadied enough for me to start the engine, I knew that, even if I discounted the danger, it had been a wasted trip. Klugg's tales of Stone Warrior Island were nothing more than nightmarish, sexually oriented figments of a maniac's mind.

Before I reached the outskirts of Sequim, I had pretty much relegated the memory of Marvin Klugg and his poor abused sister to the deeper recesses of my mind. Unfortunately, I have not been as successful in forgetting his account of what happened to him on Stone Warrior Island.

Sleep did not come easily. Excitement played across my nerves like summer lightning. From across the fog-laden straits, the banshee wails of foghorns pierced the night as freighters crept through the thick, drifting banks of mist toward Seattle.

As I lay there, restless, my thoughts turned, as they often do, to the precious memories of my lovely Laurie and to that one shining moment of happiness that she provided in my life.

My reminiscences faded as I drifted off to sleep. It had been quite a Tuesday and I slept well and deeply. Not once did I start awake, the sweat heavy on me, groping my way back to reality from the horrible dreams that have plagued my nights since she went away.

Chapter SIX

Evie awoke me at 7:20 A.M., tugging at my pajama sleeve. She stood by the bed, looking highly annoyed.

"Linc, that Mr. Mayfield's secretary is on the phone. She wants to talk to you. She sounds a bit snooty, if you ask me."

The lady, a statuesque blonde as I recall, sounded as cool and unflurried by dawn's light as she had the day before in Mayfield's office. Without wasting any time on amenities, she informed me that my plane left at 10:18. She broke the connection without a goodbye, placing me neatly at my peg in the Mayfield hierarchy.

Evie rushed for the kitchen, starting breakfast to a syncopation of crashing pots and imprecations directed at Mayfield's secretary. Evie doesn't admire arrogance.

While she was delivering her impassioned diatribe on the subject of my new employers, I managed to stagger out of bed and dress. After my midnight rendezvous with Klugg I could have used another two hours of sleep. Plucking my old duffel bag out of the junk heaped at the bottom of my closet, I began to pack, cramming it with work clothes and the usual socks and underwear.

The shifting about of clothes in my bureau drawer brought my elderly, nickel-plated revolver into view. I paused, staring at it, toying with the sudden inclination to take it with me. After all, I was going to be two hundred miles from help, and besides, the North Woods had several animals large enough to be troublesome.

The gun was a small .32, its plating chipped and scarred by many years of abuse. It had only the six bullets that were loaded in its chambers. The revolver had come into my possession during my last year in college, bought from a guy who was hard up for cash.

It would have to be checked through in a separate bag, and with the firing pin removed. I didn't know about the regulations concerning the transportation of handguns into Canada. How the bag managed to slip by at the airport without being spotted is a mystery to me. An old canvas bike bag served nicely to stow the weapon.

I slipped the vial Rod had borrowed from Levinson into my specimen case and fitted it into the duffel bag. I locked the bag, slung it over my shoulder, and carried the two pieces of luggage out to the pickup.

When I came back into the kitchen, my breakfast was waiting. Evie was stirring about back in her bedroom. I wondered if she had decided to forgo the strain of saying goodbye, but when she heard me pushing the chair back from the table, she appeared in the doorway.

The stiff-upper-lip attitude she displayed in awakening me had disappeared, and her face was a tragic mask. Tears glistened in her eyes, and to tell the truth, she almost had me ready to sit down and have a good cry with her. As I pulled away from the house, my rearview mirror framed Evie, standing in the driveway, bawling. Evie doesn't like saying goodbye.

I had the darnedest feeling that all the pain of the past two years would end at Stone Warrior. I guess a man's premonitions aren't worth very much, eh?

Chapter
SEVEN

I dislike being confined in the elongated tube of a commercial airplane and viewed the trip with displeasure, but despite my reservations, the Wednesday morning flight from Seattle to Regina went quickly. There were surprisingly few passengers, and I had a row to myself. The jet arrived in Regina on schedule, allowing me time to claim my luggage and find the Nord-Can plane for the flight to Saskatoon. The afternoon was well advanced when, with cramped muscles, I slipped into a phone booth in Saskatoon.

Mustard Chambord, Mayfield's pilot, answered on the second ring. I expected a rough, growling voice, the kind I associated with a rough-and-tumble bush pilot. Instead, the man spoke with a rather clipped, odd accent that was, no doubt, French Canadian.

Chambord was all apologies as he told me that the flight north would have to be postponed a day. After depositing me at Stone Warrior he would be flying another bush pilot farther north with a fuel pump for a plane grounded in the Great Slave Lake area. He expected the replacement part to arrive during the night.

It was not displeasing news, for it gave me a few hours to make like a tourist, wandering around Saskatoon. I hate to admit it, but this was the longest trip I'd ever taken. All too early that Thursday morning Chambord called to say that we would leave at two o'clock.

Midafternoon found us flying two thousand feet above the pool-table flatness of central Saskatchewan. Soon the dusty, west-facing windows of the plane framed a crazy-quilt pattern of prairie fields beginning to give way to gentle rises. In the distance, past Chambord's shoulder, were the first intermittent clumps of trees that grew larger until they became a blanket stretching all the way to the Arctic tundra.

The French Canadian, his silvery hair a startling contrast to the tanned leather of his genial face, twisted about in his seat to peer at me. The weathered face wore a warm smile. Chambord had a French accent that is music to the ears. I knew if I stayed around him for long I would start imitating it.

"How do you like the flight, Linc? Is this the first time you have ever been up in a float plane?"

Feeling as naive as a country yokel, I nodded. It was an honest answer as long as a consideration of the takeoff wasn't part of the question. The high-winged pontoon-equipped plane must have plowed up the river for five minutes, smacking the wave tops with bone-jarring wallops before it broke free of the water. Compared to the jets, the awkward crate seemed to be crawling rather than flying across the landscape.

Chambord winked at me. He must have found me a simple book to read. "Don't try to kid me, my friend. You have another thrill coming if the wind is kicking up at Stone Warrior. Landing a pontoon plane in a chop isn't exactly like floating down to a feather bed. But we'll survive—I guarantee it."

He laughed uproariously and tapped the hard-muscled shoulder of his silent, dour-looking copilot, who had been introduced as Earl Higgins.

Higgins offered a few choice obscenities in riposte, pulled his bill cap lower over his face, and slipped down still farther in the seat, his eyes closed. Higgins had deigned to notice me only once.

Early in the flight, when I queried Chambord about the odd name Mustard, the copilot had quickly answered without looking at me, "If you ever watched him eat, you wouldn't have to ask. That Frenchie would put mustard on ice cream."

Mustard grimaced at the scowling Higgins and continued talking at a near shout above the roar of the plane's engine. Sliding his shirt sleeve up, he squinted at his watch. "We should be down on the water at Stone Warrior within two hours. When we get there, we'll stretch our legs a bit and give you a hand starting the damned generator. I've never seen one of those sons of bitches that isn't so balky but what a man can use all the help he can get, especially after it hasn't been run for seven or eight months. Besides, I want to check the planking on the dock before the big plane brings in a heavy load."

The consideration shown by the friendly French Canadian was reassuring. "You won't find me turning down help, Mr. Chambord. But will you fellows have enough time to get where you're going before dark? I wouldn't think that landing one of these things on water after nightfall would be much fun."

Mustard turned to regard me again, his bright eyes watching me through lids slitted against the glare of sunlight lancing into the small cabin. "Hey, young friend, you forget. You've arrived in the land of the midnight sun. This time of year we only have four hours of darkness."

Chambord spent many hours flying small planes across this lonely but magnificent land of cold, clear lakes and untouched forests without any company in the cockpit. Like most people who spend a great deal of time alone, the French Canadian aviator, with a listener available, rambled on at great length about any subject that presented itself. I offered him more opportunities by asking him if he had known Mayfield long. He replied with a minutely detailed recitation of the relationship between them.

Mayfield was a steady customer who never made unreasonable demands, which was more than he could say for most clients in an area where every item had to be flown in on the frail wings of small planes. Most summers, there was a constant stream of visitors in and out, businessmen whose expenses were taken care of by Mayfield.

After a while, Chambord's intermittent monologue faded into the background, and I sought the view sliding past beneath the window. Below, the last of the open prairie had disappeared, and now the plane was over a solid carpet of green forest. With ever greater frequency, lakes both large and small appeared under the wingtips. Low-lying rocky ridges, looking like grayish rips in the nubby greenish fabric of the forest, ran in a northeastern direction.

As the aging sun drifted down across the western sky, the deep blue green of the woods below brightened to a kelly green in the yellowing sunlight. Many miles of forest had slipped behind the plane since the last sign of civilization marred the greenery below. There were no roads, no houses— none of those scars that mark the presence of man. It was easy to grasp some concept of what the term wilderness really meant.

I started, realizing that Chambord had asked me a question. Embarrassed, I wondered how long he had been questioning me.

"I'm sorry, I . . . I wasn't listening. The drone of the motor and the warmth of the sun in here is making me drowsy. What did you say?"

Higgins, who had been slumped in his seat all through the talkative pilot's constant chatter, pulled the cap from his face and peered around his seat at me. "Now you understand why I'm able to sleep when I'm flying with old motormouth here."

It was the sort of remark to be spoken with a smile when it was said about a man with whom one flew all the time. The copilot's face yielded no indication that he was joking.

Mustard ignored his surly companion and repeated his comment. "I said you will have an easy job up there. The only time you work up a sweat is when we have to unload the tanks of propane for cooking and the drums of gasoline for the generator. Usually there's only the pilot and you to handle those babies, and the sons of bitches weight over four hundred pounds apiece. If you lost control of one of them at the wrong time, you could sink an airplane right there at the dock or maybe lose a drum of gasoline in fifty feet of ice water. May-field said that he had about eighty gallons of fuel left from last summer. That will be far more than enough to run the generator until we fly in the first load.

"He keeps several canoes stored on the island, and we will bring in the aluminum fishing boats on the first or second flight. He stores them in Saskatoon during the winter. He doesn't want to take a chance of having them stolen.

"Mayfield has had trouble in the off-season with thieves. In this country it has to be some low-life bastard in a float plane who helps himself. That's always a problem with owning a place in a remote spot. It doesn't matter if it's in the States or up here in Canada. Some bastard is always around to steal you blind."

A frown settled on his leathery face. "Of course, that's the least of it now. We have real trouble brewing."

The recumbent Higgins snarled from beneath his billed cap. "Christ, Chambord! You're gonna scare the shit out of the kid with your wild tales."

"I just wish they were wild." He fixed his earnest eyes on me. "It started summer before last, Linc. Three guys from California—you know the type—big, meaty men with lots of gold chains, expensive watches, and fingers full of diamond and ruby rings—showed up here in midseason without reservations, wanting to be flown in for a week's fishing. They tried all the outfits, including us, without success. But then they lucked out—or, at least, it seemed so at the time. Frank Rodgers had a cancellation on a freight job heading for Great Slave. He flew those fellows in to a little lake north of Wollaston—water brimming with hungry trout that would hit anything.

"Frank agreed to pick them up in ten days. When he returned on the agreed-on date, he couldn't find hide nor hair of them. Their camp was still there. Although animals had been into it, there wasn't any sign they had had trouble. Except for what the scavengers had done, the camp was in perfect order. A couple of Mounties arrived the next day, but they had no better luck than Frank.

"Finally, near the end of the season, two planeloads of police were sent in for an intense search. They found the bodies about a half-mile back in the woods. They had been shot in the back—executed in cold blood. The corpses were stripped —no rings, no watches, no wallets.

"Of course, it caused a real stir. But you know how it is— people soon forget.

"Then, last spring, a man from Vancouver vanished. He had planned to meet some friends from Winnipeg at a private fishing camp, but when they arrived two days later, there was no sign of him. No trace has been found—no body, no luggage.

"We became involved last fall. Right at the end of the season, two Texans came rolling into Saskatoon. They were hell-bent on getting into the woods for a last bit of fishing. They hit the bars in Saskatoon for a week, flashing a couple of rolls of bills that would choke a horse. One of the stupid bastards bragged that he had twenty thousand dollars on him. That late in the year, most of the pilots are busy closing up camps and flying out equipment.

"One morning, we had a call for an emergency blood run up to Lake Athabasca, so I got in touch with the dummies and told them we would take them in and pick them up a week later when we made our final swing through the camps we service. Earl flew them in.

"The same thing happened as with the guy from Vancouver. There was no sign of them or their camp. They apparently never had a chance to build a fire their first night. It was on a lake about a hundred miles northeast of Stone Warrior. The Mounties made a quick search before the lake iced over, and they drew a blank. I don't want to scare you, young man, but—"

Chapter EIGHT

Earl Higgins's sarcastic words cut the pilot off. "Why don't you just admit to him, Mustard, that we have goddamned sea monsters living in these lakes that come out and devour the tourists."

Once again, Chambord ignored his copilot's remarks. "You should keep your eyes open, Linc. The world has changed to where you can't be too careful. It doesn't matter where you live."

The plane continued to inch its way across the tree-carpeted world below, and I was glad that Chambord was passing the time with talk, even if he was trying to pull a greenhorn's leg with his scary tales.

The bush pilot shifted conversational gears, quizzing me about my background. He did it in such a quiet way and with such apparent interest that, despite my resolution to reveal nothing about myself while in Canada, he soon knew about my attending Oregon State and transferring to the University of Washington. I told him about earning a degree in entomology but very little about growing up in Astoria, Oregon.

Chambord looked confused. He would soon be asking questions about why a college graduate was working as a handyman. To forestall his queries I made up a story about having taken a job in the timber industry but finding I didn't like it and deciding I needed time to find myself. I didn't want to lie but I didn't want to unburden myself to strangers, either. Trying to divert his attention, I began to ramble, telling silly stories about the tourists in Olympic.

For a moment it seemed Chambord had been taken in by my glibness, but the shrewd, calculating eyes had read the sudden confusion in my face. He was sharp enough to understand that there was a sore point in my life.

As much could not be said for the recumbent Earl Higgins. Abruptly he sat erect, pushing the long-billed cap away from his suddenly interested face, and turned to study me. He was a heavyset, muscular man of about forty with the kind of florid complexion that indicated an overfamiliarity with alcohol. His hair was cut so short it was little more than a fuzz covering his head. Its blondness showed glints of red in the flashes of sunlight peeking in under the wing. His mean brown eyes held me in their gaze.

"You mean you're up here in Canada just screwing around? Hell, I thought you were some guy really down on his luck, to have to take a butt-licking job two hundred miles from the ass end of nowhere at the beck and call of some rich bastard. Christ! You're something else."

He ignored Mustard's frantic attempts to interject a conciliatory note into the conversation.

I couldn't believe what I was hearing. A minute before, it had been a great adventure, and then this guy, whom I hadn't said a word to, started in on me. He was nothing but an over-aged bully, twice my size, who thought he had found an easy mark. I sure as heck didn't intend to justify my actions to some guy I had never seen before, so I turned away and stared out the window.

When he saw that he couldn't goad me into a response, Higgins turned away to stare moodily out the windshield, ignoring both Chambord and me. His outburst effectively killed all conversation in the cabin. There was no more talking as the plane continued to wing its way north.

Some sixty minutes later Chambord banked the plane into a shallow turn, pointing with one finger down and across the face of the bellicose copilot. "There's your home for the summer, young fellow—right down there."

As we passed the lake off to the east, banking more heavily into the long, sweeping turn, an irregularly oval sheet of water came into sight. A single island, shaped roughly like a teardrop, lay pretty much along the center axis of the lake and closer to the southwestern end. The size of the island, heavily forested except for a single area of exposed rock, was a surprise. Somehow, I hadn't been able to grasp the extent of twenty-four acres surrounded by water. The two houses were not immediately apparent as the island diminished behind us. The horizon returned to its natural position as we flattened out for our landing approach.

A brisk late-afternoon breeze was blowing across the open expanse of restless blue water. Along the boundary of the lake, treetops were swaying in the steady western wind. The plane skimmed in over the tall spires of the spruces on the northeast shore of Stone Warrior Lake, heading for the touchdown onto the heaving surface. Solid jolts pounded through the small craft as its pontoons kissed the wave tops before the Cessna settled onto the choppy surface, slowing abruptly in the grasp of the water.

Chambord revved the plane's powerplant and plowed twin frothy furrows down the lake toward the island, lying several hundred yards ahead. He rounded a point of land, and there were the waiting houses, silent in the afternoon sunlight, tightly clad in their winter wraps. They looked strangely alien in the harmony of forest and water.

The structures, two-story affairs of peeled logs with steeply pitched shingle roofs, lay on a sloping shelf of gray rock, bare except for the occasional small shrub that clung to it. The granite slab slanted down from the low crest of the island to disappear under the crystalline water of the lake. The shelf, maybe a hundred and fifty yards wide, terminated abruptly about twenty-five yards above the houses. The granite face encompassed an acre to an acre and a half of exposed rock. It was sharply delineated by the dark tangled mass of brush and thick timber that cloaked the remainder of the small island.

Wood shutters shielded the windows of the two boxy structures, sealing eight months of darkness within their quiet interiors. The buildings looked exactly alike, with the exception of a front porch on the one to the left, Mayfield's house.

A floating dock, a weathered platform of gray wood atop a flotilla of rusting oil drums, rocked ponderously in the lake waves at the foot of the barren rock face before Mayfield's house. A bare flagpole, its limp hoist ropes stirring in the breeze, stood on the slope above the dock, rearing its peeled log trunk, like an accusing finger, toward the sky.

As Chambord completed his approach and gunned the engine to move in toward the dock, there came into view, beyond the second house, the warped remains of a basketball backboard, its post still standing but tilted precariously forward, the netless rim orange with rust and encircling a patch of empty sky. I wondered vaguely how many times the players had become swimmers when the ball scooted down the steep grade into the water.

At the last moment, the French Canadian swung the plane sideways and cut the engine, using the wind's push to drift to a jarring stop against the dock. Higgins swung the door open and, despite his bulk, leaped gracefully onto the heaving platform while Chambord ran through the routine of shutting down the powerplant.

Quickly the aircraft was secured fore and aft, and the three of us stood on the float, glancing up at the shuttered houses, which cast lengthening shadows across the smooth granite surfaces that formed the bones of the island.

Without a word, Higgins stormed off the dock and hurried toward the dwellings. He quickly circled the two log buildings, stopping in front of Mayfield's home to yell at Chambord.

"No problems. Looks like they came through the winter okay. No signs of break-ins. Let's start that damned generator and get the hell out of here. Tell the kid to hustle his ass up. He'd better watch us start that son of a bitch to running."

Without waiting for a response, the burly copilot disappeared in the direction of a low, unpainted shed behind Mayfield's place. Feeling useless and foolish, I watched the hostile Higgins until my reverie was interrupted by Chambord.

His face held an apologetic smile. "I'm sorry about Earl, Wilhite. He is a strange duck—not the greatest fellow in the world—but he is a hell of a pilot. Up here in the woods, being able to handle a plane well is a lot more important than having a nice smile. Usually Earl flies freight, and Reggie and I ferry people."

He trudged up the rocky face toward the shed into which Higgins had disappeared, with me trailing behind. At the top of the island's crest was a squat, bulky object, maybe ten feet across and twelve feet high, swathed in layers of stained canvas. My bewilderment was momentary. It had to be the satellite antenna, heavily shielded against the ravages of the Arctic winter.

By the time the pilots checked out the wiring, connected the fuel line between a fuel drum on the rack and the generator, and coerced the balky motor into turning over and coughing to life, thirty minutes had passed. Higgins's already savage mood wasn't helped by fooling with the machinery. With the generator finally running smoothly, the burly aviator grinned at me, a mocking smirk, really, and headed for the dock.

As I started after him to retrieve my gear from the plane, Chambord caught me by the arm.

"Linc, these people that are using Bengston's house this summer—the Delvecchios—are supposed to fly in day after tomorrow about noon. Since Earl and I will be north of here, Reggie—he's our other pilot—will be bringing them in the big plane—the Beechcraft. You can be on the lookout for them.

"I don't guess there's any advice I can give you about getting things opened up. Hell, the only reason that I know how to start that damned generator is because there isn't a fishing camp in the whole North Country that doesn't have one of the bastards, and every one of them is as contrary as hell. You probably know as much as I do about getting things in shape.

"I'll be back here ten days from today, flying the Beechcraft. I'll have a load of gasoline and propane and some of the food stores, so you had better be ready for a good afternoon's work.

"One last thing, Linc. Mayfield doesn't have a radio transmitter. He did at one time, but he got mad at some of his guests because they were using it for personal messages, so he finally sold it. Personally, I think it was a stupid thing to do. Too many things can go wrong up here in the woods—especially when you have a group of older men.

"You might remember this. If there's trouble—I mean the kind where you need immediate help—light a signal fire down by the dock. Build as big a fire as you can. If you hear a plane coming over in the daytime, light it and put green brush on it to produce plenty of smoke. If it's at night, have a stack of nice dry driftwood to throw on it. That stuff burns like crazy. A large fire is pretty much of a universal distress signal in this country. It is best to be prepared because you can never tell what might go wrong in the woods."

Mustard Chambord extended his hand to shake before heading down the grade to the aircraft. Higgins was awaiting us, hands on hips, legs braced wide apart, before the open door of the cockpit. At his feet lay my duffel bag and the faded canvas bicycle bag in which the revolver was packed.

He yelled at me in that whiskey-roughened, hateful voice. "Hey, kid! Here's your stuff."

He wound up and threw the bicycle bag as hard as he could, sailing it over my outstretched arms. It skidded to a stop against the foot of the porch. Picking up the duffel bag he hefted it above his head. Smirking, he threw it barely far enough that it landed mostly on shore but with the rear edge in the water.

He was laughing hard and loud as he clambered through the narrow opening into the cockpit. Chambord untied the fore and aft lines securing the aircraft and, raising his arm in a last farewell, followed Higgins into the plane.

The engine came to life with a roar that overwhelmed the hushed tones of wavelets lapping the shores of Stone Warrior Island. The Cessna turned in a flurry of blue smoke and crawled out into the open water of midlake with Higgins as pilot.

It roared down the lake in front of me, throwing rooster tails of spray high into the wind and struggled into the air, disappearing over the tall trees at the end of the lake. I waited, unmoving, until the sound of its engine faded to inaudibility, and then retrieved my duffel bag.

I sank down onto the dock, drained suddenly with the excitement of the trip behind me. Several minutes must have passed before it dawned on me that something was wrong.

For a moment my mind sought a reason for my uneasiness, but then I realized it was the quietness. The only sound was the soft play of water teasing the bare shore, but overriding that was a wrap of eerie silence that Stone Warrior Island wore like a shroud.

Reluctantly I rose, turning to face the empty houses.

Chapter
NINE

Their desolate facades were enough to send me hurrying up the granite slab, anxious to be sheltered behind civilized walls. On the porch there was a sickening moment of uncertainty before my fingers closed on the key ring in my pocket. I opened the front door, aware of the musty, confined air rushing out past me.

The interior of the narrow room was dark behind the heavy wood shutters over the windows. It was of an odd shape, unusually long with three windows piercing the long wall toward the other house. The chamber's opposite side was an unbroken expanse without doors. The only doorways were the one on to the porch and another at the far end from where I stood. It led into the rest of the house. To the right of the front door, a smoke-darkened fireplace took up most of the front wall, precluding a window that would have looked out on the porch and the lake beyond.

The space was sparsely furnished with a single upholstered chair whose fabric confessed to hard and careless use, a battered game table shoved into the corner, a wooden end table, and an extra-long sofa. It was a place for kids and roughhousing, toys, and games—not a traditional living room. Surprisingly enough, there was no television set.

I made my way through the darkened area and stepped into the kitchen, brighter because of the light filtering through its ill-fitting shutters. At the rear of the kitchen another doorway opened out on to a large sunporch. The glassed-in space held a cozy warmth, the residue of the day's sun heat that had penetrated its many dusty windowpanes. The left side of the porch had been partitioned off to form the small cubicle that was to be mine.

The windows were without shades or drapes. It looked as if the handyman was to be one of the sources of idle titillation for the guests—either that or dress and undress in the dark. A single bed, more like a cot, a chest of drawers, and an upright closet-chest left little room in which to move around.

I reentered the kitchen. The room was dominated by two huge upright freezers and an equally large refrigerator, gleaming white boxes lined up in a row. A butcher-block table in the middle of the room served as a work table and a place for a quick cup of coffee. Next to the door from the living room, a narrow staircase with a stoutly built banister climbed to the upper floor. To the side of the staircase a passageway provided access to the other half of the downstairs. The short corridor opened into the sizable dining room, housing a long refectory table sandwiched between twin hutches.

A doorway at the front of the dining area discharged into a huge room that was obviously the activity center of the residence. It shared the front of the building with the room I had first entered but was over twice as wide. This area was furnished as a luxurious den, full of leather furniture squatting on a thick beige carpet, with a massive stone fireplace and a well-stocked bar, flanked by a large projection television. On the long interior wall was an array of storage cabinets whose glass faces revealed several multiband radios and cassette players. I leaned over to pull a cassette player from the cabinet, only to discover that the sliding glass panel was locked. My entertainment for the next ten days would consist of reading and watching television.

At first it puzzled me that there was no passageway between the living room and these delightful quarters, full of the smells of leather and polished wood. But then the answer dawned on me. Mayfield had built his imposing vacation chalet both as a family retreat and as a place for conducting business. The den was the rallying point for his associates. Here they could be isolated, cajoled, wined, and dined. It was a luxurious oasis for weary tycoons while the wives and children had the rest of the island as their domain.

I turned back toward the stairway, determined to explore the rest of the house before dark. The crated safe was at the top of the stairs, resting a couple of feet back from the topmost tread, its gray steel sides peeking through raw wood crating material. On the second floor, a hall ran the length of the building with bedrooms and a bathroom opening off each side. A pull-down staircase in the ceiling led to the attic, empty save for a color television and six double decked bunk beds, clustered around the stairway. No doubt, it served as a children's dormitory when the house was full of guests.

It was growing late, and by the time my tour ended back in the kitchen, the room was quite dim. Casually, I flipped the switch for the overhead light fixture. It was such a habitual act that it took several seconds to register that nothing had happened. My suddenly interested fingers flipped the switch again, and then several times in growing exasperation. Still nothing!

Tugging the beaded chain switch on the light over the sink brought the same result. Now, no longer casual at the lack of response, I opened the refrigerator door and turned up the thermostat. There was no welcome hum to pacify my anxious ears.

"Oh, no, not this," I thought. "Something's wrong with the blasted generator."

Yet its steady rhythm was clearly audible from inside the house.

Was my welcome to Stone Warrior to include living here for ten tiresome days without lights or power? However foolish it seemed, the thought of wandering around this lonely wilderness home in a primordial blackness, unrelieved by some distant glow that promised the presence of civilization, was a disquieting one.

There had to be oil lanterns stored somewhere. After what Chambord had said about generators, there must be times when it went on the blink. I needed to search the storage sheds behind the house for oil lamps before the long-lived northern twilight gave way to night.

I hurried out to the porch. The sun, now a low-lying ball of fiercest red, nestled on the dark comb-edge of pines and spruce that bordered the dusky far shore of the lake. The blues of the lake and greens of the high timber were gone now, and both water and forest were shrouded in a purplish haze. The wind had dropped, and a long bright streak of crimson ran in a wavering line over the cold waters of Stone Warrior Lake from sun to shore.

I was reluctant to move toward the shed, dreading the discovery that Mayfield had no emergency lights. Instead, I walked down to the dock and sat, peering morosely at the darkening horizon of trackless forest. To my left, in the woods beyond the Bengston home, I could see two goshawks stirring around their high nests as they began to settle in for the night. The gentle swaying of the floating platform in the glassy swells soothed me, so I stretched out flat. The warmth of my sweater felt good in the damp air flowing across the water. The gentle breeze fanned the flushed heat from my tired face. The sensation of motion faded away.

I awoke abruptly and sought my watch. Thirty minutes had passed. The sun was out of sight now, leaving the western sky a crazy quilt of purple clouds, trimmed in irridescent gold, splashed about a pinkish-orange horizon. My stupidity in falling asleep had cost me precious minutes. I was bewildered. How on earth could I, as anxious as I was about the lights, have gone to sleep?

I trotted up the grade between the two houses to the generator shed. Its rhythmic pulsing was comforting. It seemed alive and familiar, a parody of the prenatal heartbeat.

The interior of the shed was so dim it was difficult to see what might be tucked away in there, but luckily, I noticed a large pasteboard box in the corner. One of the flaps was up, and I saw the distinctive top of an oil lamp. I tugged the carton free of the clutter around it and dragged it out of the shed to where I could see into it. The contents confirmed that there were times when the generator proved less than reliable. The carton held several dust coated lanterns and an assortment of candlesticks, ranging from cheap tin chambersticks to a tall and ornate but tarnished bronze pair that had seen far better days. There were dozens of candles, ranging from elegant tapers to squat plumbers' candles.

Grabbing two of the oil lamps, I held them up to the fading light and saw that their reservoirs were full of oil. As I slid the box back into the shed my gaze chanced on the electrical conduits from the generator. They ran along the wall to a metal box that I had not noticed during my time in the shed with the pilots.

Knowing nothing about electricity but my curiosity piqued, I set the lamps down and opened the metal box. It contained two circuit breakers. The feeble light of a match revealed that one was marked Bengston and the other Mayfield. Uncertainty caused me to hesitate, not sure whether to fool with them. Then I thought, "To heck with it. Things couldn't get much worse."

The switches snapped shut, one after the other. Nothing happened. I started to push them back to their original positions but decided to wait until morning to study the problem. Slamming the covers shut, I grabbed the lamps.

As soon as I stepped out of the shed, I could see the glow of an electric light in the kitchen and breathed a sigh of relief. The circuit breakers had done the trick, after all. Placing the lamps back in the carton, I hurried down the slope toward the front porch.

Entering the dark front room, I groped along the wall until my hand found the light switch. The living room came alive with a soft glow. For the first time since landing, I relaxed, soothed by the comfortable familiarity of artificial lighting. My first few hours on the island had created a peculiar tension in me.

I felt tired after the long Thursday—too tired to cook. Dinner was no more than a quick snack concocted from the canned goods stored in the cupboards. The eating took as little time as the fixing had. My appetite appeased, fatigue began to take its toll, making it hard to keep my eyes open. The dirty dishes remained in the sink to await the priming of the water pump on the morrow. The urge grew strong in me to take a last look at my surroundings from the porch before retiring. I experienced a fleeting moment of hesitation before opening the door. After all, a nice well-lit living room has a familiar comforting feeling to it the world over. I wasn't sure how I would like strolling around Stone Warrior in the dark.

The round bowl of night sky was cloud-free and moonless, and a far-flung sprawl of stars glittered above the far rim of the lake. The water heaved fitfully along the island's edge. The pure ebony of the sky was unique—the first time I had ever seen the heavens without the glow of artificial lights somewhere on the horizon. It was an unsummoned and vivid reminder of the distance separating me from my fellow man. The bush pilot's comment, "two hundred miles from the nearest help," crept unbidden into my thoughts.

Uncomfortable with the memory, I peered down the shoreline toward the tip of the island. The ominous mass of thick woods behind the bare shoreline was a ragged black wall against the night sky. Remembering Klugg's story stirred a need in me to search the woods' silent front for movement. Annoyed with myself, I moved across to the other end of the porch toward the Bengston house.

It was uncomfortable walking those few steps, as though eyes were watching me from that impenetrable barricade of trees. The disturbing thought caused me to turn for a second look, first at the woods and then at the rock slab beyond the building. The scattered dark shapes, which had been low shrubs growing in isolated pockets of soil when viewed in the afternoon, huddled like phantoms as immobile as stone on the rock face. I knew I was being ridiculous, letting my fantasies run wild like that.

My imagination was certainly yielding to the isolation and to Mayfield's book of supernatural nonsense. Taking a deep breath of the oxygen-rich air, I stepped across to the rail facing Bengston's house. Fear arced through me like an electric current, leaving me weak in the knees.

Chapter TEN

The house next door, which should have been a bulky silhouette against the star-filled sky, was marred by bright streaks of light outlining the shuttered window of one of the second floor rooms. An electric bulb was burning in that tightly sealed, supposedly deserted residence.

Blinking my eyes did nothing to wipe away the unwelcome sight. The night, so hushed only moments ago, now seemed noisy with the sound of the water lapping on the lake's margin. It was easy to wonder if the splashing wavelets masked other sounds—sounds that one should be aware of.

I forced myself to look away, scanning the ground stretching beyond the ends of the Bengston house, but my gaze hurried back to the shuttered window. Nothing had changed. The pencil strokes of light were unwavering in their intensity. Nothing was moving between the window and the source of the illumination. With a shudder, I retreated into the dubious comfort of the Mayfield living room, softly closing the door behind me and locking it.

Flipping off the light switch, I stumbled through the dark into the kitchen to peer at the suddenly sinister residence through the shuttered window above the sink. No quick explanation came to mind.

Who in the devil could be in Bengston's? Could it be some vagrant who had wintered on the island? But why, if the visitor was willing to announce his presence by turning on a light, didn't he come out into the open? No one could be on Stone Warrior without knowing that a plane had landed and someone had remained behind. It didn't make sense.

Fear and indecision held me in the unlit kitchen for several minutes. Then I remembered something that Mayfield had said. He had told me to check both houses after the electricity was restored on the off-chance that switches had been left on when his group departed the island last fall. I tried it on for size. It was the simple and obvious explanation—a switch not turned off. I wished the light would just go out, and, just as quickly, hoped to heck it wouldn't.

There would be no sleep for me until the mystery was solved. Unbidden, the stories of the island's past came to mind—of the deaths, the terror, and the supernatural things that were said to have walked the island. Angrily, I rejected the nonsense. It was embarrassing for a college-educated man in the twentieth century to allow such wild tales to linger in his mind.

Stone Warrior had lured me north with the promise of adventure, but it had not been my intention to receive my full share the very first night. Unfortunately, the only thing to do was to go next door and flip the light off.

A search of the packed duffel bag, conducted in the dark, yielded my flashlight. From the canvas bike bag I extracted the .32, reinserted the firing pin, and loaded it. A lot of folks back in Washington would have been getting their jollies if they could see me arming myself to walk next door and turn off an electric switch.

I slipped out the front door into an outdoors that hadn't become any more cheerful during my brief time inside.

The confidence developed inside those four walls vanished in a twinkling. The dark encirclement of trees, the bare stony slab, faintly reflecting the night sky, and the sullen, heaving surface of the lake were like a vast arena awaiting another of those ancient bloody dramas that had been played out more than once on the death-ridden island.

At that moment, I started to dislike Stone Warrior Island, a feeling that was to grow ever more intense. It seemed always to be waiting and watching. Waiting for what?

Cautiously, I moved toward the Bengston place. It was probably no more than fifty feet from door to door, yet it took forever to cover the distance. The house sat, enigmatic, passive, behind its shuttered windows, its barely visible entrance beckoning me to—what?

The house lacked a porch, so the wood treads rose abruptly to the front door. I mounted the three steps as quietly as possible, and rapped tentatively on the wood panel. There was no answer to my knock—nothing but the indefinable and ominous rustling around me, cloaked in a night that was electric with patient expectancy. With a cold chill playing along my back, I struck again at the door, this time much harder than was my intention. The hollow reverberations caromed through the structure's empty confines. The alien sound of my fist had surely been loud enough to summon out whatever might be lurking within its walls.

Feeling foolish at pounding on the door of an empty building, I slipped the key ring from my pocket and began trying the keys in the lock. The third one fit, and the lock turned as easily as if it were freshly oiled. The latch clicked, and I pushed open the door. It swung back and met the wall with a soft thump.

Staring into the dark tunnel of the hall, I called, my voice low, "Anyone here?" and then again, louder, "Hey . . . is anyone here?"

My words carried through the night-veiled spaces with the same hollow resonance my fist had produced. The response was the same; the house remained mute, unchanging.

Snapping on the flashlight, I stepped through the doorway and carefully eased the door shut behind me. The light beam probed a long, straight hall, devoid of furniture.

The two structures weren't built to the same floor plan after all.

At the far end of the passage, a full-width stairway disappeared upward into the shadows cast by the flashlight. Unsettled by the unfamiliarity with the arrangement of rooms, I was sorely tempted to abandon my investigation and retreat to the friendly confines of Mayfield's. After all, it wouldn't break him to have a light burn for a few hours extra. The trouble was I would know what a chicken I had been. So, it was full speed ahead and damn the ghouls and whatever lurked inside.

The air in the hall had a closed-in staleness that was unpleasant to the nose. The two doors on the right side of the passage were shut. On the left was an open doorway, black and gaping. I hesitated, reluctant to expose myself to its menacing obscurity. But then, annoyed again at my timidity, I stepped inside and swept the room with the torch's rays. This living room, unlike Mayfield's, was obviously used as a family center.

Farther down the hall, another opening on the left, near the stairway landing, led into the kitchen.

Reaching the foot of the stairs, I thought to myself, *Oh, boy, this is where the real fun starts*.

There were three steps and a wide landing where the stairs reversed their direction to complete the journey upstairs. I crept up those first steps to the landing and paused there, listening. The silence in the building was absolute. There were none of the strange noises with which older houses complain of their age in the dead of night. There were not even the teasing sounds of busy teeth where rodents live out their lives in the walls.

Uneasy with the stillness, I started to climb the rest of the stairs, staying close to the widewall to lessen the inevitable protest of the treads under the sudden stress. My foot was on the top step when, from somewhere below me near the bottom of the stairs, a board popped.

I froze for a split second, turning slowly to scan the steps below me. Empty! It had been a compressed board belatedly releasing the strain of my weight.

The air was even more fusty on the second story, and the passage held an uncomfortable warmth from the day. Halfway down the hall, on the right side, the unshaded glare from an electric bulb spilled out on to the dust-frosted floor.

Embarrassed but unable to stop myself, I pulled the nickel-plated revolver from my belt. The cold, deadly weight of the weapon a comfort in my hand, I crept toward the lighted doorway, my throat dry. It might not have bothered Rod or someone like him to stalk through that lonely dwelling, but I was flat-out afraid and willing to admit it.

Taking a deep, shuddering breath, I stepped through the doorway into the light. The harsh glare concealed nothing in the tiny bedroom.

It was unoccupied. The drawers of the small white dresser and chest were pulled open to reveal empty interiors, and the mattress was bare under the brightness of the naked bulb in the overhead socket. The glass shade from the light fixture rested on top of the chest. A small closet space to the side was doorless and open to scrutiny. The floor beneath the old-fashioned iron bed was bare except for a thin film of dust and a few dust devils tucked against the legs.

Sighing with relief, I backed out the doorway and, without thinking, flipped the light switch. Instantly the bedroom and hall vanished into a stygian gloom. Startled, I spun the cool cylinder of the flashlight in my hand, feeling for its switch. It came close to crashing on to the floor. Although my panicky fingers were like ten thumbs, I finally located the button.

I should have checked the rest of the upstairs, but the panic had been too strong. I was anxious to get out into the open air.

The trip down the stairs went much faster than the trip up. A current of moist outside air brushed me as I reentered the downstairs corridor. Startled, I directed the flashlight beam down the long hall. Where the front door should have been was a dark rectangle of night. Somehow it had swung open during my exploration upstairs.

I tried to remember if I had closed it firmly. Either way, it had opened itself or had been opened. The flowing air would have been noticeable if it had come ajar before I climbed the stairs. The last thought of lingering to make a thorough examination of the place vanished with the discovery of the open portal.

I did pause at the entrance to the living room and, sliding my hand along its side, found the light switch. The room burst into view. It had about the same dimensions as Mayfield's den except for the den's greater width. At the far end was a fireplace of the same stone as the one at Mayfield's, and next to it was a twenty-five-inch console television. Near me at the back of the room was a long sofa. Large recliners, worn and dissimilar in style, flanked the sofa along the side walls, together with an odd assortment of straight-backed wood chairs from long disbanded dining room sets. The house was probably the final depository of all the discarded furniture from Bengston's Seattle home.

Somewhat tranquilized by the sight of such an ordinary, back-home room, I flipped off the light and left the dwelling, locking the door behind me. Twenty minutes later, I was sound asleep on a porch with walls of windows that looked out onto the rock and woods of the island of the Stone Warriors.

Chapter ELEVEN

The sun on my face, boring in through the east-facing windows of the sunporch, awakened me. Its rays were already warming the small room, making it uncomfortable under the blankets. I knew it was late because the sun was high enough to have topped the crest of the ridge behind the house.

Thinking that had I been back in Sequim this fine Friday morning I would have been making my weekend plans, I straightened my legs, pushing my feet down into the coolness in the corners of the sheets. I sensed immediately that something was wrong. They stung! Pulling my legs free of the sheets, I stared at my feet in bewilderment. They were filthy, and there were several tiny scratches on them. I tried to remember. Had I gotten up and gone to the bathroom during the night? I had been dead tired by the time I got in bed, but still, I wouldn't have thought I would be so exhausted I couldn't remember getting up—and why hadn't I slipped into my shoes? It was strange.

My watch's dial settled into hazy focus—9:04. I shot out of bed, hastily pulling on my clothes. If the Delvecchios arrived on schedule they would be landing in twenty-four hours, and the Bengston place wasn't ready for them.

I stepped out of the cubbyhole and stopped, unable to believe my eyes. The door leading outside from the sunporch stood wide open. The key was in the lock. It had been opened from the inside. I had to have done it, but why couldn't I remember? Would I have left the back entry open, especially after getting the scare of my life next door? Even Marvin Klugg hadn't mentioned that his spirits had him up running around in the middle of the night without knowing it.

I had a hard time making a joke out of it. I had lain there unconscious and helpless for hours, vulnerable to whatever might have found its way through that door.

More than a bit disturbed, I secured the door and tried to stir up some enthusiasm for my first day's labors. A breakfast of canned bacon and powdered eggs proved filling, but not very appetizing. It seemed unlikely that eating would be one of my favorite sports for the summer if much of it was to come from cans.

Trying to put the thoughts of what occurred during the wee hours behind me, I hurried outside, squinting in the glare off the bare rock. The sky was a deep blue, unsullied by pollution. A scattering of white puffy clouds completed the picture postcard look. The wide, unbroken reach of water displayed a stately procession of whitecaps, prompted by the steady wind sweeping across the watery plain from the west.

Alan Mayfield could never be accused of being anything other than a meticulous man, not if that carefully detailed and sequenced list of chores that he had given me in Seattle was any example. Linc Wilhite was about to spend his first full day on Stone Warrior Island as a househusband.

The afternoon before, when I explored the house, it really hadn't appeared all that large, but after I had been working a couple of hours at Mayfield's first task, vacuuming and dusting every square inch of the place, from the first floor to the attic dormitory, it seemed the size of a palace.

Midafternoon found me back in the generator shed, rummaging through stacks of boxes piled high along the back wall, looking for a fresh bottle of window cleaning solution among the supplies.

My schedule began to fall apart. The trouble was that I kept stopping to look through the small but intriguing cartons containing the odds and ends of clutter from Mayfield's years on the island. One little gem I pawed through contained everything from the ridiculous to the sublime and from the obscene to the sacred, with its Fred Flintstone and Barney salt-and-pepper shakers lying next to a sterling silver soup ladle and several other badly tarnished silver serving pieces. Deeper in the carton, a ceramic statue of the Virgin Mary rested atop the deck of dog-eared playing cards decorated on their backs with coyly-posed nudes. Piling a few candles for emergencies atop the box, I set it down outside the sun porch door, with the intention of polishing the silver pieces when I had time.

The last vestiges of Friday's extraordinarily reluctant dusk was fading into night as I finished the final window and hurried out to the shed to store the cleaning supplies. Only then did I realize how dead tired I was. I managed to choke down a canned meat sandwich and headed for bed. I doubt that the Bengston house could have furnished any spectacle as an encore to Thursday night's performance that would have kept me awake a minute longer.

I don't remember my head hitting the pillow, but I don't think I will ever forget waking up in the predawn darkness.

I was lying with my body turned toward the windows, away from the doorway that led toward the kitchen. There was an interval of knowing something was wrong before I woke up enough to open my eyes. I had been frightened the night before when I saw the light in Bengston's, but it was nothing like this.

The cobwebs of sleep disintegrated in a split second, and I was terrified. There was light in the small chamber, a wavering yellow-tinged light. Burning candles were illuminating my quarters. In the reflection from the window glass, I could see that they were resting on the chest of drawers. I needed to turn and look, but I was too afraid of what I might see. When I finally did move, it was with an explosiveness that shot me upright in the bed, my back against the wall, spinning around to stare at the source of light. I was so darned scared my teeth were chattering.

There, on the chest of drawers, were two tall bronze candlesticks, the ones I had seen in the box in the generator shed, each with a long, lighted taper in it. They flanked a small upright object that stood between them. I squinted in the uncertain light, and then I recognized it. It was the small ceramic figurine of the Virgin Mary. Someone—or something—had made a bizarre shrine on the chest while I slept!

All around me were the windows, with their reflections of that horrible little shrine, masking whatever might be watching outside in an impenetrable nothingness. I forced my gaze beyond the candle to the doorway filled with a formless blackness.

Chapter
TWELVE

I don't know how long I lay there, too scared to move, but I'm sure it must have been ten seconds. I couldn't decide what to do, which way to turn, facing dark rooms that might hold who knows what horror. I was so distraught that I toyed with the idea of leaping through the closed window. It was not the thought of injury but the idea that I might be placing myself in the hands of God knows what lurking in the darkness that deterred me. I tried desperately to remember where I had put the bicycle bag with the gun.

Slowly I came to my feet, but once standing, without thinking, I leaped for the light switch. Then, unable to stop myself,

I raced barefoot through the house, downstairs and upstairs, turning lights on and off as I went. Nothing had been disturbed, and the doors and windows, all except one on the upper floor, were locked from the inside.

I had to force myself back to the cubbyhole with its burning candles and the small Madonna. That was when I saw the writing. The figurine was sitting on a sheet of paper, marked with bold strokes from a felt tip pen. Not until I had freed it did I realize the slashes of ink formed a crudely printed message. For a moment I thought I was going to pass out. It read: *May God have mercy on your soul.*

I was so shocked that I was capable of only the slowest physical movements. I blew out the candles, collected the figurine and tapers and carried them across the sun porch to the back door. I opened it, oblivious now of what might be waiting outside, and deposited my load in the carton resting against the rear wall of the house. Locking and bolting the door, I returned to the cubbyhole, folded and refolded the sheet of paper with absurd precision, and carried it into Mayfield's den. I set it afire and watched it turn to ashes in the fireplace.

I sank into the recliner, the one in which I had been reading earlier in the evening, to await the dawn. I was acutely aware of the sounds of the building, cooling in the night air. Idly my glance fell on the tiny pile of ashes and suddenly I shot upright in the chair. The words on the paper—they were verbatim what old man Klugg had said to me before he went back into the store. It meant I had written the note myself—it had to be me. It was beginning to look like the Kluggs were about to send me off the deep end. I leaned back, closed my eyes and tried to remember if I had dreamed during the night.

The next thing I knew the sun was up, bright against the granite beyond the window. With the rising of the sun came the joyous thought that it was Saturday and the Delvecchios would be arriving and I would be alone no longer. I opened the front door and breathed deeply of the breeze coming off the lake. All was quiet except for the sound of the running generator.

Its steady beat drew a pang of guilt from me. Mayfield had given strict orders to run it only twelve hours a day and to make sure that Bengston's relatives understood this. They would have to realize that electricity was a luxury in the wilderness.

I started toward the shed and then changed my mind. It was time to get to work—to avoid a lot of remembering and wondering about what had happened the first two nights. I decided to have the Delvecchios' place ready for them. They would appreciate having the house aired and their deep freeze and refrigerator ready when they arrived. Mayfield surely wouldn't begrudge a bit of extra gasoline to get their equipment down to reasonable operating temperatures. Crossing to the Bengston residence, I entered the hall, leaving the door ajar to allow the breeze to freshen the musty interior.

The place seemed different, more pleasant, in the bright light of morning. Two sets of footprints marred the light film of dust on the stairs, reminders of the unpleasant journey upstairs night before last.

I had switched on the appliances and was turning to leave the kitchen when the front door slammed. I leaped out into the hall and looked down its length. The door was closed—just the opposite of night before last when it had swung open during my investigation of the upstairs. My feelings toward the Bengston domicile underwent another change.

I stalked out of the building, my anger rekindling because the bands of tension were about me again.

It was foolish to be upset about a door. Only—it didn't seem that there was enough wind at the front of the building to slam it. Perhaps Stone Warrior Island was home to the first haunted front door in parapsychological history. I could see Hollywood doing a flick about it. *The Door that Came from Hell*.

The remainder of the morning flew by. That done, it was time to see about clearing the protective wrappings from the satellite antenna. Mayfield was probably right about the Easterners needing television to feel that all was right with the world.

Activating the canvas-shrouded instrument atop the rocky crest, which I had feared might be difficult, turned out to be a piece of cake. Soon the white dish of the antenna was gleaming in the bright morning sun. I connected the cable clamps to the base terminals and jogged back to the house with crossed fingers to check the controls on the TV in Mayfield's den. A hammer-and-saw man isn't of much use when high tech electronics go on the fritz.

I flipped the control switch, moved the directional knob, and saw the arrow on the dial start to revolve. It worked, thank God.

The next item on Mayfield's list was priming the water pump. It must have been my lucky day because it started on the first try. I'd put off doing it yesterday because I knew what a hassle these babies could be. The pump began the task of filling the long-dry water tank, an eleven-hundred-gallon redwood container that stood atop the island's rocky spine thirty yards beyond the Mayfield home and supplied household water to the two residences.

Back inside, I sought a small screwdriver to tighten a connection on the back of the antenna control. In the course of my search I opened a drawer in the den and found, instead, a folded red and white Canadian flag. The flag fluttering in the breeze atop the flagpole would serve to announce that Stone Warrior Island was in business for the summer. The flag raising was a job quickly done. Despite the squealing protest of the rusted pulley atop the pole, the bright banner was soon rippling in the steady wind, a brilliant swatch of red and white against the deep azure of the sky.

With everything in readiness for the arrival of Bengston's relatives, I sank down by the base of the flagpole to soak up the heat of the bright midday sun. It had about reached its apex, and the shadow of the flag flapping in the steady wind stroked my outstretched legs with its dark caress.

If I do say so, young Mr. Wilhite had done a pretty fair morning's work and was feeling rather confident about himself. The initial chores Mayfield had assigned me were finished, and the sense of loneliness that pervaded Stone Warrior had slipped from my mind.

I decided to invest some time in walking the circumference of the island, but that idea turned out to be a bad one. It wasn't quite the stroll I envisioned. Two hundred yards of hard going was enough to persuade me to turn back. Stone Warrior had no beaches. The heavy brush cover that crowded the fringes of the dense woods ran right down to the island's bare granite rim, which plunged abruptly into the deep, clear water. The lake was at its highest level of the year, and the smooth rock strip was quite narrow. At times it was necessary to struggle along through the tough brush that bordered the granite or swing back into the dense timber out of sight of the water. The great expedition would have to await another day.

An alien sound caught my ear as I was retreating toward the house, sweating, my skin stinging from being scratched by the tough brush. Pausing by the flagpole, I listened intently. A faint throbbing was discernible in the distance through the wash of the waves and the rippling of the flag overhead. It grew louder by the moment and was soon recognizable as the sound of a plane's engine.

Before long, toward the southeast, a glittering speck appeared against the sky, quickly growing larger. Gradually the silvery craft lost altitude as it banked toward Stone Warrior Lake. It was a two-engine job, its pontoons easily visible below the fuselage. It had to be Chambord's Beechcraft, bearing the Delvecchios.

Not wanting to be caught standing on the shore, gawking at my new neighbors like a nerd, I retreated to the porch. I guess it isn't hard to tell how shy I am.

The plane flew past, directly above the far shore. After making a long, sweeping turn north of the lake, it glided down onto the surface, dropping with a huge splash into the sharply pitching waves. The Beechcraft lost the momentum of its landing and, its engines roaring, plowed awkwardly down the lake, the pontoons sending white sprays of water past the tail of the glistening metallic craft. As it came even with the dock, the plane turned and slowly approached, lurching sluggishly in the grip of the ever roughening waves.

The Beechcraft's movements made me aware that the wind had been steadily freshening for the last two hours. It was beginning to look as if the later part of the afternoons were always this way at Stone Warrior Lake. The plans I had made back home for canoeing up and down the lake like some frontier character out of *The Last of the Mohicans* didn't include a desperate struggle to stay afloat in a chaos of wind-churned seas.

I ducked inside, shutting out the sight of the plane drifting in against the dock. The Delvecchios would have to wait a while to see their fellow castaway. Besides, it was time to make an inventory of the pantry supplies.

There was nothing in the stored foods to make me think the menus would be any better until Chambord ferried in the perishable stores for the freezers. It was a pretty safe bet that the steaks and similar goodies would arrive only when the boss did.

As I worked, the sounds of the Delvecchios' arrival floated through the closed window of the kitchen: the excited whoops and yells, the shouted commands, the thud of running feet, and the scuffing of boxes. The clatter of the plane's pontoons bouncing against the fenders of the landing stage supplied a counterpoint to the bustle of human activity.

Still reluctant to intrude on the boisterous scene outside, I found the hammer and, climbing the stairs, set to work uncrating the safe. It turned out to be a more tedious job than it first appeared. The strongbox was sealed with a combination of staples, steel banding, and nails, but, finally, it was freed.

As I tottered downstairs shortly after three o'clock, my arms overflowing with the crating material, the whine of the plane's props turning over drifted into the house. The engines awoke to a splattering of rapid backfires. I squeezed through the front door with the tangle of banding and wood strips to find the Beechcraft about fifty feet out from shore, swinging its tail toward me. The prop wash of the engines swept over me on the porch.

A tall, big-boned man, clad in a loud sport shirt, stood balanced on the slowly heaving dock. Unaware of me, he was watching the plane as it moved away, waddling through the rough water toward its takeoff point.

The plane reached the middle of the lake and taxied sluggishly, its wings dipping crazily, down the choppy surface toward the southern end. About a mile and a half below the island, the twin-engined craft turned and began its straining, jolting run to gain takeoff speed, bouncing wildly, throwing towering sheets of sparkling water into the air. Finally, it broke free of the water's rough embrace and rose awkwardly into the air. The sound of the laboring engines rumbled across the lake as the plane disappeared over Stone Warrior's northern rim. My respect for bush pilots increases every time I watch a takeoff run.

The sound of the Beechcraft receded quickly. Delvecchio, sensing that he was being observed, turned and saw me standing on the porch. After a momentary hesitation he raised his arm in casual greeting.

As I approached, he smiled, revealing brilliant white teeth, contrasted against his smooth olive complexion. He outweighed me by forty pounds and was at least three inches taller. He was a man of forty-five who wore his age well.

Delvecchio hurried forward in ground-devouring strides, his arm extended long before he reached me. Swallowing my hand in his own, he said, "Hey, you must be the college guy that Gene was telling me about. I'm Pete Delvecchio. Glad to know you. Your name is . . . ah . . . ah, Willhoit?"

"That's Wilhite. Linc Wilhite. I'm glad to see you made it all right. I did my best to get your place aired out this morning, but I only arrived myself late day before yesterday. There hasn't been much chance to organize things yet."

The big man roared in a booming voice that was flavored with more than a trace of an Italian accent. "Hey, forget it, guy. After all, there's only one of you, and I brought a hardworking wife and a bunch of kids. Don't you worry about us. We'll have this place squared away in jig time. Just you wait.

"By God, this is beautiful country, Willhoit. I thought northern New York was great, but I've never seen anything like this. You know, if that bunch of characters back in Syracuse could see me now! There is no other place on earth that has the woods and the fishing water this country has—and without people bumping into you all the time. That's the trouble with New York. Every place you go there are swarms of them. Even when you think you're in the deep woods, you bump into a bunch of wiseacres."

I looked beyond Delvecchio's imposing figure to the bulky pile of nondescript boxes and cartons on the dock. His family must have brought enough gear to spend the whole summer, rather than a month. The canoe was the real showstopper of the pile. It was a brand new birch bark job, a gleaming white number that pretty obviously had never touched water. A garish red and blue logo on the side near the bow proclaimed it to be a "Genuine Indian Joe" product. I wondered what Delvecchio would think if he knew that Mayfield and Bengston had a whole shed full of canoes on the island. He didn't seem to know a heck of a lot more than the typical tenderfoot wandering around Olympic National Park.

"Mr. Delvecchio, I would be happy to give you a hand with carrying your gear inside. I don't have anything to do that can't be put off until later."

He shook his massive head emphatically. "No, no. Like I said, the unpacking will keep the kids and me busy for the rest of the day. One thing a man learns, my boy—keep youngsters busy, and they stay out of mischief.

"Hey—look there!" He pointed toward the Bengston house, where a tall, Junoesque blonde about his own age had emerged to pose on the steps, arms akimbo, eyeing a boy of some ten or eleven years, who was trudging across the rock face, carrying one small box. I expected Delvecchio's wife to lapse into a Wagnerian aria at any moment. She sure looked like Brunhilde—if Brunhilde ever wore slacks.

Without preamble, Pete Delvecchio grabbed me by the shoulder and propelled me toward her. A second look at the scowling Amazon convinced me she could also portray a female warden in a Nazi concentration camp movie.

Delvecchio roared in my ear. "Hey, Dolores! Here's our neighbor. Come over here and meet him."

The big blonde hissed at the small boy who was just passing her, wearing a woebegone expression. "Rick, you might as well quit sulking. The sooner we get all the stuff in, the sooner you can explore the island. I told you that."

Giving him a backhanded pat on the butt, she came down the steps into the bright sunlight, squinting nearsightedly through the glare.

Delvecchio yelled at her. "Dolores, why in the name of God don't you put on your glasses so you can see where the hell we are? I want you to meet young . . . your name is Willhoit, right?"

I hoped the Amazon had a lot better memory than her husband. "I'm Linc Wilhite. I'm glad to meet you, Mrs. Delvecchio."

I gave her my best courtly bow, just in case the family were into "old country" etiquette. Sudden recognition crossed her face, a countenance suddenly wreathed in smiles. "Oh, you're the college kid that Gene told us about. I'm so glad you're here. Daughters get fidgety, you know, especially in the wilds like this, without any boys about."

Chapter
THIRTEEN

After a bit of small talk about the vagaries of the trip from the East, Mrs. Delvecchio retreated toward the steps, pleading the need to unpack their baggage and start on the house cleaning. Inspired, no doubt, by my woeful tale of powdered eggs and canned bacon, she promised several times that a dinner invitation would be forthcoming as soon as she had things organized well enough to find the pots and pans. The temptation of fresh food was too great for me to play hard to get.

Delvecchio watched his wife's massive buttocks sway back and forth up the steps and through the doorway and commented, "That's a fine woman, Willhoit. It hasn't been easy. I'm a pharmaceutical supply salesman back in Syracuse, and God knows I've had my ups and downs with the job over the years. You'd think it would be a steady business, but it isn't —too damned much competition these days, and too many new products.

"I'll tell you another thing. Raising kids today is a hell of a job. That little woman has been the glue that's held this family together through thick and thin. By the way, I want you to meet the younger members of the Delvecchio clan."

He roared again, "Rick! Get your little fanny over here!"

The boy, having absorbed the admonition from his mother, had increased the size of the loads he was ferrying into the house but had compensated by walking even more slowly, managing to scuff his feet on the granite with every step. He looked speculatively at his father as though judging whether it was safe to ignore him and keep walking, then set the carton of bedding down, tugged at a pair of shorts that threatened momentarily to depart his slender hips, and skipped across the intervening space to stop obediently in front of his hulking father, eyes downcast.

Delvecchio ruffled the boy's tangled hair with a beefy hand. "Rick, I want you to meet Willhoit—Mr. Willhoit to you, buddy. He's going to be our neighbor for the next three weeks, and I've got a hunch that if you treat him okay, this guy can probably show you something about fishing this country."

The boy's answer was to make a face at his father and then look at me, his face pink with embarrassment. His reply was barely audible. "Hi, Mr. Willhoit."

Squeezing the boy's slender body against his own, Delvecchio said, "Actually, his name is Rico, but kids these days don't like the names their fathers give them. He wants to be called Rick, so what can I do? Now, get your little butt moving and pack those boxes into the house for your mother— you hear? When Papa gets through talking, he'll give you a hand."

As the boy turned to leave, his father gave him an open-palmed whack across his small bottom. Apparently, the Delvecchios were butt patters from way back. The youngster, eager to escape, ran back and picked up the box, continuing his measured procession toward the house, a fascinated observer of his shadow, writhing along the ground before him.

Delvecchio watched his son's lackadaisical portage with fondness until the boy disappeared into the interior. He gave me a big wink as though to assure me that the boy was actually a real go-getter when he wasn't putting on an act for strangers.

My new neighbor pivoted in a circle, his eyes scanning the area around the dock and along the slab, and then glanced toward the second floor of the Bengston dwelling. His very glance seemed enough to produce results.

One of the upstairs windows opened, and a young, long-

haired blonde girl, about fourteen, leaned out, vigorously
shaking a small rug against the side of the house. She was
unaware of our scrutiny, her eyes tightly shut against the dust
from the rug.

I gawked, struck dumb by the familiar gesture. It was the
way Laurie always acted, squenching her eyes when she
shook out a rug. Not that this child looked at all like her.

Even now, when I picture Laurie, it is as I saw her the day I
met her, sitting on her porch. She had luxuriant, light brown
hair, which she always wore in girlish pigtails, and a nice,
pixieish face, but, in honesty, she wasn't a beauty. Laurie
wasn't particularly well built, and she always dressed conser-
vatively in sweaters and lacy blouses. She had a smile that
would explode in a sunburst of joy, the kind of smile that is
contagious. When she grinned, her light green eyes would
dance with delight, and dimples would deepen in her cheeks.
She had a way of cocking her head to listen, as though she
were hearing the most important words in the world.

That was my Laurie.

Delvecchio's voice blasted me out of my reverie. "Hey,
Teresa! I want you to meet someone."

A scowl flitted across the attractive little face as she looked
down, startled. Her voice, thinned by the steady wind, protested, "Papa, it's Terry. Honestly!"

Delvecchio shook his head emphatically. "Okay . . . okay
. . . excuse me for living. It's Terry—Ricky, Mickie, Terry.
Tell me, Wilhoit, why are they ashamed of their names?

"Anyway, Miss Delvecchio, I want you to meet Linc Willhoit. He's the college guy that's going to be staying here this
summer."

One hand whisked the dangling rug back through the window with alacrity while the other hurried to smooth the wind-
tossed hair. A soft smile bloomed on her fresh young face as
she called down to me, "Hi, Linc. Glad to know you. I'll run
down and introduce myself properly when I can get away
from these slave drivers."

It wasn't the kind of little girl's greeting that I expected.
Maybe the invigorating atmosphere of Stone Warrior was
making me look younger or the young lady had some unusu-

ally precocious ideas. Perhaps New York girls are a bit more mature in their mannerisms than western girls.

Further speculation on the regional mores of nymphets was brought to a halt by Delvecchio's trumpet of a voice exploding in my ear again. "Listen. As long as we're talking names, I'd better tell you straight out—I want to be called Pete. Don't you give me any of that Mr. Delvecchio bullshit, buddy, until you can show me that you're a better man than I am."

He looked at his watch. "Hey, now, I can't stand out here shooting the breeze all day. I have to get busy and stow all this junk away, especially my worry case."

He pointed toward an oversized black attaché case which rested near the steps, its chrome latches glittering in the strong sunlight. "We call it my worry case—my wife and I—because I have to be so damned careful with it. It contains my samples of what they call controlled substances—you know —narcotics. I've also got a few compounds in there that are toxic as hell if you overdose on them. I meant to leave the damned thing at the office before we took off, but I forgot. I sure wasn't going to risk leaving it at the house, so there was nothing to do but drag the damned thing all the way up here with us. I'm always worried about losing the son of a bitch. I'd be busy for a month, making out reports for the cops.

"By the way, what's your line of work? You know, what did you study in school?"

"Forest entomology—the study of insect life in the forests. I had hoped to gather some specimens for my collection up here, but so far, things have been kinda hectic. Maybe after I get settled into a routine I will have time to work on it."

It was rather apparent that Pete didn't think too much of devoting one's labors to bugs. He had started to walk away, his attention focused on the black bag, when he remembered something and turned back toward me. "By the way, Willhoit, I don't plan on giving these kids of mine any time to get bored during our month here. We'll be on the move every minute. This is going to be an experience they'll tell their grandchildren about. As a matter of fact, the day after tomorrow I plan to take the whole crew across the lake to the mainland and do some camping out in tents. We didn't fly three thousand miles to sit on our buns in a damned house. I made sure we brought everything we need: tents, sleeping bags, gasoline stoves—the works.

"Hey, any advice you can give me is welcome because—I admit it—I don't know my way around a real wilderness, but I want to learn. Hell, I spend a lot of time outdoors—hunting and fishing—in New York, but I figure that isn't anything compared to this. I wouldn't want to run into any trouble by not knowing what I'm doing."

I could recognize a trap when I saw one. As a new employee at Olympic, the tourists had done the same thing to me. A little advice here and there soon ended with them walking away and leaving me to babysit their kids. Old Lincoln was in danger of becoming scoutmaster to young Rick.

"Listen, Mr. Delve—Pete," I protested. "You probably know as much about this country as I do. This is my first trip up here, too."

My attention was distracted by the sight of Terry leaning out the upstairs window again and spreading her arms in a gesture of despair, as though to sympathize with me for being in her father's clutches. Delvecchio, sensing my distraction, reached out and grabbed my shoulder, spinning me in the direction of the dock.

"Hey, Linc, don't pay no attention to the girl. What do you think of that canoe there? It's genuine birch bark, you know. I bought that baby in Saskatoon. The man in the shop guaranteed it was made by real Indians. The bush pilots tried to talk me out of buying it—said that they had plenty of canoes here on the island—but I figured since I had made this long a trip, I wanted the kids to experience the real McCoy. With these damned aluminum and canvas jobs they have today, there's no way they can get an appreciation of what it was like for the Indians who lived here in the old days. Well, I guess I'd better get that baby in the water and let it soak. I'll see you later, guy."

I smiled at his retreating back. These people were exactly like the tourists back at Olympic. The gift shop owners could sell the poor devils anything. If I had brought along some mugs labeled Stone Warrior Island, Brunhilde would have owned a dozen before dark. It was a sure bet that the lake was about to see the first birch-bark canoe that had ever plied its surface.

An hour later, shortly before seven o'clock, I remembered that the Delvecchios hadn't been told Mayfield's rules for the generator. They wouldn't realize that the island didn't have twenty-four-hour-a-day power like Syracuse. Delvecchio was no longer in sight, so the only thing to do was walk over and tell them.

I had crossed the open space between the two houses and was at the foot of the steps when my Wagnerian neighbor popped out the front door as if she had been shot through it. She confronted me, arms on hips and legs widespread.

It was hard to avoid the impression that she was barring my way, despite the smile and quiet, "Yes?"

Dolores Delvecchio didn't seem particularly interested in my twice repeated explanation about the electricity. She appeared more concerned with what sounded like a donnybrook among the kids within the house. I decided it might be better to explain to her husband and, without thinking, mounted the first step.

Her hand came up hard against my chest. There was no question about it now. She had hurried out the door for the specific purpose of barring me from her home.

I thought *To heck with this!* and, mumbling something to the effect that I would talk to her husband about it later, retreated to the friendlier confines of my own dwelling.

I wondered if I had inherited a family of snooty people who thought they were better than the hired hand. Of course, Mrs. D. would be perfectly willing to talk to the help sometime tomorrow when she discovered there was no power.

Not anxious to get rebuffed again, I decided, on my own, to try to remember to turn the power on by seven each evening. After all, with four mouths to feed, it would take the Delvecchios much longer than it did me to prepare meals.

I walked up the slope to the shed to switch on the generator. From the open window of their kitchen came the clash and rattle of pots and pans. Mama Delvecchio was preparing to cook the first family meal on Stone Warrior.

They were apparently a little more sophisticated about portable electrical systems than Mayfield had given them credit

for. I was no more than out of the shed when their house came
alive with lights flaring on and off all over the building. It was
Saturday Night Live at the Delvecchios.

It seemed likely that the Delvecchios might be a bit more
obtrusive than Mayfield had supposed. Not that Pete Delvecchio didn't appear both enthusiastic and pleasant enough, but
the family would probably want to keep as many of the comforts of civilization around them as they could. Mustard
Chambord's ancedote about Mayfield getting angry over the
use of his short-wave radio didn't bode well for the future.
The new neighbors might well be viewed by my boss with the
same jaundiced eye.

From somewhere behind me, I heard a strange whirring
noise and spun around in time to see the antenna disk, a dark
circle against the fading light of late afternoon, slowly rotat-
ing toward the south. The Delvecchios had managed in six
hours to discover and exploit all the island's civilized amenities. I decided it was time for me to attend to my culinary
duties.

Rising from the table after another delightful repast of
canned goods, I wandered restlessly through the silent house.
With the coming of dark the memories of what had happened
Friday night became vivid again. I admitted to myself I was
going to put off going to bed as long as I could. It took little
time to discover that my fears about a scarcity of reading
material were ill founded. Scattered in small drifts throughout
the bedrooms and in the den were dozens of paperbacks of
every genre, from smut to Spock. I chose a Dorothy Sayers
mystery and looked for a good spot to curl up.

The choice was easy. Mayfield's luxurious den offered posh
leather chairs and good reading lamps. Besides, Linc Wilhite
would probably be an infrequent visitor to the den, once the
boss and his bigshot buddies arrived.

Despite the convoluted plot twistings of Sayers's tale, the
temptation grew strong to close my eyes and drift off to sleep
under the bright circle of light that was the sole illumination in
the dark room. I was tempted to remain there and sleep in the
chair with the light on, but I knew if I did I would dread that
cubbyhole the rest of the summer. Delvecchio had said he

wanted new experiences. I was willing to share mine. At ten-thirty I knew I could put it off no longer. I headed for bed.

I moved across the living room to check the front door and then for several minutes stood watching the bright spills of light streaming from the windows in the other residence. The Delvecchios apparently didn't care for Stone Warrior's brand of darkness.

Even if they did cause some headaches during their stay, it was nice to have other people close at hand.

Later, in bed, the memory returned of how the Bengston residence had looked the night of my arrival, vacant, with that solitary light shining from the upstairs bedroom, beckoning me into its silent chambers. As unpleasant as such thoughts were, it was better than thinking about the door to the sun-porch that had stood open all night and much, much better than remembering the burning candles and that figurine. I slept very poorly, coming awake time after time, bathed in sweat, listening, looking.

Chapter *FOURTEEN*

By breakfast time I felt much better about the scares I had experienced. There is something about having other people around that does wonders for one's sense of perspective. Though I had been shaken at finding the back door wide open, leaving me vulnerable in a strange house in strange territory, I had obviously been so exhausted after the trip that I had wandered around dazed after going to the bathroom—dazed and confused by the unfamiliar surroundings. The adventure with the candles and religious statue needed more thought. I had not dreamed it. The Madonna and tapers were there to see, resting in the carton outside the rear door. I must have written the note since it had Klugg's words on it, and if I did that I must have set up the candles. But why?

Sunday midmorning found me tired but busy at another of Mayfield's high-priority jobs—replacing the weakened boards of the deck. This had to be done before the plane arrived with the drums of fuel. Besides, it would keep me within sight of the Delvecchios if they needed help.

It was a slow, awkward job because of the difficulty in getting at the nails holding the old, half-rotted planks. Another gourmet breakfast of powdered eggs stirring uneasily in my midriff did little to help. The morning was well along when, startled, I looked up to see Delvecchio standing over me. His approach had been masked by the hammering and the clanking of the steel drums supporting the platform as they jostled against its underside.

The interruption was welcome since my hand was trembling from all the nail driving. Delvecchio looked down at me, a more distracted man than the happy warrior I had seen the day before. His salutation seemed forced today, unlike the spontaneous greeting of yesterday.

"Hey, Willhoit, I see you're hard at work. You're just the kind of guy I'd like to take back to Syracuse with me. Know what I mean?"

I decided to give it one last try. "That's Wilhite, sir."

He shrugged as if to ask, "What's in a name," and continued, "Have you ever been in upstate New York, guy? Some fine country back there, I tell you."

"Afraid not, Mr. Delvec . . . er, Pete. The only time I like to see snow is when I drive up into the mountains to ski."

Delvecchio, wearing a pair of polyester slacks and a Godawful Hawaiian shirt, seated himself beside me, letting his sandal-clad feet dangle over the edge of the boards, barely above the slow heavings of the subdued lake. He grew silent, as though he was trying to reach some sort of decision. His mind made up, he stared hard at me, his smile fading into a somber, haunted look that aged his craggy face.

"To tell you the truth, buddy, now that I am here, this trip doesn't seem as good an idea as it did when we were planning it back in Syracuse. The oldest—she's been in the hospital for over a year. We thought when she got out it would be good for her to look forward to a trip to some faraway place, rather than just going back home into the same old grind.

"I thought this place would really be great—all the fresh air and none of those heartless punks around to make thoughtless remarks—the good, clean water to swim and fish in—all the land on earth to camp in. But it's beginning to look as if old Pete made a hell of a mistake. It's been nothing but sheer hell since we walked into that house over there.

"I guess it would have been better to have stayed home in Syracuse. At least it couldn't be any worse. There's probably a sense of security in coming back to an old familiar place. Sure, young kids can adjust to a change of scenery—maybe even look forward to it—but when they're older, about grown, they get settled in their ways like adults. All she wants to do is get back to what she knows—what she remembers.

"Well, whether we screwed up or not, we'll have to make the best of it for these four weeks. It must sound odd to hear a salesman say this when he faces pressure having to find new customers and make new sales every day of his life, but it's not that easy to stay relaxed when you're dealing with your own family.

"I'm a family man. Sure, I may go out hunting and fishing with the boys once in a while and raise a little hell on occasion—a few beers and all that—but I'm a damned good provider. You know what I mean?

"I love my kids. I try to do what's right for them. But how in hell does a man always know what is right? Damn it! There's so much pressure on the young ones today, with all the drugs and drinking and the sex and being asked to make adult decisions before they are out on their own. Hell, you're young. You tell me—how in the name of God does a man know what to do?"

I wondered for a second if it was a rhetorical question or if he expected a reply. But Delvecchio was peering expectantly at me. He wanted an answer. I felt like laughing or something. It was ironic that he would query me, of all people, about youngsters who had problems during their teen years.

He had come to the right source to find out about screwed-up teenagers and, for that matter, screwed-up adults. My relationship with my father had cost me the joys of youth.

I was a subservient child in an unpleasant home in Astoria, anxious to please. It was my fate that in me, the younger son, my father saw the academic bent that could grant him a second vicarious chance at whatever thwarted dreams he nurtured. It was my fate, and perhaps my mother's, that somewhere along the way he transcended the bounds of normalcy and drove me finally to a nervous breakdown. He took my youth from me, but he gained nothing by it.

My father crushed an eight-year-old Linc who played too long at his first birthday party, who wet himself and endured a public humiliation by his dad before his thoughtlessly cruel playmates. When I was sixteen he brutally whipped me before my girlfriend and her father because I couldn't protect her from the sight of a rape committed by my father's drunken twenty-one-year-old second cousin during a double date. That was the first time I tried to fight back. A fractured jaw was my reward for that.

I still remember clearly the night I wrecked the car, swerving to avoid a deer on a dark, rain-swept road. Afterward, Father called all my friends' parents and told them what had happened. He made sure that I would never be allowed to drive any of my friends' cars.

But Pete Delvecchio didn't want to hear about my problems, so I shrugged and replied, "I don't know what to say, Mr. Delvecchio. I can't help you. Shoot, there are people who will tell you that I'm just as fouled up as anybody. All a man can do is what he thinks is right, and he can't be held accountable for more than that."

My new neighbor came to his feet with an infinite weariness, leaned over, and gripped my shoulder with his powerful hand. "Hey, young fellow, I didn't mean to wish all my troubles on you. It's just that life gets a little discouraging once in a while. A man has to be a tough paisano to survive."

Delvecchio was struggling to shake off his feeling of despair. "Well, if you miss us tomorrow, we'll be camped out on the mainland—somewhere along there on the south end where the map shows a creek coming in. I plan on camping out for three days and doing some stream fishing.

"I didn't know the sun comes up in this country as early as it does. We were up most of the night. The sky was growing light before two-thirty, so I imagine we'll be on our way by four or so. I'm going to find out if the money I forked out to teach the wife and kids to handle a canoe was worth it. The swimming lessons will come in handy if they capsize the damned things. So either way I win, eh?"

He started to walk away but paused. "Listen, Willhoit, the little woman plans to have you over for a get-acquainted meal tonight. I thought we should all get to know each other a little better before the Delvecchio clan disappears into the woods. She'll probably come over or send one of the kids to let you know as soon as she's sure she can put a decent dinner on the table.

"Well, see you later, buddy. Save some room for the wife's cooking. It's nothing fancy, but she makes the best damned pasta in Syracuse."

Grinning at his ill-concealed pride in Brunhilde, the big man shambled back up the slope and disappeared into the shadowed interior of the Bengston home. There was weariness in every step, and his shoulders were sagging. I wondered what his problem was—all that talk about his kids. He obviously had slept very little the night before. Maybe Rod was right; he contended that every family had its share of troubles. It was just that outsiders didn't always know it.

Picking up the hammer, I turned my attention to the stubborn decking. Boards were more easily dealt with than human frailties.

Early Sunday afternoon found me clinging perilously to the steeply pitched roof of the Mayfield chalet, replacing weather-damaged wood shingles. I scrambled about my precarious perch, trying to hang on to the hammer and push the bundle of shingles ahead of me without plunging to the granite below, cursing Mayfield for not having a metal roof like most vacation homes in Washington.

From time to time I would pause to watch the pair of goshawks in their high nest beyond the Bengston place. Despite the thick woods there were surprisingly few birds visible. I thought I saw several belted kingfishers and a couple of Trail's flycatchers as well as a few others that I was unfamiliar with. I wasn't even sure about the identification of the flycatcher.

My lofty perch offered an excellent position to observe what was happening with the neighbors. There was very little activity, especially considering that they were to be off on their camping trip at dawn's first light. Midway through the afternoon, Rick and Terry climbed the slope to the satellite antenna, circled it a couple of times in a cursory inspection, and then wandered over the granite ridge to disappear into the dense woodland beyond. Precocious Terry, noticing that I was watching them, waved vigorously just before they vanished among the trees.

Still later, Delvecchio himself came out and charged up the grade between the houses without noticing me watching him from my lofty aerie. He went into the low shed where the canoes were stored and, a few minutes later, came back down the rocky pitch, his head hidden beneath a red canvas canoe carried atop his shoulders. He placed it in the water, where it rested next to the birch bark canoe, floating some ten yards from the dock in a tiny indentation in the shoreline.

With half the roof repaired, I was about to call it quits when the two youngsters reappeared and trailed single file past the antenna. Rick stopped and looked up at me. "Hey, mister!"

I yelled back, "Yeah, Ricky, what do you want?"

"What will you do if a bear gets after us?"

"Don't worry. There are no bears in this country."

It didn't satisfy him. "But what if there was?"

"Well, I've got a pistol to protect us. I would shoot him."

His "Oh" suggested I had given the right answer. He marched on into the house without acknowledging me further.

Terry stopped, obviously prepared for a lengthy conversation despite the handicap of elevation and distance, but her plans were thwarted when her mother came out onto the front steps and yelled at her, ordering her to start sweeping. Terry stalked angrily past her statuesque mother, her face red, and disappeared inside.

Mrs. Delvecchio remained outside, looking up at me until I disappeared across the roof peak and cautiously slithered down the steep incline to where the ladder rested against the far side of the building. As I descended it, it shuddered under my weight and that of the wood slabs balanced on my shoulder.

Rounding the corner of the house, I dumped the shingles by the porch and looked up to see the stately Dolores come off her front steps and stride purposely toward me. Unlike the watchdog belligerence that she had exhibited earlier, she had a pleasant smile on her attractive face.

My dinner invitation was on its way.

Chapter
FIFTEEN

I found myself sitting on one of the thigh-high boulders scattered over the flat granite shelf at the tip of the island, my feet bare inches from the tiny wavelets rolling up on to the rock. It was full dark, and a cold breeze was finding its way through my thin wool shirt. I must have been sitting there a long time, for my buttocks ached. Shivering, hungry, and weary, I climbed to my feet, overwhelmed by the desire to be inside and tucked into the warmth of my bed.

When the Delvecchios saw the lights on in the Mayfield house, they might decide to come over and apologize. If they did, it would be a futile quest. Their excuses were going to fall on deaf ears. We might be stuck on Stone Warrior Island together, but they were no longer welcome around me—not after what they did.

Mrs. Delvecchio had been all smiles when she met me with her dinner invitation. What a hypocrite she turned out to be! To this day, her words and that purr in her voice remain crystal clear in my memory.

"Oh, Linc, we do want you to come over and have a bite to eat with us as soon as you clean up. I know you must be too tired to fix yourself much of anything after scrambling around on that roof all afternoon. Besides, I'll admit to being a little selfish in asking you. The kids will enjoy it a lot more if they have someone younger than Pete and I to be with while we're here. It won't be anything fancy—just some good, solid Italian cooking."

Of course, the invitation was enough to cause me to revise my earlier impression of the lady, who had practically thrown me off her steps. Gullible as always, I felt pleased to be making friends so quickly with the family. She departed with my assurances that the generator would be turned on immediately, in case she needed extra time.

Pete Delvecchio was standing at the front door, waiting for me, when I arrived. Grabbing my arm in his big mitt, he propelled me into an interior filled with the roar of the television, the shrill chatter of female voices, and the rattle of kitchen utensils.

"Hey, guy, chow is almost ready," he announced in that stentorian voice of his. "If you're like most fellows your age, you're more interested in food than small talk, so let's go right on into the dining room."

While we sat at the table talking, the mouth-watering aroma of cooking food drifted in from the passageway. Terry appeared in the doorway, suddenly shy, looking domestic with a long blue apron tied about her waist. It didn't take long to discover the source of her shyness. Her father kidded her incessantly in my presence. Thinking back to the conversation we had that morning about his troubles, I decided that Papa Delvecchio didn't understand how sensitive a girl could be at that age. It probably caused a lot of the hassles in their household. Terry finally gave up trying to squeeze into the conversation, cast me a last appealing look, and vanished in the direction of the kitchen, only to reappear a moment later to set out a carafe of wine and a small bowl of grated Parmesan. She muttered, "The rolls," and scurried out again.

Mrs. D., resplendent in a white peasant blouse and dark skirt, dashed in, carrying a big bowl of fettucini and a bread basket. Placing them on the table, she called sharply to Rick, who grudgingly abandoned his post in front of the television and appeared at the door of the dining room.

"Rick, run upstairs and tell your sister we're ready to eat."

He had been gone from the room less than a minute when

his shrill, excited voice called from upstairs. "Mom! Mom! Come here—quick!"

Her face chalky, Mrs. Delvecchio let the wicker basket of rolls crash onto the table, sending the brown rounds scattering across the white tablecloth. She ran heavily down the hall as Pete Delvecchio shot to his feet and, yelling, "Pardon me, Willhoit," rushed from the room.

The house jarred with the weight of running footfalls in the hallway above my head. Then, Terry and Ricky, their faces intense, careened past the doorway, racing for the front door.

Seconds later, their mother, breathing heavily, poked her head into the dining room. "I'm sorry, Mr. Wilhite, but you have to go home. We can't feed you now."

I tried to grin, not sure whether she meant it or even how to react to her unexpected comment. No one had ever invited me to dinner before and then thrown me out. I decided to make a joke out of it. "Sorry, ma'am, when you invite a Wilhite to dinner, you have to feed him before you get rid of him."

Then Pete Delvecchio appeared beside his wife and swept her out of the doorway with one arm, shouting, "Don't waste time arguing with the goddamned idiot, Dolores!"

He glared at me. "Go home! You can't stay here. Get the hell out, like she asked you!"

Whirling, he pounded down the hallway after his wife and out the front door, leaving me alone, reeling from the impact of his words.

Waves of humiliation came crashing down on me. I tried to tell myself that it didn't matter what these rude slobs thought, that they were like—like my father.

I knew I had to get out of there. All I could think of was my father—those god-awful memories of a life of bitter humiliations. I remember grabbing a chair and throwing it out of my way, but what happened was just what Dr. Molloy had said would occur if I were put under too much stress. I blacked out. I must have fled from the house and down to the rocky point immediately. I vaguely recall running out the front door.

Obviously, several hours had passed while I sat on that boulder in deep emotional shock. A glance at my watch confirmed that it had been five hours since dinner was scheduled at the Delvecchios'.

Reluctantly I headed back along the boulder-strewn shoreline to the house. My quarters were dark, but the other dwelling displayed several lighted windows. Apparently my neighbors had resolved their problems—never mind that they had talked to me the way you wouldn't talk to your pet dog.

Reaching the bare rock, I moved cross-slope, keeping the Mayfield residence between me and the Delvecchios'. They were not going to have the pleasure of seeing me slinking back into my own place. I unlocked the front door as quietly as possible.

Later, in the unlit living room, I sat before a small fire of damaged shingles and crating from the safe. Sitting in the dark, watching the moving brush of firelight painting its quick strokes on the far wall, I unwound a bit. My thoughts turned to the puzzling chain of events that had occurred with the Delvecchios that afternoon.

In retrospect it seemed that the ruckus had little if anything to do with me. The woman might have been truly distraught when she asked me to leave. Maybe my reply had been too flippant, or it seemed to them like I was being a smart aleck. It had all happened so quickly I hadn't known what to say. Nobody had ever ordered me out of their house before. It would take more thinking about it to decide whether Pete Delvecchio could be excused for what he said in the midst of that bizarre scene.

Whatever happened, they were going to have to make the first overture. After all, an invited guest had been insulted, and it was their place to explain why.

Despite the drained feeling that followed my emotional outburst, my stomach was grumbling at being neglected since lunchtime. Reluctantly, I left the warmth of the flame-lit living room to find something that would ease my hunger pangs without the need to be cooked.

I stumbled about in the shadowy kitchen, lit only by the distant fireplace, for some reason unwilling to signal my return by switching on the lights. Peanut butter and jelly, spread on the last of the cold hard biscuits from breakfast, established a truce with my stomach. The food so revived my flagging energy that I went into the den and mixed an old-fashioned.

Back in the front room, the last of the flames still licked

fitfully at the glowing remnants of wood in the fireplace. I dropped into the big chair by the window, where by sitting upright I had a clear view across the sill into the Delvecchios' living quarters.

The dim overhead globe was the only light burning there or, at least, the only one I could spot. Pete and his wife were sitting on the sofa in line with the window, intent on the television at the far end of the room. They had recovered in a hurry from whatever had upset them that afternoon—a lot bigger hurry than I had.

The variations of light from the television reflected against their faces and the cream-papered walls of their quarters. By leaning forward, it was possible to see the upstairs windows, where lights went on fitfully as the kids moved about the residence.

With the fire nothing more than a few glowing red coals, I yawned loudly and stretched, peering out for a last look before going to bed. The drink had wrought its effect on me, and now my only thought was of climbing into the sack for a good night's sleep.

The act of standing up brought the blonde head and shoulders of the precocious Terry into view. She was curled up in the big recliner at the side of the room, near the doorway to the hall, as engrossed in the boob tube as her parents. Beyond her, in the dark hallway, I thought I saw some movement, no doubt the boy wandering around during a commercial break.

Why should I let the Delvecchios hurt my feelings? The man was a loudmouth, unable to get along with his kids by his own admission, and without the slightest idea of how to be courteous to visitors. They were a family with nothing better to do than stare at the TV or argue with each other.

My anxiety somewhat alleviated, I headed for the dubious comforts of my little cubicle on the many-windowed porch. Despite its exposure to the night sky, the sunporch was as dark as the kitchen.

There was no inkling anything was wrong in my cubbyhole until I felt for the blanket to pull it down and discovered several shirts and pairs of jeans lying across the bed.

My mother's injunctions about putting my clothes away had stuck with me over the years. Even in this tiny space, the only clothing not stowed away each day was my pajamas. In addition to the clothes on the bed, most of the rest of my gear was strewn about the floor.

My resolution not to reveal myself to the neighbors was forgotten. I turned on the light, revealing the room to be in a shambles. All the drawers were standing open, and the duffel bag was draped across the chest of drawers, emptied of the dirty clothes I had been stowing in it.

Remembering the revolver, I frantically sought the bicycle bag. It had been tossed into the other corner of the tiny cubicle. I slipped my hand inside. It was empty!

They had taken my revolver! It had to be the Delvecchios; no one else was on the island.

Hoping against hope that they had done no more than examine it and put it down somewhere in the house, I hurried out of my quarters toward the kitchen. As I did, I saw it, in the spill of light from the cubbyhole. The revolver was lying in the middle of the sunporch floor. With suddenly awkward hands, I flipped open the cylinder and muttered, "Thank God." The six blunt-nosed rounds still rested safely in their chambers.

My return from the island's tip must have surprised them in the act of rummaging through my belongings. Could they have ducked out the back way when they heard me unlock the front door? I started toward the rear entry to check it out, but stumbled over something in the shadows. My groping hand closed on my specimen case, open on the floor. I couldn't believe their arrogance. Rising to my feet, I grabbed the doorknob.

It wouldn't open. Fumbling in my pocket, I extracted the key and fitted it into the lock. Even unlocked, it still wouldn't yield to my tugging. Chagrined, I thought of the hand bolt and slid it back. The opened portal revealed empty ground between the house and sheds. I relocked and bolted the door.

This was another explanation that they owed me. It might be petty of me, but Mayfield would hear about everything that had gone on.

The need to sleep was still strong. Hurriedly, I tidied up my quarters and climbed into bed, but not before secreting the revolver under my pillow and shoving the specimen case into the far corner under the bed to conceal it from any future forays by the Delvecchios. It would be hard to spot unless an intruder knew where to look.

Once in bed with the covers over me, feeling the dank, woodsy smell of chilly air across my face, I slid my hand from under the blankets and trailed it across the top of the old antique wooden box, perhaps the prize of all my possessions. I was glad they hadn't damaged it.

My fingertips traced the gouges in the smooth, worn top where my name was etched into the wood. The touch of that fine old chest was a security blanket to me—you know, like it was something I could count on, something that would never betray me. While I was still in high school, first interested in entomology, Dr. Harmon, our next door neighbor, had given me the antique specimen case. He had used it as a college student.

Self-conscious about my need for a symbolic amulet, I tucked my hand back under the covers. Sunday had been a disaster. Soon I was sound asleep.

Chapter *SIXTEEN*

It seemed no more than a few minutes before the obnoxious clamor of the alarm clock intruded on my rest. I must have slept deeply, yet there was little energy in my awakening. It was 6:00 A.M. and as cold as the devil in that tiny room. The many windows were misted over, casting a frosty gloom over the cubicle.

Monday was the sort of day that prompted my thirty-second dressing drill, perfected in two years of chilly mornings in the Grand Tetons and at Olympic. The fury of my quick dressing warmed me enough to face the prospect of dashing out the back door to the shed to shut down the generator for the day.

Back inside, I made my way into the living room. Opening the front door to allow the chilly air to dilute the acrid after-smell of the burned-out fire, I looked out on to the damp boards of the porch. At 6:00 A.M. in this northern latitude, the sun was usually well above the horizon, yet the light was subdued, almost like dawn. The lake lay quiescent under a low-lying blanket of fog that hung just above the mirror-smooth darkness of its surface.

It was the first time the island had been completely free of wind. The fog bank was all around the place, so wet that moisture was dripping from the eaves. The Bengston house was a gloomy, silent hulk looming out of the thick mist, its dark windows opaque screens masking the interior. Beyond the building the border of dense growth faded in and out of view through drifting patches of fog. It was like a setting for a Poe short story. Shuddering, I retreated into the front room.

It was a good day for some gourmet breakfast goody that could make me forget the surrealistic landscape awaiting me beyond the log walls. The nearest thing I had to exotic was canned pancakes.

I had awakened, gripped by a fatigue that contradicted what had been an uninterrupted night's sleep, but the moving about, preparing breakfast, slowly brought me out of my strange lethargy. Since the weather was doing little to invite me outside, it appeared to be a good day to tackle the job of painting the kitchen and sunporch. I headed up the grade, hoping that the paint would be easy to locate among the untidy stacks of supplies in the shed. The fog was lifting rapidly, forming a thin haze overhead, pierced by a faint and watery sun whose ennui appeared to match my own.

Framed by the doorway of the shed, the Bengston residence appeared lifeless under the anemic midmorning sun, its windows tightly closed. Apparently Delvecchio had managed to herd his family into the canoes for their little expedition without creating enough disturbance to awaken me. it was best that way, with them leaving so early. I wasn't sure I was ready yet to meet them face to face, even to hear an apology. Now there would be three days to forgive and forget.

I brought the paint down the hill by the direct route between the two homes. A glance at the tiny bay beside the dock where the canoes had been drawn up the night before confirmed that the Delvecchios were truly gone and not sleeping late. The tiny inlet's surface, dark green under the haze, was free of the small craft.

Once again, the strange, brooding presence of Stone Warrior Island was mine alone to experience. It was odd how quickly the island could impose its unpleasant mood on me after the others departed, leaving me alone to sample the atmosphere of the death-haunted strip of land.

Having exhausted all the rationalizations for not starting the painting job, I buckled down to the task before midday. For some reason I found myself half-expecting—even wishing—to hear Pete Delvecchio's shouted commands, the kids' protests, and the general excitement of the clan returning—especially after our talking about his offspring's not being overjoyed by the challenge of roughing it in the wilderness.

The painting was finished by midafternoon, leaving me with nothing to do but eat a bit of lunch and then prowl restlessly through the house, unwilling to read or watch TV.

There was something about the ambience of the place that was bothering me. The light conditions had changed since breakfast. Curious, I walked out onto the porch.

The breeze was returning, gusting but steadily building in velocity. Even as I watched, the surface of the lake grew more agitated. The wind carried the faint musty smell of rain. A watery sun was still visible in the southwestern sky, but the high haze had thickened appreciably. Off to the west, a low battlement of darkish gray clouds stretched along the horizon. They were the first clouds I had seen at Stone Warrior that held the threat of rain. There was more movement about the island now. It looked alive, with the pines and spruces in constant motion.

Watching the commotion about me, I perceived that the uncanny silence that had bothered me from the moment of my arrival had vanished and that the wind now carried a strange unceasing note, a tone that shifted continuously in pitch and volume. There was no mystery about what was causing my now unrelenting, newly sensed aural companion. The humming was the result of the sharp wind whipping through the tops of the thick stand of timber.

Still, I was puzzled. The wind had blown often since my arrival. Why was the strange humming audible for the first time? The trees on the island were exposed to the air currents whenever they swept across the lake.

The gusts soon settled into a steady breeze, and the wailing grew constant, a single monotonous note. Could the bizarre effect somehow be due to the weather change? Stone Warrior's dark forest, singing its mournful dirge, held me a moment longer, feeling the chill, and then a shudder ran through me, sending me back to the cubbyhole for my light jacket.

Far and away the most strenuous job on Mayfield's list was cutting and stacking twelve cords of firewood. After the spring thaw he had flown in a crew of loggers to fell standing dead trees on the main shore and float them out to the island in rafts. This timber was to be cut and split for the woodpile. It seemed a good time to locate the logs and get an idea of how hard the job was going to be. Any task that would distract me from the change in the atmosphere of the island would be welcome.

I chose to take the long way around, following the shore—a route that appeared easier to traverse than at the other end of the island because of the gentle slope of the land. The rocky tip served as the pointed tail of the teardrop-shaped island. It was a bare, almost flat granite surface that slipped under water at the slightest of angles.

Donning my jacket, I set off, passing the rocks where, the night before, I had sat, brooding about my treatment at the hands of the Delvecchios.

Passing the point, I worked my way down the island's far side. The logs had been drawn up above the waterline and lay, tumbled at odd angles, on the sidehill. Cutting and splitting the wood would be a simple task, but carrying it across the ridge, armload by armload, would take several days and plenty of energy.

Standing down by the water's edge, I scanned the hillside above me, anxious for a look at the island's insect life. The more I looked the more puzzled I became. Nothing was moving—no insects, no birds, no small animals. I scanned the tops of the trees carefully. I had not seen a great number of birds around the house, but it defied the bounds of reason that they would be on only the windward side of the island. When I entered the woods beyond Bengston's the morning after my arrival, the gnats had been swarming around my face, and I had seen a few flies and a couple of small anthills, but this hillside appeared devoid of insect life.

About halfway up the slope, a short distance beyond a pile of dead brush in a tiny clearing, lay a tight clump of shrubs. Determined to flush out something in the way of native fauna, I advanced quietly up the hill. Stopping twenty feet short of the clump, I squatted, looking for a pine cone to heave into the shrubbery.

The underlying carpet of pine needles was stained by some brownish substance that had matted the needles together. Noticing the same darkish crust on the cone I had been reaching for, I seized a fallen branch and flipped it aside, uncovering an odd little cylinder some three inches in length that had been concealed by the cone. The shriveled brownish object had a faintly unpleasant odor. Gingerly I picked it up to examine it more closely.

I let out a yell and threw it as far from me as I could. I had picked up a human finger by its mangled end!

Close to being sick at my stomach, I reeled back down the hill to the shore. I was so stunned I stood for several seconds before I realized what I must have found.

Obviously there had been an accident among Mayfield's logging crew. He must have known about it. The least he could have done was warn me. An additional moment's reflection showed me how silly that was. He could have had no idea what happened to the man's finger or that I would find it. The logging crew must have looked without locating it. A chain saw could flip a severed finger thirty or forty feet.

Whatever the explanation, the discovery had effectively quenched my enthusiasm for further exploration. Returning along the shoreline, I found sizable heaps of driftwood scattered along the exposed rim of rock that separated the water from the brushy fringes of the woods. Memories of last night's crackling fire prompted me to carry an armful of the weathered gray wood back to Mayfield's for the evening. I resolved to start on the woodpile bright and early the next morning.

If only the long-idle chain saw would start without a hassle, the task would go quickly, but its use would demand extra care. This was no place to have an accident. The sharp steel teeth could chew their way through a log—or a human limb—in split seconds. The finger I had found was mute evidence of that.

After returning to the house I wolfed down the larger part of a canned picnic ham, and afterwards, sitting at the table and nursing a cup of coffee, I watched the log siding of the Bengston residence redden in the glare of the setting sun that had finally found an opening under the haze. Despite the coffee, my limbs were heavy with fatigue. Staying awake had never been a problem with me, but Stone Warrior Island's air was like a mind-numbing sedative.

Trying to shake off the drowsiness, I decided to build a fire. With a chilly wind still whipping across the island, there were worse things than curling up in an easy chair and watching the flames do their dance in the fireplace. Besides, with darkness coming on, Stone Warrior needed some life and movement, even if it was no more than flames caressing a log. With night would come loneliness and an awareness of the two hundred miles of unforgiving wilderness that separated me from civilization.

The front door opened to a world of wild, glaring, crimson light. The sun was a fierce scarlet ball just above the horizon, shining through the lower fringe of the haze that had kept its filmy embrace about the island all day long.

The side windows of the other building were blinding, blood-red rectangles reflecting the rays of Monday's dying sun. The green of the surrounding brush and thick timber looked black under the ghastly illumination. A coldness worked its way along my spine, prompting me to bring the wood into the house as quickly as possible. Before closing the door, I paused for a last look at that tossing, indifferent aquatic field before me, with its inky, troubled waters stirring uneasily under the strange sky. The disquieting requiem in the island's trees was louder now as the building wind tormented their tops.

The driftwood sprang into fierce life, and I slumped back on the sofa for a minute to relax before having another go at the Sayers novel. Sleep must have overtaken me almost immediately.

My eyes opened to find the room still warm, but the flames had diminished to a bed of glowing ashes. The furnishings were barely discernible in the faint light, and the kitchen beyond the doorway was pitch black.

The outside world was filled with sound. As the webs of sleep fell away, my mind, more alert, began to make sense of it. The wind, a steady breeze when sleep had overcome me, had freshened. An odd, pattering noise added a rhythm to the turmoil of the storm. My momentary confusion quickly vanished. It was the distinct sound of wind-driven rain splatting against the bare surfaces of the slab.

My mouth must have sagged open during my nap because my throat was dry and scratchy. Thirst led me, still half-asleep, into the dark kitchen, stumbling over to the sink to draw a glass of water. My nose, pressed against the cold glass as I stared into the darkness, tingled to the unique smell of wet granite.

A brightness flared before my startled eyes. Directly across from me a light, gleaming wetly on the granite surface, had come on in the other kitchen. The Delvecchios must have noticed the rain coming and raced back across the lake, abandoning their plans to spend the night in tents.

I peeked through the rain-streaked glass into the lighted room. From my vantage point no one was visible. A shift of position brought their living room into view. Its three windows were ablaze with light.

I hurried back into the now dark front room. Only the faintest glow betrayed the dying embers in the fireplace. Staying well away from the glass to avoid light reflecting from my face, I peered through the curtains of hard-driving rain, feeling like a Peeping Tom, but receiving a certain smug satisfaction from the scene before me.

There was a sense of déjà vu about what I saw. The Delvecchios were framed by the window, engrossed, as usual, in the television. I sure had them pegged. These were the kind of people I had read about that were truly addicted to the tube. They probably enjoyed the test patterns.

The family were seated just as they had been the night before, with Papa Delvecchio nearest the window, seated on the sofa. No wonder the kids were antsy about their dad! I had heard of old-line Italian families in which the father was a rigid patriarch. Apparently, Delvecchio had assigned everybody a seat for TV viewing and expected them to stay there.

I shook my head, suddenly appalled at my hypocritical judgment of Pete Delvecchio. Rigid? The man was a reed in the wind compared to the unbending martinet that is my father. Whatever their trouble, the Delvecchios were too much of a family to be involved in the kind of traumas I had endured.

My troubled family life had come to an end, a violent end, one winter night a few blocks off the Oregon State campus. After graduating from high school, still desperate for some crumb of love, I bowed to my father's demand that I undertake a college major for which I had no aptitude. Fruitless study, endless worry, and constant frustration could not stem the tide, and early in my third year, he received the notice of my academic probation. Three nights later, miserable and frightened, I sat across a motel restaurant table from my father and my distraught mother, who couldn't summon the courage to meet my gaze.

It had always been the same. While Father raged at me, she would mutter in intercession, but when he turned his wrath on her, she would look at me with tearful eyes in a mute plea for absolution before shrugging and hurrying after him like a beaten puppy.

That night his accusations began quietly enough, but before long his shouting was the only sound in the hushed dining room. Abruptly he leaped to his feet, reached across the table, and pulled me upright by my hair. "I wish to God you had died the day you were born, you worthless bastard!"

Turning to my mother, he screamed, "My God, Vivian, how could you produce something like this?"

It was the insult to Mother that sent me over the edge. I was confined three months before fully understanding that I had battered him with a chair until his arm and cheekbone were broken and he lay unconscious with a severe concussion. I have not seen him since.

Eleven months later I was released, the nervous breakdown cured, the pain sealed away. I wonder how my life would have developed if I hadn't met Laurie.

No, it was not a charitable attitude I had toward the Delvecchios. Those who live in glass houses have no business throwing stones. I headed for the sunporch.

Putting on my pajamas, I returned to the kitchen to prepare the coffee pot for breakfast. When I finished I flipped off the light, knowing I could not resist a final peek at my neighbors.

A family who could sit as they did for hours on end was beyond my experience. The temptation to return to the front room for a last guilty peek at them proved too great to resist. Linc Wilhite was acting like some nosy crone whose chief recreation was watching the goings and comings of her neighbors.

They had not moved, still staring with rapt attention at the flickering tube. Shifting my position to the side of the window brought Terry into view. She was tucked into the chair again, her head and body relaxed. Yet her eyes were wide open, turned toward the TV set. Idly I wondered where the slow-moving Rick was, and then one of the upstairs lights came on.

"Ask and you shall receive," I said aloud.

Grinning at the inaccurate quotation, Stone Warrior's resident Peeping Tom headed back to bed, pausing by the kitchen window for a last glimpse. Delvecchio-watching had replaced the football game as my favorite Monday night viewing.

From the kitchen window most of the young blonde's upper body could be seen clearly, curled up in the recliner, her cheek resting against its back. But from this position I could no longer see her face, only the back of her head and a little of the side of her attractive little face. Some sort of brown object, barely in view, rested against her knee.

Unable, for the life of me, to figure out what it could be, my curiosity mounted. I started to get a kitchen chair to stand on, but hesitated, ashamed of my abject curiosity.

Then I thought, "Don't be a hypocrite, Wilhite." I grabbed the chair and climbed on it.

From that height, looking downward, the brown object was identifiable as the top of Rick's head. He was sitting on the floor, leaning against Terry's knee.

Remembering the lighted room upstairs brought a momentary surge of indignation at the waste of electricity. But what the heck? The generator didn't cost any more if it ran one light or twenty. A random thought flitted through my mind. Oddly enough, the light burning upstairs was the same one that had frightened me the first night alone on the island.

Chapter
SEVENTEEN

I awoke Tuesday morning, startled, knowing that something had disturbed me. My mind was so dulled by sleep that several seconds passed before I realized it was some change in the outside sounds that had roused me. The rain had stopped while I slept, and now only the diminishing wind remained. The numerals on my watch face fixed the time at 3:00 A.M. I took a deep breath of the damp, chilled air flowing through the narrow opening of the window and rose on my elbow to peer out across the bare rock grade.

Dawn light, more subdued than usual, was giving substance to the shrub-dotted slope. The sky was a dark, metallic gray with a heavy cloak of low-hanging clouds casting a dismal sheen over the wet granite stretching beyond my quarters.

Snuggling back into the warmth of the blankets, I was content to let the chilly air drift past my face. My limbs had grown heavy again when the idea—an absurd idea—began to work on my mind. Could the television fanatics next door have sat up all night watching old movies?

As foolish as the notion was, it brought me out of the warm bed and into my jeans. Slipping my feet into cold tennis shoes, I stalked into the kitchen, but once there tried to resist the impulse to glance out at the other dwelling, keeping my eyes riveted on the floor of the dimly lit room.

The words tumbled out, spoken aloud, "What in heck is wrong with you? If you're stupid enough to climb out of a warm bed to check on the neighbors, go ahead and do it. They're not going to bite you."

Determined to put an end to my asinine curiosity, I peered through the gray world toward their living-room windows. The panes of glass framed a pitch-black interior. The Bengston house was without signs of life. I crossed the living room, faintly illuminated by the pale glow of the cloudy sky, eased the door open, and stepped out onto the porch.

The lake was a sullen, gunmetal color, reflecting the dismal sky. In the fragile light of the rain-drenched dawn, it was hard to see how much wind was at work on the water, but the waves still slapped against the rocky shore. The lake, the shiny wetness of the granite slab, and the dank woods formed a forlorn, dead landscape. There seemed to be no other existence but the dreary world of Stone Warrior Island.

My gaze swung past the dock toward the watery indentation lying in the deep shadows of the high trees. It was too dark to see if their canoes were drawn up on shore. I debated whether to walk down to the tiny bay where they had floated. After all, something might be wrong. Perhaps they had returned last night for some other reason besides the weather.

Delvecchio had struck me as the kind of man who, if he changed his plans, would have felt the need to barge in last night when they returned and explain why they had decided to abandon the camping trip.

I cautiously descended the rain-slicked wood steps and walked quietly across the open slope with the dank breeze against my face. Behind me, the blind, unshaded windows of the Bengston house followed my every movement. There was a crawling at my back. It was a silly thought, but in that ghostly light, the place looked sinister. The temptation was strong to abandon my errand and return to the familiar comfort of the cubbyhole.

From the vantage point of the dock, the indentation where

the canoes had been beached was plainly visible. The shad-owed surface of the tiny inlet was unmarred.

The canoes couldn't have sunk. Pete Delvecchio might have left them upright on shore to fill with water, but he had exhibited enough sense the day before to draw the small craft far enough out of the water to prevent their sinking.

Maybe the family hadn't noticed the rain until the last min-ute and had been routed by its onslaught, abandoning their tents and gear on the mainland. Then, with the rain stopped, they had gone back as soon as it was light to salvage what they could.

I stole another glance at the Bengston residence. That had to be it. The windows were tightly closed. The house had been shut up all day yesterday, so it would have been unpleas-antly warm when they returned. They naturally would have opened the place up last night and would not have closed it up again unless they were going back to their camp. While I didn't care for the feeling of loneliness that being alone on Stone Warrior Island engendered, the knowledge that my odd neighbors had returned to the mainland brought a sense of relief. Three days of solitude until Chambord's return no longer seemed like such an unpleasant interval.

Comforted by the satisfying click of the lock behind me and drowsy again, I retired to my bed on the sunporch, which was beginning to have far too many windows for my comfort. It already had too many bad memories for me—memories of flaring candles in the night and cryptic messages.

I awoke for the second time Tuesday morning to a room filled with light from a bright morning sun. The clouds had disappeared, leaving an unblemished royal blue sky, a blue so intense that it looked as fantastic as something out of a science fiction movie. The sense of foreboding that had led me out-side in the gray dampness of early morning had disappeared, leaving me anxious to be about my chores. Stone Warrior Island was certainly showing how effectively it could affect the moods of its residents.

It took an hour of sorting through a year's accumulation of junk in the shed to find the chain saw. Coaxing the darned thing into running proved as difficult as the generator had. At last it surrendered to my persistence and roared to life, quickly settling into a high-pitched whine.

Turning it off, I slumped down beside the shed for a moment and watched the steady procession of waves across the open lake. The forest on the other side looked unfocused through the diaphanous veils of steaming vapor rising from the sodden forest floor. That far shore was as remote to me as the surface of the moon.

The dully gleaming, deadly looking metal bar of the cutting tool caught my eye, leaving me uncomfortable with the thought of how a blade capable of slicing through dense wood as if it were butter could devastate human flesh. Unbidden, the memories of the severed finger came to mind, and each time it did, my mind's eye shaped that shriveled flesh more horribly than the time before.

Rising, I grabbed the saw and a gallon of gasoline and set off across the ridge to where the great pile of downed logs awaited me.

The sun's heat worked its way through my shirt as I topped the rocky spine of the island. Already the air was far warmer than at any time since my arrival. The night's weather front was bringing unseasonable warmth to Stone Warrior. For a moment I considered going back and opening the windows at Bengston's, but the memory of what they said to me was still too fresh.

I worked steadily through the morning and into early afternoon as the chain saw sliced through log after log, reducing them to fireplace length. Later would come the more arduous task of splitting the wood and lugging it across the knoll to the site of the woodpile.

Five hours passed before the aching muscles in my back and arms convinced me that it was time to stop for the day. It was the kind of fatigue that leads to accidents. This godforsaken island was certainly the last place on earth to be if a running chain came in contact with the fragile flesh of one's leg.

I plopped the saw and gasoline can down on top of a large log jutting out over the steep rock pitch by the water's edge and climbed a short distance up the hillside to flop down and drink the last of my thermos of coffee.

With the high, whining pitch silenced, the quiet in the dense grove was startling. I thought about yesterday's walk around the island tip—how I had made my grisly discovery while trying to catch a glimpse of the island's wildlife. As hard as it was to believe, apparently all the birds had left the island. Could it have something to do with the sound produced by the wind? With the heavy timber and the garbage available during the summers, birds should have been there in large numbers.

Sitting there, turning my head from side to side, searching the treetops above me, I became aware that other sounds were missing, too—the rustling of small creatures on the forest floor and the whirring and buzzing of insects about me. Gradually my ears recovered from the raucous assault of the chain saw, and I knew the silence was not absolute. Above me, the trees softly hummed their funereal air.

I drank the last of the coffee from my thermos and rolled onto my side, eyeing the tall, spindly trunks as they climbed into the sunlight far above my head. Useless, undernourished trees grew by the tens of thousands on Stone Warrior Island, spreading like a malignant growth atop its rocky hide.

A few steps into the island's ill-formed woods carried one into a deep twilight where the fanciful might expect to see the trolls and ogres of childhood fairy tales. Only the lofty sun-stained crowns of the trees hinted at a brighter world.

Fatigued from the wood cutting, I stretched out on the ground, trying to relax, but a vague anxiety thwarted my efforts. If only there were some natural sounds besides that god-awful, eternal humming, something that bespoke of small living creatures.

My skin crawled. The feeling of being watched touched me like a revulsive caress. My efforts to shake the feeling only intensified the chilling awareness.

Three times I reared up on to my elbows and scanned the woods around me. There was nothing to see—only the shadowed emptiness under the forest canopy. I jumped to my feet, suddenly antsy. My intention was to pick up the chain saw and gasoline and take them back to the shed, but it seemed foolish to haul extra gear across the island when it would be needed again tomorrow. So, leaving my tools lying on the overhanging log, I took the long way home around the rocky tip of the island.

My euphoric mood quickly vanished when I reached the dock, and my gaze was drawn to the spot where the Delvecchio canoes had been. It would have been no surprise to see them drawn up on the rock again, but the tiny bay was empty.

Back inside the house, I renewed my assault on the ill-treated Sayers novel. At home I was an avid reader, but here, my attempts to read found me either falling asleep or too restless to concentrate. The same thing happened again. My gaze strayed often from the book, inspecting the nooks and crannies of the den.

Twice my reading was interrupted by a trip into the kitchen to stare out at the Bengston domicile. The windows were still shut, and there was no movement inside or outside the big log structure. It was deadly quiet around the sealed house.

Back in the den, I noticed a pair of powerful binoculars resting on one of the bookcases. Except for the aborted trek the morning after my arrival, I had made no attempt to explore the island. The time had come to brave the brushy barriers and hike the circumference of my estate, using the binoculars to try to locate the Delvecchio camp on the mainland. One never knew when there might be a need for some kind of emergency communication—at least that was the story I tried to sell to myself.

With the binocular case slung around my neck, the great exploration got underway. The afternoon was well along, and the sun was low enough that the shadows were quite elongated.

I paused by the flagpole, binoculars in hand, anxious to get a close look at the goshawks and their nest. I found the nest without trouble but failed to spot the birds although I spent several minutes in a futile quest.

Beyond Bengston's, where the woods grew down to the lake shore, the light effects were striking. The sun was bright against the spindly tree trunks nearest the water's edge, but its light was quickly absorbed by the thickets of crowded spruces climbing the rising ground. The effect was of sun-painted pickets enclosing an enchanted woods under the spell of eternal twilight. It looked like some kind of fairyland.

I had gone only a few yards before it became apparent that the journey was going to be more work than fun. Walking was extremely difficult because the trees and the brush grouped around their bases were no more than six or seven feet from the water. Between the woods and water a scant strip of glass-smooth rock dipped into the water at a thirty-five-degree angle. Many spots were so steep that they could be crossed only by moving fast across the granite; to stop was to slide into the water. The shoreline was spotted with deadfalls and piles of driftwood that necessitated a detour back into the dense grove.

I struggled along the obstacle course that was the shoreline, stopping every few minutes and using the binoculars to search the forested shore across the lake. My visual search was done with great care; I methodically scanned every foot of the far side.

The wind had dropped, as it did every day at about the same time, yet it was still strong enough to create a chop on the surface. The heat was quite noticeable, unseasonably warm for this northern climate.

Nearing the southwest end of the island, I stopped on a spur of rock that jutted out from shore. From that vantage point, almost all the west and south rims of the lake were visible. Again, my search was painstaking. The binoculars found the mouth of the one small stream that ran into Stone Warrior, but there was no sign of my neighbors' camp.

I tried to remember. Had Pete said they planned to stay by the mouth of the stream, or had he said upstream? There was no camp in sight: no canoes, no tents—only the somber green forest enclosing the clear depths of the lake. They must have gone far enough up the creek to be out of sight.

As I was turning away, a limb snapped sharply somewhere behind me. My heart was in my throat for a second. A backward glance at the brightly lit trees, with the shafts of sunlight falling in between them, revealed nothing.

Chapter
EIGHTEEN

I grimaced at my show of nerves and spoke aloud, "Wilhite, you're getting spooky."

Undoubtedly the sharp sound had been that of a dead limb, making its final plunge from one of the tall conifers to the forest floor.

Giving up the search for the Delvecchios' camp, I continued my journey of exploration but was soon brought to a halt. Ahead of me, Stone Warrior's rocky perimeter abruptly changed to a low cliff that continued as far as it was possible to see. My only choices were to turn back or to cut across the ridge top to the other side of the island. I chose to climb the ridge.

A half-dozen steps into the forest brought me into the area of perpetual twilight. A jungle of trees, no thicker in girth than my thigh, were all around me, so close together that it was necessary, at times, to twist sideways to pass between them. There was a gloominess and a smell of moldy, stagnant air that surpassed anything in the fern-choked rain forest of the Olympic Peninsula.

At that moment the noise came again—another sharp, breaking sound, as if something had put weight on a dry branch somewhere behind me. I spun around, trying to spot the source, but it was a futile effort in that thick growth. The countless stunted trunks made it impossible to see farther than twenty or thirty feet.

My heart was pounding, and my breathing was quick and shallow. I longed for the comforting weight of the revolver, but the possibility of encountering dangerous animals had appeared so remote that it seemed foolish to bring it along. At that moment, it was under my pillow back at Mayfield's.

The woods were silent save for Stone Warrior's windsong, faint now in the light breeze. Ahead of me, farther up the hillside, the bright green of sunlit spruces indicated a partial clearing. The tree trunks were much larger and farther apart. The area along the crest was sunny, open ground with a scattering of large trees and tall shrubs.

It was impossible to move without broadcasting my location because of the thick carpet of dead branches and needles underneath. Stopping frequently to listen for furtive noises behind me, I reached the crest and paused to catch my breath.

The clear field of vision made me feel more secure and willing to concede that my imagination might have parlayed two falling limbs into a pursuer. Still, the exploration of Stone Warrior Island had lost its appeal. It was time to get back to Mayfield's, and by the quickest route—along the island's spine. As I turned for a last look before heading home, I thought I saw from the corner of my eye, a human form, someone with long hair, crouched behind a tree trunk!

I looked again—along the slope, quite a ways below and ahead of me. There was nothing to see but the countless tree trunks.

I remained in place, scanning the woods. It had to be my imagination. I was the only live person on the island—but what about those sharp sounds I had heard while scrambling up the hillside?

Then it dawned on me. If I had seen something, it was between me and the houses. Discretion being the better part of valor, I headed down the far slope toward the water. I started walking, but soon I was racing downhill at full speed. My foot hooked under an exposed root and sent me sprawling, sliding along the slick pine needles in a cloud of fine forest debris. I lay there, half stunned. Somewhere behind me, a cannonade of breaking twigs broke the silence.

Pulling myself upright, I stumbled the remaining distance to the shoreline, clutching at low-hanging limbs to save myself from plunging into the lake. Clinging to a tree trunk, gasping for breath, I stared upslope, my ears straining. Only the kiss of water against the shore disturbed the woods. Back in the dark thickets, nothing moved.

An involuntary yelp escaped me as my weight came on my right foot. My ankle had turned awkwardly when my foot hooked the root. Gingerly I put weight on it again. It hurt, but not as badly as before. It was a minor ankle sprain.

I had not chosen the best time to be unarmed and unable to run.

A sturdy tree limb lying nearby made a usable if clumsy crutch to support my tender ankle. It was a difficult enough trip with two good legs. With one, it became a nightmare.

My gaze shifted constantly between the timbered hillside above me and the treacherous underfooting. Once I stopped, sure that I had seen movement on the slope—a flash of white. The wind was rising, stirring the tops of the trees. The sound of the waves slapping the shore was growing in volume. It was becoming too noisy to hear whatever might be in the dense grove above me.

Just when it seemed my flight would never end, the results of my morning's labors came into view along the shadowed sidehill, not forty feet ahead of me. Elated to reach familiar ground, I limped quickly toward the log pile, ignoring the protests of my ankle.

After pausing briefly to rest my throbbing leg, I resumed my trek. My ankle needed to be rested as soon as possible. Before I had taken a half-dozen steps, I remembered the chain saw. The more I thought of it, the more I decided my eyes had deceived me back on the ridge top. Still, it wasn't a bad idea to carry the saw back to the shed and tuck it away out of harm's way. I looked back toward the water's edge where I had left it. There was nothing on the tree trunk!

Blinking my eyes in disbelief, I rushed toward the log overhanging the water, willing the chain saw to materialize. My hands slid frantically along the top of the trunk like those of a blind man. It was a stupid act because its full length was visible. There was nothing on it—no saw, no gasoline.

Fear slammed into me like a fist. A quick search around the down timber yielded no clues as to the fate of the equipment. I wanted desperately to believe that a falling limb, an animal, or some quirk of the wind had somehow swept the saw and gasoline off the log on to the steep, stony rim and into the lake.

The memory of the horror movie about a chain saw massacre swept through my mind. In my imagination the saw was ready to come alive with a roar, with me turning to face a grinning maniac on the slope above me, the ultimate butcher's tool in his hand. Lincoln Wilhite had been seeing too many of the wrong kind of movies.

Then I was running up the hill, ignoring the pain of my sprained ankle, desperate to get into the open. I don't think I can claim bravery as one of my major assets.

Twenty minutes later, I was sitting on the porch steps, the revolver shoved into my waistband, embarrassed at its presence and my own behavior. I had been terrified when I dashed into the house, fleeing from the bogeyman. Now, with a couple of shots of Mayfield's booze warming my insides, I was feeling sure of myself once more, scornful of my earlier fears.

The rapid swing of moods between abject fear and sleepy contentment was a developing source of worry. It wasn't hard to believe that Stone Warrior Island was toying with me— playing with my mind, terrifying me one minute and lulling me into complacency the next . . . readying me for what?

Chapter *NINETEEN*

Unwillingly, my thoughts returned to the family next door. The closed-up building would be like an oven in the warm weather. Maybe it was time to forget yesterday's unfortunate episode. After all, they hadn't been given a chance to explain, and if we hadn't had that run-in, I probably would already have gone over and opened some windows to keep the place comfortable for their return.

Good thoughts turned to good intentions, perhaps thanks to the Wild Turkey, sending Stone Warrior's good samaritan into action. I started to walk right in, but the lifelong conditioning that one doesn't enter others' homes uninvited asserted itself. The sound of my knuckles against the door produced the same odd reverberation it had the first night.

Nothing stirred in the interior.

A second rap, much louder this time, produced no better result. I was feeling sillier by the moment, pounding on the door of a vacant building, carrying a stupid gun in my belt. Why was I knocking? I knew they weren't home when I walked over. Why didn't I go on in?

I vented my embarrassment by shouting at the empty house.

"Hey, is anybody home?"

It met my inquiry with a stony indifference.

"Please . . . is anybody here? I don't want to bother you but I wondered about opening the windows."

The building, Stone Warrior Island, and the whole world remained closed against my pleas. Suddenly, I felt like a complete idiot standing there, begging them to answer me, angry with the Delvecchios for being the kind of people they were, and knowing I was venting my frustration on an empty house. Turning away, I scurried back to Mayfield's, my tail between my legs. Was this the guy that had told Evie how cool he was going to be hobnobbing with the rich and famous?

Later, with the sun a stark iridescent disc in that relentlessly cloudless and strangely colored sky, I sprawled on the dock's rough boards, my earlier fears forgotten, doing a little fishing to supplement the dried and canned diet. My fishing line drew a nubby crease down the wavering red path of sunlight on the dark water. Rafts of water fowl rested on the surface near the mainland shore. It's strange that none of them were close to the island. Up near the north end of the lake, the dark surface held a huge float of what looked like Canadian geese. They formed a ghostly patch of white, drifting through the purplish mist thickening over the lake's surface. My reverie was interrupted as my line twitched and began moving steadily toward deeper water.

Only the slightest incandescent sliver of sun was visible

above the fringed silhouette of the shore when I lifted the dripping stringer with two fat lake trout from the water and ambled up the grade.

Depositing the trout in the kitchen sink, I rushed out back to start the generator. It coughed once but failed to catch. Again and again it refused to start. Darkness was rapidly setting in, honing my nerves to a fine edge.

Finally it came to life, ran smoothly for a hopeful few seconds, then coughed again and shuddered to a stop.

With daylight at a premium, I worked desperately over the generator, trying to check it out like a car motor. Luckily, my first guess was the right one. If the fuel intake hadn't proved to be the problem, there wouldn't have been enough light for a second try. Where the fuel line entered the filter, the copper screen was clogged with fragments of insect nests and bodies. It seemed likely that they had found their way into the disconnected fuel line during the off season and built a nest. Another puzzle! The clogged line offered ample evidence of a healthy insect population on Stone Warrior. What had happened to them?

By the time the tubing was reconnected and the engine primed again, the daylight had vanished, and the sky was deep purple, with a cloudy ornamentation of stars visible overhead. A last desperate try at starting the generator brought it to life. I sighed in relief.

I stepped out of the shed, shutting the door behind me, and gaped at the Bengston house in amazement. The monolithic darkness of the side wall was interrupted by the startling brightness of a lighted upstairs bedroom. The kitchen window flared with light even as I stood there, frozen in my tracks.

God! The Delvecchios were home again. It was beyond belief! How on earth could they have returned without my hearing them—unless they had come back while my ill-fated expedition was under way. But that didn't make sense, either, because I had knocked on their door after my return. First they had showed up at home Monday when they were supposed to be camping, and now Tuesday night!

Had they followed me around the island? Could that have been what made the noises? I was suddenly very uncomfortable in the near-darkness and hurried in the back way, locking and bolting the door behind me. The pain in my ankle, almost forgotten in my earlier euphoria, was back, dull and throbbing.

Twenty minutes later, I was at the table, a barely touched plate of food before me, cooling quickly. I had been ravenously hungry earlier, but after seeing the lights next door, I felt a glacial cold tying my stomach in knots.

There was no rational explanation for their behavior. Was it for my benefit? There must be an answer. The Delvecchios acted as if they wanted to stay out of sight. Maybe they had a good reason to hide—but from whom? With a name like Delvecchio, the guy could be in the Mafia. Possibly they had seen someone on the mainland shore—someone they believed to be after them. But if that were so and they were cornered here, why, for goodness sake, wouldn't Pete Delvecchio have come to me and asked for my help to escape in the canoes?

That line of speculation didn't make any more sense than anything else about them. But it was coming to the point where I had to have some answers or end up as crazy as they were.

It was humiliating for a grown man to sit in the dark, picking at his food, afraid to turn on the lights. At last, disgusted with myself, I rose, slid the dirty dishes into the sink on top of the uncleaned trout, and stalked from the room. The thought of standing at that window, cleaning trout and watching the strange goings-on next door, was more than my ego—pride —whatever you want to call it—could tolerate at that moment.

My restless wanderings carried me through the house—upstairs and dôwn, in and out of every room. I tried to tell myself it was to walk off my frustrations about my neighbors, but in truth, it was as much to check the locks on the windows.

I had had one bad experience with my neighbors and that was enough. I would have to corner Delvecchio and demand an explanation for the family's bizarre behavior. Back home in Washington, it would have been none of my business what they did, but cooped up on a tiny bit of land hundreds of miles from anywhere, people need to feel comfortable with each other. My plan was to stay up and wait for them to start for the canoes—even if it was two or three in the morning. He might tell me to go to hell, but at least I would have put to rest what was becoming an obsession.

Buoyed by my newly found resolution, I slumped on to the sofa in the living room, a vantage point for watching the up-stairs rooms of the house next door. The upper story was in darkness.

It was 11:20 when I settled in, determined to remain there until morning, if necessary.

The minutes of watching became hours, yet the Delvecchios never stirred. Each remained in his or her assigned place in the living room, absorbed in the old "tellie."

My time was divided between sipping coffee and serving as audience to the sideshow next door. Somehow, Pete Delvecchio's profile was different tonight. In a sudden bright burst of light from the screen, the reason became apparent. The puzzling glints against his face were reflections from his perfect white teeth. His lips were drawn back in a grin and his teeth were showing. Beyond his shoulder, the blond amazon Dolores wore the same foolish smile.

It was hard to credit what I was seeing. The smiles lingered on their faces as if they were pasted on. Whatever was on the tube was a source of continuous hilarity.

Finally, disgusted with myself for peeping and at them for their idiosyncrasies, I retired to the den, hoping to distract myself with some late news. The screen blossomed into washes of color that stabilized into the image of a musta-chioed gent, waving his hands toward a sale-priced waterbed. A spin of the dial conjured up a forecaster audibly marveling as the colorful weather map before him underwent electronic transmutations. The sound was faint and distorted, and the weatherman began to disappear under the onslaught of a newsroom snowstorm.

Without thinking, I reached forward and adjusted the an-tenna control, bringing the TV weatherman in out of the cold. It didn't take long to find out that nothing had changed in the outside world. The newsman who followed the forecaster rat-tled off the usual dreary narrative of violence, suffering, crime, and war. I waited out the end of the news program to take a good look at the sexy looking anchor lady before turning off the set.

The realization didn't hit me until that moment that my fooling with the antenna had probably disrupted the Delvecchios' viewing. Mayfield must have worked out some system with Bengston to handle the conflict, but he hadn't told me.

I headed back into the living room to see if my mistake had interrupted the Delvecchio clan's entertainment. Not to worry. They had not budged from their seats.

The binoculars would have been just the thing for taking a really close look at Pete Delvecchio, still sitting there with that constant smile on his face, but it was an idiotic idea. The thought of that much intimacy was unbearable, even though he would never know.

A light came on in the bedroom directly above where they were, sending me to the kitchen window to see which of the kids had gone upstairs.

I was flabbergasted. Both youngsters were still in the room, sitting exactly as they had the night before. Terry, wearing the same soft blue sweater, was curled in the big recliner, her feet tucked beneath her, her face half concealed by her light blonde hair, her head resting against the chair back. The boy was sitting on the floor, as before, leaning his shoulders against the chair, his tousled head cushioned against his sister's leg. The upstairs bedroom was still brightly lit!

Without conscious thought, I raced up the narrow stairs and burst into one of the rooms facing the Delvecchios'. The lighted bedroom—or, at least, all of it that could be seen—was empty!

From this angle, all four members of the family were visible, still intent on the television. By shifting my position, the lower half of the television screen came into view.

The picture was rolling, the sort of quick roll that gives no hint of the picture. One of them would surely go over any moment to tune the set. The seconds grew into a minute and then another. *My Lord*, I thought, *those suckers are all too stubborn to get up and adjust the thing.*

I hurried back downstairs. My neighbors were giving a fair imitation of being refugees from a science fiction movie. It was time to do some serious thinking about the Delvecchios and me.

They had me slinking around in the dark, refusing to turn on lights, and scampering from window to window, peeking at them—not really the ideal environment for a guy who had put in some time getting his head straightened out.

I had grown quite frightened at something I didn't understand. It was becoming impossible to huddle in the dark, hoping everything would be all right.

The living room window drew me like a magnet. Somebody must have finally given in and adjusted the set because they were still watching. It was almost one o'clock in the morning. What in the heck could they be looking at now? It was probably some West Coast movie or a program from Hawaii.

Suddenly it was the most important thing in the world for me to know what they were watching. I stampeded up the stairs and hurried to my vantage point. Never, as long as I live, will I forget my emotions as I peered down into that room.

At that instant, I knew that something was wrong next door —terribly wrong.

They were sitting there, husband and wife on the sofa, the girl curled up in the chair, the boy resting against her knee, totally absorbed in the television set.

The problem was that the TV continued to roll relentlessly in a mindless whirl.

Chapter
TWENTY

Sagging against the window frame, I sought within my mind for some explanation. Could the Delvecchios have placed mannequins in the living room chairs? Why would they do such a thing? The idea was too absurd to contemplate.

There would be no more sneaking around in the dark, peeking at them. The people next door were going to reveal their secrets . . . one way or the other.

Storming downstairs, I shoved the revolver under my belt, dug out my flashlight, and hurried out the front door. Concern about the gun brought me to a halt halfway across the pitch. The appearance of a wild-eyed, gun-toting handyman, pounding on the door in the middle of the night, might scare the pants off them. Even as I hesitated, the kitchen light flared to life. My fear transformed itself into anger again. Whatever was happening in there was insane.

They could think what they wanted about the gun. It was time to bring matters to a head. I hammered at the door, no longer caring what they thought of me. The Delvecchios were going to give me a reason for what was happening in that madhouse.

There was no response to my pounding.

The doorknob turned easily, and a feeling of relief washed over me. Somehow I felt better, as though the unlocked door excused my breaking in on them without permission. The door swung back on its noiseless hinges.

A wave of heated air swept past me. The house was stifling hot from having been closed up all day, and the warm air had

a strange unpleasantness about it. My nose crinkled in dis-
taste.

"Hey . . . is anyone home?"

No answer.

"Hey, for gosh sake, quit kidding around! Can I come in?"

The shadowed hall yielded no answer. Somewhere behind
me, I sensed some slight movement and turned, but the
ground outside was clear down to the water's edge. The passageway was dark except for the light streaming out of the
living room. The bright reflection from the corridor wall
shielded my view of the unlit stairway at its far end. The only
sound in the house was a faint scratch of static from the TV.
Otherwise, it was as quiet as a grave.

Choking back another shout, unwilling to do anything to
disturb the house further, I started cautiously down the hall,
my footfalls hollow in the empty space.

I paused at the open door of the dining room. It was impossible to pass that dark, menacing gap without examining its
interior with the flashlight.

I froze in my tracks, the hairs on the back of my neck
rising, bewildered by the scene before me. There were clean
plates on the table, together with a heaping bowl of pasta. A
smaller bowl, filled with some green vegetable, looked as if it
had been upset and rerighted, leaving a widespread stain on
the tablecloth. Several glasses lay on the floor, and one was
overturned on the table, resting in the middle of a large red-
dish blotch. The dining room had to be the source of the
stench, but why would the Delvecchios have allowed food to
rot that way? Surely one of them, even young Rick, could
have found time to clean up the mess.

I was no longer sure that I wanted to know the answer to
the Delvecchio puzzle.

Two more steps brought me near the doorway to the living
room where the Delvecchios were sitting. I had been mistaken
about the smell emanating from the dining room. Here by the
living room, a dreadful, gut-wrenching stench assailed me,
gagging me. Involuntarily I spoke aloud, "My God! That
smell—it's horrible!"

I wondered if they had left meat out to spoil in the kitchen.
It was a rotted, dead smell.

I paused, psyching myself up to bursting in on them, uncertain of how they would respond. Again there was the feeling that watching eyes were gently stroking my back. The flashlight's beam revealed nothing but the night-filled rectangle of the doorway. Damp night air was drifting down the hall, diluting the odor somewhat.

Taking a deep breath, I stepped into the living room. It was like passing through the portals of hell.

The stench was staggering—the ripe, pungent odor of death. I was standing by the sofa, looking down on the grossly swollen features of the man and woman—their eyes open and bulging, lips drawn back from their teeth, their rigid faces a fish-belly white, lightly tinged with blue.

To my left, the girl Terry looked toward the television with dull, lifeless eyes. The light, stronger here, struck her stony, drained face, revealing the purplish cast of her skin more clearly. Her lips were drawn back in a hideous snarl. The boy sat on the floor, his head tilted back. His blind eyes, their pupils huge black pools of nothingness, stared in eternal wonder toward the ceiling.

The television supplied the only motion, with its endless rolling.

My skin crawled in arrhythmic waves, and my heart pounded so hard and fast it left me breathless. Waves of nausea flooded over me, and only revulsion at the thought of collapsing on the floor with those corpses looming over me gave me the power to stay on my feet.

They should be examined to determine what had killed them, but I couldn't stand the thought of touching the cold, putrid meat of the cadavers. God! I wanted to bolt from the room, but the hall behind me seemed filled with unimaginable terrors. It was impossible to turn away, leaving those dead, bulging eyes at my back. At that moment my terror had me very close to the quicksands of madness.

A soft, wavering moan floated in the air. Frantically, I sought its source, then realized it was coming from me—a horrible—almost inhuman—sound. If my sanity was to be preserved, I had to get out of there.

Starting toward the door, I heard a loud click and whirled in time to see the television screen go blank. The same glance found the power cord at the base of the TV running to a timer plugged into the wall socket. This bit of rational observation, somehow, gave me a hold on my sanity. My gaze remained on the timer, finding comfort in it.

Then it, the television, the rotting shells of human flesh, and the room disappeared into a void of blackness.

How long I stood there only God knows—maybe seconds, maybe a minute—trying to stop my senseless keening. Some primordial sense of self-preservation drove me toward the doorway, careening off its framing, reeling across the corridor and crashing into the wall. Despite my thrashing about the darkness of the hall in a mindless frenzy, I retained possession of the flashlight and found the switch.

Its beam lighted a path to safety through the open door. Fleeing the monstrous shadow of my running body, I tumbled down the steps and sprawled full length on the cold granite, my stomach heaving.

Scrambling to my feet, I raced for Mayfield's, ignoring the pain in my ankle. Only after the door was slammed and locked did some semblance of rationality return to me.

With reason came the memory that my so-called sanctuary had stood wide open for the last fifteen minutes. Still too upset to think of turning on the lights, I freed the revolver from my belt and searched the shadow-filled dwelling from top to bottom, flashlight in hand. Several times I was perilously close to firing at my own moving shadow.

The absurdity of my behavior gradually sank in. There couldn't be anyone inside. Only four people had been on the island besides me, and now all four were stone dead.

I stopped short, frightened by my choice of words. Aloud, unable to stop myself, I whispered, "Why in the devil did I say that? Stone dead—Stone Warrior?"

Ashamed of the unreasonable fear that boiled just under the surface, I stormed out to the porch, forcing myself to glare at the Bengston residence. Underneath the bravado, terror gnawed at me like a rabid beast.

A single light was on in that charnel house, and it was in the upstairs bathroom. Despite my discovery that timers were responsible for the lights going on and off next door, I couldn't shake the feeling that someone was slinking through that deathtrap, flipping the switches. The devices must have been placed all through the building. For some unfathomable reason, the Delvecchios had set their lights to respond in a timed pattern during the evenings.

The bathroom light went off, and the corpse-laden structure was dark and silent, silhouetted against the coldly glittering night sky.

Determined to subjugate my fear, I walked down the grade to the dock and settled down, cross-legged, the gun in my lap, facing the mausoleum that only days ago had been a luxurious vacation home. A solution had to be found for the horrible thing that had happened in there.

A family had died inside that building, and there was little question but that death had been instantaneous—or nearly so. No bloodstains or any other visible signs of violence marked those poor souls. There had to be an explanation for their deaths that made more sense than the idiotic legend of Stone Warrior Island.

The most probable cause was a leak in the line or a valve of the propane system, allowing gas to overcome them before they realized what was happening. But why wouldn't they have noticed the fumes?

It had to be something like that, but my sense of smell is quite good, and I had failed to detect any trace of gas. With the house closed up, the odor should have lingered. Maybe it had happened two days back—on Sunday night after I went home. The Delvecchios had planned to cross to the mainland Monday morning, but they hadn't been in sight since our ill-fated confrontation Sunday afternoon. The gas might have had time to dissipate, leaving only the nauseating smell of decaying flesh. That must be the solution!

Somehow, that theory seemed too pat, yet it couldn't have been food poisoning or botulism. They would have had more than enough time to seek my help after it first affected them. Whatever had happened had caused a loss of consciousness before they were aware of their danger.

Carbon monoxide! Why hadn't I thought of it before? That would explain the lack of odor. It was a common enough accident. Perhaps the vent of the stove or water heater had become blocked during the winter. That was the most sensible possibility of all! The victim loses consciousness without being aware of anything except being drowsy.

But, what about the use of the timers? Maybe they were used extensively in the East. People around Seattle were beginning to buy them to turn their house lights on at random intervals as a protection against burglars. It was an hypothesis that fit the facts. But who did they expect to commit the burglary—me?

Appeased by the neat solution, I grew sleepy in the aftermath of the emotional turmoil the night had brought. Mayfield's blasted book about Stone Warrior Island has to bear much of the blame for my irrational terror that night. If it hadn't been for the wild tales, I might have forced myself to remain in Bengston's house long enough to investigate, instead of running away, frightened to death.

One problem remained. There were no means of notifying the authorities in Saskatoon about what had happened to the Delvecchios. Until the police could be notified, those bodies would have to remain in place, decaying, for another week.

My long vigil continued until the stars above the island's crest grew indistinct in the light of Wednesday morning. That was when the idea hit me. There was a way to signal passing planes that help was needed. A universal distress signal is to fly the national flag upside down. Of course, the Canadian flag didn't look a great deal different flown either way, since the only change would be the upside-down maple leaf. Still, it was better than nothing.

The rusty pulleys on the flagpole complained loudly as the night-dampened flag came down. The harsh squealing prompted me to glance uneasily over my shoulder, cursing myself for not oiling the hoisting hardware when the flag was put up. I thought of the old saying, "Making enough noise to wake the dead," and shuddered in the dawn chill, but the cold air was not the cause.

The flag was quickly reversed and run back up the flagpole. While securing the rope to the cleat, I remembered what Chambord had said about signal fires. That was another thing I should do. One of my morning tasks would be to collect driftwood for one. If a plane passed within fifteen miles of the lake, the pilot should be able to see the smoke.

I returned to the house with an easier mind, sure that the mystery of the unfortunate Delvecchios had been solved. Locking the door, I hurried through the place, my anxieties put to rest, anxious to be nestled under the covers.

I never made it to bed in the cubbyhole. The revelation came as I was slipping on my pajamas. My "boudoir" had far too many unshaded windows for my peace of mind as well as harboring some unpleasant memories. There would be no more sleeping in that tiny cubicle—at least not until the bodies of the Delvecchios left the island. Gathering my blankets and pillows, I returned to the living room and made a bed on the long sofa.

Despite my exhaustion, falling asleep proved impossible. Time after time, drifting toward the final, hazy moments of consciousness, I would think I heard something outside the window and bolt upright.

Two hours later, with the rosy early-morning light bringing substance to the furnishings of the room, I gave up and dragged myself into the kitchen to make a cup of coffee. Instant coffee and fatigue are not the best of companions for a queasy stomach. It tasted awful.

Later, back in the front room, I sprawled on the sofa, thinking about the good times I had experienced with Rod and Evie. Somewhere along the line, the mournful windsong of Stone Warrior Island lulled me to sleep.

Chapter
TWENTY-ONE

I awakened with a start, struggling to disengage myself from the blanket, wrapped tightly around me. Remembering my circumstances, I ceased moving and listened with a fierce intensity.

Save for the sustained pedal-note of wind in the treetops, all was quiet. It was a stillness that shouldn't be listened to for too long, else my imagination, working overtime as it was, might begin to add the excited whoops of Rick Delvecchio, the girlish greetings of his sister Terry, and the booming bass voice of their father, with his clipped Eastern accent. Vaguely apprehensive, I came to my feet.

The sun had a midmorning strength, reflecting into the shadowed living room. My sleep must have been light, for fatigue still gripped me. My head hurt, and there was a sweaty stickiness around the elastic band of my shorts and under my collar.

I tottered into the kitchen. Despite yesterday's unaccustomed hard labor with the woodcutting and my inability to eat last night, my stomach gave little indication it wanted food. A forced breakfast did little besides draw tighter the bands of tension and hone the steel edge of my headache. The forgotten and now smelly lake trout caught my attention. I dragged them from the sink, intending to bury them in the woods.

As I worked at the sink, my eyes lifted, unbidden, to focus on the rustic abode that served as the grisly crypt for four rapidly deteriorating bodies. Morbid fascination drew my attention, like a magnet, to the darkened living-room windows. The glass panes revealed nothing, hiding Pete Delvecchio's puffed face, distorted in a grotesque death rictus, and his bulging eyes, forever watching the cold electronic world of the television.

Shutting my eyes, I broke the hypnotic spell of the window, anxious to flee the mustiness of my gloomy quarters.

From the front porch, I surveyed my surroundings. The sky was unlike anything in my experience—an incredible royal blue, incandescent, without a cloud to mar the effect. The scene looked unreal, like the background of a garish travel poster. A strong, chilly breeze stroked Stone Warrior's surface, creating small broken ridges of white water. The sound of the waves slapping the shore was loud enough to muffle the hum of the wind in the timbered mantle of the island. The cool, moist air was gradually dulling the sharp edge of my headache.

While I had the courage of daylight in me, it was time to

make a decision on what I should do. Unless a passing plane became aware of the situation on Stone Warrior Island, a very unpleasant five or six days remained for me. My first priority should be to collect wood for the signal fire. There was always the chance of a bush pilot passing overhead.

A second idea came to mind. With so many watermelon-size rocks strewn around, it would be easy to lay out a distress sign on the exposed granite face. If an aircraft flew over during the daylight hours while my chores took me away from the house, the pilot would be able to spot the plea for help from a couple of thousand feet up.

I turned for a last look around before going in to get into my work clothes. The alarm bells went off. There was something wrong—something was missing.

I eyeballed the scene, scanning the water's edge from the small basin where the canoes had rested to where the rocky shore disappeared behind the trees down toward the point of the island. Nothing appeared to be out of place.

Still puzzled, I stepped back into the house. My movements were lethargic. The slowly accruing fatigue was draining the strength from me. The loss of appetite wasn't helping.

It dawned on me, as I started down the steps, that I didn't have my revolver with me. Embarrassment did not deter me from reentering Mayfield's to retrieve it. I tried to kid myself into believing that I still might encounter a dangerous animal, but the truth was that I had begun to frighten myself with another absurd fantasy, a visualization of the Delvecchios issuing single-file from their house, their arms rigid at their sides, eyes rolled back in their heads with only the whites showing—like zombies. I damned myself for every one of the seven times I had seen *Night of the Living Dead*. My predilection for monster movies was exacting a belated price from me.

In the act of stepping off the porch, I knew what was wrong with the scene before me.

With the strong wind whipping across the foreshore of the island, the Canadian flag should have been a dancing splash of color on the flagpole. There was no flag. The pole was a bare needle, launching itself toward the gaudy unnatural blue of the sky. A tangle of weathered hemp rope lay around its foot.

From the base of the flagpole, I turned a full 360 degrees, searching for the splotch of red and white that would mark where the banner had fallen. The wind direction suggested that it should have landed in the bushes at the edge of the slab next to Bengston's. My gaze probed the brush and lower branches of the conifers, even skipping along the foundation of the building, but avoiding the door, left ajar the night before in my panic. No flag was visible.

The wind must have veered since early morning. The pennant could have been blown out into the lake, where it became waterlogged and sank.

I picked up the rope end, wondering why it had parted. It had been neatly severed, like a knife had been used on it, rather than shredded as might be expected. The breeze must have sawed the rope across a sharp edge on the pulley until it parted. Since there were no coils of rope for repairs in the shed, my distress signal would fly no more even if I found it.

Flag or no flag, it was time to get to work if I was to finish in time to work on the sign. With the chain saw gone, my efforts would be confined to splitting and stacking the wood already sawed to length. Once I crossed the ridge and plunged into the timber on the eastern hillside, the wind quickly disappeared. Only the eerie humming overhead remained as evidence of the breeze. As before, the dark silence of the woods was undisturbed by birds or insects. Despite the bright sun climbing toward its zenith, the sidehill, under its dense cloak of attenuated tree trunks, remained dim and damp.

Though my renewed confidence vanished as quickly as the brilliance of the day had fled upon entering the grove, I plodded down the grade, determined to think only of the wood splitting. Once in view of the timber rounds, cut the day before, I paused to scan the ground around me in the forlorn hope that, somehow, I had tucked the chain saw out of sight and had forgotten about it. There was no sign of it. I had to face up to the truth. It had fallen from the log and tumbled down the steep incline into the lake. No doubt it had been precariously balanced and a falling branch had dislodged it.

Mayfield impressed me as a man who would extract the cost of a replacement from an employee's wages.

I started to work splitting wood, pausing from time to time to scan the quiet forest around me. With the gun in my belt, yesterday's events seemed far less threatening—even silly.

Three hours of hard work produced an impressive heap of firewood. The tenderness in my ankle was soon forgotten. Climbing the slope time after time, my arms filled with split logs, I found myself able to look down at the Bengston dwelling without emotion. At last, with a full cord stacked near the antenna, it was time to take a break.

I will admit to experiencing a few qualms coming downhill between the two houses, but once inside Mayfield's, the tension eased. The cool air inside felt pleasant against my sweaty torso. Loading a glass with ice cubes and instant tea, I crossed to the sink to fill it with water. The water ran clear for a second or two. Then there was an impolite burp from the faucet, and a couple of spurts of heavily discolored water splashed into the glass. The spout managed a dying gurgle and went dry.

I slapped the faucet in frustration. It looked as if Linc Wilhite had still another problem.

The water supply for the two houses was stored in the big redwood tank, standing on a framework on heavy beams just this side of the ridge some forty yards north of the woodpile. The residences used a gravity-fed water system because of having to depend on the generator for power. Each evening the water pump kicked in automatically and refilled the tank through a pipe that ran out on to the lake bottom.

I tried to remember if the water pump had come on last night. Even if it hadn't, the system had run long and hard that first morning when the power was turned on. The five of us could not possibly have exhausted its capacity in that short a time. Either the pipe had developed a blockage, or the tank was leaking.

I splashed the glass of dirty water into the sink and headed for the rear of the house, dreading what I would find. It didn't take long to spot the problem.

A wide streak of wet granite stretched from the base of the wood structure to the lake's edge. It was impossible to know

how long it had been leaking. Water had been available at
breakfast, but, of course, it could have been losing water at a
slow rate during the night.

I trudged up the slab to the tank. Viewed from close up, the
trouble was easy to spot. The cleanout plug at the bottom had
somehow come loose. It dangled limply from its chain. It was
likely that the contractions and expansions of the wood reser-
voir in the warming air of spring had loosened it enough that
the weight of a full tank of water popped it out. Luckily, it
was easily fixed.

The plug went back into place without difficulty. Slithering
back to ground level, I hurried to the shed to turn the power
back on so the tank would refill.

The generator kicked on immediately, and I stepped out of
the shed to confirm that the pump was running. The small
shelter that housed it was ominously quiet. The pump was
located in a small white boxlike structure of wood, tucked in
at the base of the timbers supporting the tank. Lifting the
hinged cover released the stench of burnt insulation and the
distinctive aroma of ozone.

I bent over the motor, trying to keep the shadow of my head
out of the way. At first glance, it looked okay, despite the
ominous odor that bespoke trouble. A closer look put that
little misconception to rest. A glinting strand of copper wire
protruded from the ventilating slot of the pump's motor. I
carefully pulled it free. The part of it that had been within the
motor housing was blackened, and the end looked as if it had
melted.

I slammed my hand against the pump housing in frustration. The length of wire in my hand was obviously the legacy
of some childish prank from the summer before. The wire,
undoubtedly poked into the motor in curiosity, had finally
worked its way into contact with the armature wiring. I put
my eye against the ventilation slot, trying to see within the
metal housing, expecting to find tangles of the wire, but my
shadow and the dimness within the case effectively screened
the interior.

The inside of the motor was probably a melted mess. Cursing my luck, I slid the housing cover back over the ruined
pump, wondering if Mayfield would blame me for this loss,

too. One thing was for sure; from now on, my needs would have to be satisfied by hauling lake water a bucket at a time.

Later, returning to the far side of the island, I vented my frustration on the tree rounds, working well into the afternoon, splitting and hauling loads of firewood up to the rapidly growing pile at the crest. Sometime past midafternoon, my sore ankle started throbbing again, driving me back to the house.

My sweat-soaked clothes dried rapidly, making me acutely aware of the dirt and tiny slivers of bark and wood clinging to cloth and skin. It was no longer possible to take a shower, but a dip in the lake would help.

Grabbing a couple of towels, I started out the door, but not before making sure that the reassuring bulk of the revolver was wedged into my waistband. There was no point in being hypocritical about it; the gun was going to be my constant companion whenever I was outside. Too much had happened since my arrival. I was afraid. I didn't know what of—it was all explainable—but nevertheless, I was frightened and willing to admit it.

From my vantage point on the float, I scanned the lake. Adjacent to the mainland shore, large expanses of water were crowded with flocks of waterfowl. The binoculars revealed small birds, their species unknown to me, flitting around the tall stands of spruce along the shore opposite the house. Why didn't the birds use the trees on the island? Another thing—despite their reputation, I had seen very few black flies or mosquitos on the island and none in the last few days. Even the ants I had noticed by the generator shed that first afternoon had disappeared.

No signs of life were present on the island now unless the snapping noises in the woods yesterday were something besides falling branches. I was almost ready to concede that it had been my overactive imagination that had ruined the hike. Yet . . . I could swear I had seen a figure . . . something.

With a growing reluctance to be parted from it, I laid the revolver down on the towels and stepped out of my pants.

The lake, as was its pattern in the early afternoons, was relatively calm. The dock's up-and-down motion was almost imperceptible. Resting on its weathered wood decking, striped by the new planks, I tried to keep my gaze away from the death-ridden dwelling next door.

My mood would have been better if the front door, still standing ajar, had been tightly closed. Still, it was better than the way it had been after I ran out of the place. It had been wide open then, but the wind must have partially closed it. It would have pleased me most if all the doors and windows were boarded over—just a nice way of keeping what was outside outside and what was inside inside.

Determined to quit thinking about the horrors that lay cold and lifeless within those walls, I drew a deep breath, ran the length of the dock, and dived off the end nearest the miniscule bay in front of Bengston's. To be honest, yours truly isn't much of a diver—not even much of a swimmer. It always takes me several seconds to persuade myself to open my eyes when I'm under water. I was near the nadir of my dive, still clawing awkwardly for depth, before I ventured a peek.

My plunge had carried me deeper than I thought possible. The water was icy, heavy, and dark green. The bottom was a dark, congealed mass below me, and the pressure pounded against my ears. Alarmed by the depth and with my body demanding air and light and warmth, I angled upward, pulling for the surface. At that moment, a flash of white appeared against the dark, shadowed bottom below me, and then it was gone. Breaking the surface, I swam quickly back to the float and scrambled up on to it, where I sat, puzzled.

Whatever the white thing below was, it appeared too long and narrow to be a gasoline drum that had broken free and rolled off the dock. Growing more intrigued, I left the float, looking for a large rock that would force me down to the bottom in the vicinity of the mysterious object.

If there was anything the island had, it was plenty of rocks. Soon I staggered back on to the dock, carrying a good forty pounds of granite. After a rest to recover my breath, I gathered the miniboulder in my arms and lumbered off the end of the dock with an enormous splash.

The weight took me down too quickly. My ears popping, I struggled to rid myself of the rock, which seemed to cling to me. Finally, within three feet of the bottom, it fell away, leaving me to swim awkwardly through the dark, frigid water.

Just when I thought I had missed the white object, I saw it directly beneath me, clearly—too clearly. Instinctively my hand shot out and grabbed the sunken craft to hold myself at the spot.

It was the birch bark canoe Delvecchio had bought in Saskatoon, sitting upright on the bottom, filled with seven or eight large rocks. There was a gaping hole in one side of it, starting right behind the Indian Joe logo.

Chapter
TWENTY-TWO

Suddenly frantic to be away from the strangely mutilated craft, I pulled desperately for the surface. In a fury of white water, I swam toward the dock. Even as I hoisted myself from the water, I was looking for the gun. It still lay where it had been left.

I was cold, deadly cold, and it had nothing to do with the chilly water. My God, I had been stupid. Even after finding the Delvecchios dead, I had never thought to ask myself what had happened to the canoes. My theory about the deaths of the Delvecchios needed revising—a lot of revising that wouldn't be pleasant. The picture of that grimly savaged canoe lying in its watery grave refused to fade away.

Once I was safely back in Mayfield's, my thoughts turned to the other craft—the red one Delvecchio had brought down from the storage shed. It should have been as easy to spot underwater as the white one, but there had been no sign of it. Where was it? Why wasn't it on the bottom with the birch-bark one?

One of my earlier theories about the family's deaths must have been correct. Someone—maybe a Mafia hit man—had come ashore, killed them, and slipped away again in the red canoe, sinking the white one when he realized there was someone else on the island who might pursue him. If only that sunken wreck could tell its tale!

My mind was made up in a split second. It was only Wednesday, too long to remain on Stone Warrior, waiting for Chambord's return. Since my grim discovery in the house next door, I had thought of little else but the bloated, decomposing corpses. Now I had new worries, thoughts about a killer and a missing canoe, wondering if he would return to erase the last witness to his crime.

It was time to find out if it was possible to reach cvilization using one of Mayfield's canoes. Escape lay in finding a major river close enough that it could be reached with only a few portages. With the right equipment and an easy route, I could find my way out.

I spread Mayfield's maps about me on the floor of the den. There were two possible paths. If easy portages were available, it would be feasible to go west to the Cree River, then north toward Lake Athabasca. The second possible route entailed following a string of lakes lying along the same axis as Stone Warrior to where they intersected the east-west running Fond-du-Lac River. From there, it would be possible to reach a small settlement, Stony Rapids, west of Athabasca. It didn't appear to be much of a town, but it would have a radio transmitter.

Continued rummaging in the chart drawer turned up more detailed maps, and my initial optimism evaporated. The trip westward toward the Cree River looked impossible—too many ridges to carry a canoe across. I would have to head northward. There would be portages, but most of them would be down the valleys between the lakes.

The main obstacle would be encountering patches of muskeg which might prove impossible to cross. I would just have to find detours around them.

I stared blankly at the charts, still uncertain. It was unreasonable to embark on a long, hard trip that might take two or three weeks when Chambord would return within five days, yet I was revulsed at the prospect of remaining on Stone Warrior with its horrors. The idea never dawned on me simply to load a canoe with supplies and move over to the mainland shore to await the plane. I never even thought about the implications of leaving the scene of a crime, especially when I was the only witness.

My resolution made, I refolded the maps. There was one piece of equipment necessary for a successful escape—a small canoe. The portages would prove unfeasible with anything larger than a two-man job.

Tucking my now constant companion, the revolver, under my waistband, I walked out the back door. The canoe shed, a squat, wide-doored, flat-roofed structure, lay slightly behind and to the left of the generator shed. It had been of no interest to me before, but one look at its door changed all that.

The latch, with the padlock still locked on it, hung loose at one end, attached to the door by a single screw. I lunged forward, grabbed the door, and swung it open. The sunlight spilled into the interior, falling on the front of the four canoe racks.

That's all there was to see—four empty racks.

My first thought was of Chambord and Higgins's conversation about thieves raiding the cabins during the off-season, but my gaze returned to the damaged door frame and I knew that wasn't the case here. A big chunk of wood had come away with the latch, leaving a bright scar that stood out vividly against the gray, weathered wood above and below it. It was a fresh gouge, not more than two or three days old at the most —maybe only a few hours.

I fingered the wood, not wanting to recognize the obvious, but I knew. The other canoes had suffered the same fate as the white one. They lay somewhere offshore, filled with rocks, under that icy water. There had been someone—or something—on the island. The Delvecchios had been murdered.

There was no need to worry further about whether I was doing the right thing in fleeing. I was a prisoner—intentionally or unintentionally—going nowhere, and my world had shrunk to the twenty-four acres of Stone Warrior Island.

No, that wasn't true—because nothing could induce me to again traverse the woods at the other end of Stone Warrior or to set foot in the building next door. My prison was much smaller.

Slowly I turned full circle, scanning my surroundings, staring at the open water, iridescent with the sun sheen, at the green wall of timber and brush that fenced in the rocky slab on which the lonely houses rested, and at the rocky knoll, above which the white disc of the antenna stood motionless, as it had since the Delvecchios died. I could imagine the jolt of terror that would course through me if it started to move.

The absolute horror of the island was beginning to affect me badly. Stone Warrior's mournful requiem was swelling in volume, a testament to the building winds of the lengthening afternoon. There was an awesome deadliness to the whole scene, devoid as it was of life—an ecological dead zone.

My panoramic inspection disclosed the ladder, still resting against the side of the Mayfield house, forgotten since the moment I descended from the roof to meet Mrs. Delvecchio, hurrying toward me with her unfortunate dinner invitation. I started toward the side of the building, intending to put the ladder away, but was sidetracked. I needed to check the fuel supply for the generator to ensure that electricity would be available during the evening.

As I left the shed, the task completed, my nose was assailed by the rich odor of decay. With my nerves already honed to a sharp edge by the memory of the hideous smell I had encountered when I discovered the Delvecchios dead, I froze in midstride. Rigid with fear, I searched my surroundings with fearful glances.

Chapter
TWENTY-THREE

I saw the source of the odor at once. The lake trout, their silvery sides glittering in the sunshine which was rapidly spoiling them, lay on the yellowed sheets of newspaper on which I had placed them that morning. When I stopped at the shed earlier to pick up the splitting maul, I had set the trout down and then forgotten all about them. My intention had been to carry them with me and bury them near the log pile.

Stepping back into the shed, I grabbed a shovel and, gingerly picking up the newspaper with its unsavory cargo, headed across the ridge, determined to rid myself of them. Pausing in the perpetual twilight of the tree-choked slope above the site of my woodsplitting, I sought an open spot where a small pit could be excavated without encountering tree roots. Some fifteen yards to my left was a small clearing, tightly encircled by the spindly spruces. A tangle of dead brush littered the ground at the end nearest me, brush that must have been dragged to its resting place. I felt a bit squeamish about approaching it because I had found the severed finger only a few yards down the hillside from the tangle. Nevertheless, my anxiety to be out of the somber glade before the sun had sunk much lower overcame my reluctance, and I hurried cross-slope toward the spot.

A small, squarish object protruded from under a dead branch in the piled brush. Seen closer up, it was obvious that the object was man-made.

Dropping the shovel and dead fish at the clearing's edge, I tugged the branch free of the pile of scrubwood, exposing a dirt-encrusted wallet, badly weathered by the winter. Pulling it free, I brushed the dried mud away from the cracked leather. It was an expensive item, made from an unfamiliar leather—probably lizard or some other exotic skin.

The bill compartment was empty, save for a dank earth smell. The personal papers appeared intact in the interior pockets. Unsnapping a leather tab released a deck of plastic-clad credit cards that unfolded in a shower of bright colors, reaching the ground. It was with a premonition of horrible discovery that I stood in that small clearing, ringed about by the stunted, useless trees, and furtively rifled through the papers and cards of the discarded billfold. The name was consistent on all the documents: Leroy Stearman, with a street address in Dallas, Texas.

Puzzled, I patted the water-stained leather case against my palm, wondering how one of Mayfield's guests could have lost it in this place and why he would have been carrying a wallet without money. Wondering if the brush pile concealed other puzzles, I flipped the wallet out of the way and started dragging dead wood back into the trees.

The ground that had lain beneath the piled scrub, protected from the drying winds of spring, still felt soggy. The soil had a raw, disturbed look, as though it had been turned over and then trampled down again sometime within the past few months. Two faint depressions, long and narrow, ran parallel to one another on the upslope of the disturbed ground. Quite a bit of dirt had been moved around in that small clearing, and I wondered why. My best guess was that Mayfield and his partner were using the place as a dump for their nondegradable garbage, such as plastics, foil, and cans. It seemed wiser to open a new pit for the fish on the other side of the clearing, rather than dig into the mess.

Stooping to pick up the fish and shovel, I happened to glance down toward the lake. I looked a second time, but what I thought I saw at first glance had disappeared! There had been a rainbow sheen in the slack water near shore—the kind of slick that indicated the presence of floating oil or gasoline. Excited with the prospect of having located the underwater resting place of the chain saw, I scrambled down the hillside toward the log where it had been left.

Once there, I squatted and stood and walked back and forth from spot to spot—even climbing halfway up the hill again—but I could see no further sign of oil on the surface and finally had to conclude that it had been an optical illusion.

Disheartened by my futile search, I turned back toward the clearing, determined to bury the fish and scurry back to the warmth and safety of the house. I stopped abruptly, transfixed by what I saw on the slope above me. Because of the freshly turned dirt and the absence of trees, the clearing appeared brighter than the surrounding woods. Bizarre though it might be, the glow was concentrated in the two shallow depressions, and they had a luminescent quality, made all the more vivid by the gloomy thicket that surrounded them. I had the weirdest feeling that they were there for me, beacons to draw me to them. I looked away, angry with myself for my foolishness. First, a nonexistent oil slick had sent me down the slope, and now the clearing beckoned me with its pale beacons. I tramped up the hill, staring doggedly at the ground before me.

The grove was appreciably darker than it had been when I first pulled the brush away. The sun was setting rapidly now, and the God-awful banshee cry in the treetops was building in volume. There was no longer time to open a new pit. The old dump would have to do.

I picked up the shovel and walked carefully across the damp soil to avoid muddying my shoes. The steel blade bit into the soft fill at the head of the nearer depression. The clay-like soil was even wetter than it initially appeared. The first shovelful clung, with a wet slurp, to the blade. The sharp metal edge sliced into the soggy excavation a second time, and its tip met resistance. I pulled it free, straddled the depression, and rammed it straight down into the hole. There was a hollow thump as if the blade had struck wood, but it was not the solid resistance of a tree root. Working with diligence, I soon had cleared enough of the depression to see the obstacle beneath the shovel.

About a foot and a half down, boards—one-by-sixes—ran parallel along the length of the indentation. Tattered fringes of black plastic were pinched between some of the muddy planks.

Again I almost abandoned the excavation and crossed the clearing to dig a fresh pit for the fish. But, my curiosity aroused, I resisted the temptation to start anew. There had to be an explanation for the strange depressions. Most certainly they hadn't served as garbage dumps for the houses—not the way they were covered up.

The blade, slicing away at the uphill edge of the hole, soon exposed the ends of the boards. I reversed the shovel, working the stout oak handle down past the end of one of the planks, and began to pry. It was a standoff for a moment, but then the length of wood broke with a loud crack at the point where it ran back under the soil. It flipped up free of the hole, taking a long, ragged scrap of plastic with it.

The smell of putrefaction rose from the hole in a ghastly billow, and it was like the discovery of the Delvecchios all over again.

I spun away, coughing and dry-heaving, clutching weakly

at the slick trunk of a spruce until my stomach settled down.
Unwillingly I turned back to the depression's edge and peered
down past the raw earth fringes into the cavity.

I began to shiver, swept up in an uncontrollable paroxysm
of fear. Within the cavity the partially skeletonized head and
shoulders of a person were visible. Patches and strips of
blackened flesh still clung to the emerging skull. A stained
cowboy hat, which must once have been light tan, lay crushed
under the head, which retained its covering of pale blonde
hair. A sodden red-and-black-plaid shirt covered the decaying
shoulders.

The fate of Chambord's two missing Texans was inexplicable no longer, nor did any mystery remain about the brownish stains matting the spruce needles and the fragment of
human flesh I had found. I had discovered the very spot on
which one of the poor men in those graves had been murdered.

For a moment I was remarkably calm. It seemed fitting that
the doomed men had made their way no farther than the bone-
yard that was Stone Warrior Island.

I reached for the shovel to repack the cavity, but never
completed the move.

The enormity, the hideousness of my discovery, swept over
me. I could hear nothing but the anguished moaning in the
treetops, see nothing but the growing darkness of the dank
woods, and sense nothing but the awful loneliness of those
unknown graves. Panic-stricken, I lunged free of the clearing,
fleeing up the slope, forgetting the wallet and the shovel, un-
mindful of the low branches whipping against my face.

At the ridgecrest I turned to look behind me. All was quiet.
The gathering darkness in that blighted woods and the slender
trunks in their close ranks combined to shield the ghastly se-
cret of that ground. I had no intention of venturing into the
haunted glade again.

Slowly, my panic ebbed. I looked toward the houses below.
Nothing had changed. Only the shadows of the two buildings,
growing darker and reaching farther across the nude slab of
rock, had altered during my trek over the ridge to discard the
trout.

I had to collect my wits, to understand the implications of

the gruesome discovery the tiny clearing had yielded. Was Stone Warrior Island being used, in the off-season, by a gang of murderous thieves as a base from which to ambush solitary travelers? Had the Delvecchios and I surprised them before they could get away? For a moment this seemed a frightening possibility, but then reason asserted itself.

If there were such men cornered on the island, my corpse would have been resting beside those of the Delvecchios long before this. The ancient .32 with its six rounds would have proved no deterrent against ruthless men with rifles. Besides, that theory failed to explain the silent and unknown means by which the Delvecchios had died. I couldn't kid myself. Whoever had killed the family next door—whoever was pursuing me—it had nothing to do with the bodies of those poor fishermen.

The momentary relief—the same sort of release I had experienced when I believed the Delvecchios died of carbon monoxide poisoning—lasted only as long as it took a new and more chilling thought to flash through my mind. If the deaths of the Texans were unrelated to those of the Delvecchios, it meant there were two killers—or maybe more, one of whom was using Stone Warrior as a burial ground. A plane, bearing fresh victims, might appear over the horizon at any time. If they found a witness here, they would kill again without hesitation.

I scrambled to my feet and laughed aloud—a near hysterical outburst. The thought was delicious. If there was an assassin stalking me, he would be in as great a danger as I if a planeload of murderous thieves did come gliding down to a landing on the lake.

The thought made me bold. But as I swaggered toward the gap between the houses, the sound of the running generator reminded me of the coming night and of the lights that would flash on and off, unbidden, next door. My feeling of well-being vanished, speeding me down the grade, desperate to be out of the windswept outdoors. I clambered up the porch steps, my skin crawling to the touch of watchful eyes.

The tendrils of panic entwining themselves about my mind had grown stronger in the past several hours. I wanted the comfort of lights, yet knew already that fear would make me spend another night in the dark, fighting the insane desire to steal a glance at what the lighted windows of the Bengston residence revealed. The thought that the act of throwing the circuit breaker in the shed would bring an end to the lights in the Bengston home never entered my mind.

With the sky rapidly darkening, I heated a can of soup but, after a few sips, shoved it aside. I was eating little and sleeping even less. Grabbing a fresh bottle of Wild Turkey, I sprawled out on the sofa in my new sleeping quarters, the living room, occasionally sipping a bit of whiskey as I watched the changing patterns of reflections on the ceiling from the lights in that house of the dead.

The combination of whiskey, work with the firewood, and lack of sleep made me drowsy. After several catnaps I rose, slipped out of my clothes, and dropped onto the sofa. Sleep came within a minute, erasing the longest Wednesday I had ever experienced.

Chapter
TWENTY-FOUR

I came awake, every muscle tense, wondering what had intruded on my unconsciousness. The night was as quiet as any on Stone Warrior, considering the now constant droning of the wind and the murmur of wavelets against the slab where it dipped into the lake. Then it started.

From somewhere far off came a light, quick rapping. It was barely audible and, at times, faded to nothing. Then it would build in volume again.

I came off the sofa, trying to catch my breath. For one frightening moment it seemed impossible to draw enough air into my lungs. The intervals of rapping came and went so quickly it was impossible to determine the direction from which they came.

Like a sudden clap of thunder, a tremendous slamming shattered the night, and I cried out in terror. There was no question about what it was. The front door of the ghastly building next door had crashed shut with awesome force.

I lunged for the window and stared up at the trees beyond the ebon roofline of Bengston's, wondering if the wind was gusting violently. The shadowy spires of the spruces and pines were swaying gently in the constant breeze.

"Oh, God, there is something alive in that place."

The voice startled me until I realized that it was my own. I was glad Evie wasn't there to hear me. She had often expounded the theory that it was the first stage of going bonkers —talking to oneself. But it would have been a lot worse if another voice had answered me—I'll guarantee you that.

It wasn't a joke to me, though. God, I was so scared my teeth were chattering.

I slumped on to the sofa and buried my face in my hands, afraid of not only what was happening outside but beginning to wonder if I could handle the situation. I didn't know how to fight what I couldn't see. Groping around on the dark floor, I found the bourbon and gulped down two large swallows, coughing as it seared my throat.

It had to be the wind that slammed the door. It had to be—a single hard gust, maybe. Raw fear retreated steadily before the onslaught of this shibboleth repeated over and over, sometimes aloud in a fatigue-slurred voice. Numb with exhaustion and lulled by the alcohol, I sagged sideways onto the sofa. Soon sleep swept away all thoughts.

I awakened with it still dark outside, needing desperately to take a leak. My nap must have been of short duration because the few times I've done any drinking the alcohol always has run right through me. My aching bladder forced me to rise and feel my way through the unlighted house to the bathroom.

The timer switchings next door were finished for the night, and the Delvecchio dead lay entombed in darkness only a few yards away.

Still befuddled by the lack of rest, I returned to the sofa and was almost asleep again when a sudden jarring against the house brought me fully awake. A second jolt followed the first.

This time there was sound as well as sensation—the sound of wood sliding against wood. Something heavy clattered across the log facings, and there was an explosive shattering of glass somewhere in the rear of Mayfield's.

Grabbing the revolver, I rushed through the kitchen and out onto the sunporch, hardly aware of what I was doing. Everything seemed normal until I glanced into the partitioned area that was supposed to serve as my quarters. Something glittered in the soft light from the night sky.

Stepping into the tiny bedroom, I saw a sparkling outfall of glass flung over the sheet on the unmade bed. Glass crunched with a dry crackling beneath my shoes. It had been sprayed all about the floor. There was a long object protruding through the window.

It was a flat, splintery piece of wood. I slid my hand cautiously along its weathered, prickly surface until I encountered a round dowel inserted into the length of wood. It was the ladder that had been leaning against the house. Somehow, it had become unbalanced and had fallen. Probably the combination of wind and the rain had shifted it enough that even something as minor as the wood contracting in the nighttime temperature after the warm day had toppled it. It must have rebounded off the hard surface, sending one of its side rails through the glass. Mayfield was going to decide that he had hired one of the original Three Stooges.

Grabbing a towel from the bathroom, I wrapped it around my hand, grasped the end of the ladder, and tried to shove it back through the jagged gap in the windowpane. It gave way on the second try, skidding free to land with a clatter at the base of the window.

Morning would be soon enough to find a piece of cardboard to put over the shattered window. I shut the door of the small alcove, sealing out the night air, and felt my way back to my new quarters.

For several minutes a feeling of euphoria engulfed me at having found a simple explanation for the sudden crash. Of course, it was a case of grasping at straws.

Returning to the living room, I stood, staring up at the barely discernible ceiling, my thoughts drawn back to the first incident—that slamming front door. Thinking about it, I glanced toward the window, peering with fearful fascination at the tomb of the Delvecchios, dark and loathsome in the wee hours of night.

My physical exhaustion was becoming so acute that my legs would start to tremble when I stood unmoving. I sank into the easy chair by the window, staring up at the thin slice of night sky between the dwellings, trying to think of anything but what was happening on Stone Warrior Island. The cold, indifferent sparkles of light, bright in the pristine northern sky, illuminated the lonely site with a ghostly glow.

For the next hour or so I stared at that cheerless sky, thinking. I remembered the last afternoon in Sequim, telling Evie that it was important I go to the North Woods to test myself. I grinned in the dark, thinking that I had received all the testing I wanted—and then some.

If only the Delvecchios had not died in that bizarre way, the other episodes would not have been so alarming. The canoe, resting on the bottom of the lake, could have been there for years. It might not be the one Delvecchio brought to the island. There could have been others in the past. But it was a little hard to believe that Indian Joe had done a lot of business at such an isolated private lake, especially when the brass plate on the gunwale of the canoe had identified Little Rock, Arkansas, as the place of origin.

The slamming door—its ferocity could have been an exaggeration of my frayed nerves. All noises seem much louder in the night. Besides, a sudden gust of wind could have slammed the door. I couldn't say it wasn't that.

The feeling of being watched when I hiked over the island, my stupidity in placing the chain saw where it could fall into the water, and the malfunction of the water pump were things that might be accepted as unfortunate coincidences if it had not been for those dead bodies. Although I found small comfort in my thoughts, they pacified me enough that I was rapidly drifting toward a real sleep.

A brief, unidentifiable noise intruded. I wasn't sure what it was or where it came from. It was a scraping sound, like wood being dragged across wood, yet different from the sound when the ladder slithered down the log siding. I held my breath, wide awake now, my body tense.

There was a thud against the outside of the house. It was heavy enough that windows rattled somewhere inside, but so muffled that it must have come from the other side of the building.

Instantly, I was on my feet, pawing among the blankets for the revolver. Then I remembered that I had left it on the end table. Clumsy in my fearful haste, I almost knocked it from its resting place, feeling the cold metal slide away from my reaching hand.

As I listened, weapon in hand, the noise came again, but it was different—an odd rattling that involved the whole side of the building. It stopped and started again, lasting maybe thirty seconds altogether. Then there was silence—an absolute, terrifying stillness.

Despite the chilliness of my sleeping quarters, sweat beaded on my forehead. The intense quiet vanished with the breaking of a window somewhere above me. I yelped at the suddenness of it. My finger almost pulled the trigger of the gun as it dangled, muzzle down, from my hand.

There was no long period of silence this time. Almost immediately, the crunching of glass being ground beneath weight filled the silence, followed by the squealing protest of a floorboard above my head.

Something was in the house with me—upstairs, in the dark!

I couldn't move. It was as if I was paralyzed, aware of nothing but the noises coming from the second floor. A brief pause ended in a second grinding of glass underfoot, followed by another soundless interval. Overhead, something—some creature listened as intently as I, waiting for me to betray my position.

After what was an eternity, a shrill ripple of sound ran across the ceiling—and then another. The night visitor was moving out into the hall, gliding toward the stairway, which would bring him down to the living room, where I waited, too stunned by the suddenness of the invasion to know what to do.

The vague light was sufficient to reveal the far wall and the abrupt black gap of the doorway to the kitchen. The door, standing wide open, had to be closed to shut out the dark shadows of that suddenly frightening room. I tiptoed toward it.

In doing so, I betrayed my position. The movements overhead ceased instantly—but only for a moment. They started again, moving quickly along the passage to the head of the stairs. I jumped at the sudden sound, a ponderous rumbling that was shaking the ceiling and wall. Then I knew what it was. Mayfield's newly uncrated safe was being moved. It stopped as suddenly as it started.

It was hard to think—much less act. I pulled at the door to shut it, but it moved only a few inches before catching on something. I couldn't budge it!

For one irrational moment, it seemed that whatever was upstairs had somehow seized the door. Then I understood that the rug's edge had become wedged under the wood panel. Dropping to my knees, I clawed breathlessly at the edge of the carpeting. The boards in the ceiling continued to betray the moving presence above me. Finally, the rug came free, and my fingers hit the boards of the floor, driving a splinter deep under my fingernail. With the rug out of the way, the door swung easily. I had been so intent on trying to free it that I had lost track of the intruder.

The key! What had I done with the key? The day before, I had found a wire-tied bunch of old-fashioned iron keys in one of the kitchen drawers and had tried them. I was sure I had left the one key in the kitchen door. I clutched at the faceplate of the lock.

The keyhole was empty on the living-room side. With a sinking heart, I felt for the other side of the lock—and there it was. The key resisted my frantic efforts to free it. I tugged at it. It came free, slipping from my fear-clumsy fingers and clattering to the floor.

The top tread of the stairs popped as weight was placed on it.

I sprawled forward on the linoleum, slapping my hands against its cold bareness until my fingers closed on the small piece of metal. It was too late to try to be quiet. I slammed the door and locked it. Sick with fear, I slumped against the door. My heart was beating so fast it was impossible to separate the individual contractions.

All at once it was important to have more than an inch of wood between me and whatever might be standing beyond that thin panel. I groped for the revolver, which had slipped from my waistband as I tugged at the rug, found it, and backed across to the sofa, never taking my eyes off the kitchen door, a barely visible white rectangle in the faint illumination.

My breathing gradually slowed as silence returned to the house. Both of us—victim and predator—were frozen in an instant of time. Once again the barely audible wavelets lapping the shore and the never-ending windsong imposed themselves on the stillness of the interior. It took very little imagination to believe the moaning to be the eternal lament of the damned souls that had ended their evil lives on this unholy spot.

As unpleasant as the island's dirge had become, I would have been content to hear no other sound save that. It wasn't to be.

The movements upstairs started again, moving methodically from room to room, seeking God knows what. Whatever was roaming the upper floor moved with a slow, dragging shuffle. The temptation to fire a round into the ceiling had to be resisted. Crazy as it sounds, I was afraid of angering the interloper. I kept envisioning Pete Delvecchio probing the dark spaces above, seeking me with blind eyes.

There was no comfort in thinking that the searcher might be human. A man who would sweep the Delvecchios out of existence certainly would not let me live. The events of the past two days were of a pattern. But what was the purpose? Was someone trying to kill me or drive me nuts?

After a while, it dawned on me that there had been no noise upstairs for a long time. One of the last sounds had been of glass crunching again. Did that hideous presence remain inside the walls of the Mayfield house with me?

Glancing about me, I was startled at how clearly I could view the Bengston place. It was morning, and the sun would soon be above the horizon.

Never had I been so glad to see the dawn.

Chapter
TWENTY-FIVE

Comforted by the coming of morning, I closed my eyes once more for what seemed but seconds. When I opened them again, it was to stare out the window in amazement. The sun was high overhead. I was exhausted from so little sleep and terrified of what Thursday might bring.

Remembering what had happened during the night, I glanced at the locked door to the kitchen. All was quiet beyond it.

Someone—something—had placed me in a state of siege, emotionally as well as physically. Mayfield's chores were going to have to be postponed. I needed to conserve my flagging energies for the effort to survive. I had to be prepared to attract the attention of passing planes to my plight. Driftwood had to be gathered for an emergency beacon and a HELP sign laid out on the granite face above the water's edge.

Ready to leave the house, I paused long enough to extract the key from the kitchen door and jam a sliver of charred wood in its place to prevent the use of a key from the other side. It was a relief to be outdoors, away from the dark, brooding stillness.

The seemingly never-ending breeze blew steadily in my face. Small, white-crested waves still hurried across Stone Warrior Lake toward the island. The distant shoreline remained a featureless wall of greenery, while overhead the incredibly blue and cloudless heavens continued to enclose the whole world. The unearthly look of that strange royal blue dome had grown most disturbing. It was inexplicable. Such colors simply didn't exist.

I walked a few yards down the slope and turned to face the Mayfield place. The ladder stood brazenly against the outside wall, the top rung resting immediately beneath the side window of the corner room. The glass had been broken out of the lower half of the frame, and a few glittering shards from the shattered pane were sprinkled between the foot of the ladder and the foundation. A length of two by four lay in the midst of the glass fragments.

Full of daylight courage, I started for the ladder to remove it, trapping the intruder upstairs if, indeed, he was still there. But the memory of the heavy concrete blocks, used as doorstops in the bedrooms, brought me to a halt. Anyone venturing beneath that window would be a sitting duck. The ladder would have to remain in position.

The length of wood, some four feet long, caught my eye. Three extremely large nails—really small spikes—had been driven through one end of it. It had not been there yesterday. It meant nothing to me for a second; then I understood. The intruder must have had it in the house with him. The nails seemed freshly driven—no rust around them. That rapping! Could I have been hearing the board being made into a weapon?

In that moment it became very clear. Whoever was on the island with me wanted to kill me. He had intended to lure me upstairs last night and attack me where I would have had little chance to use the gun. I stared upward at the window, wondering if I was being watched. My God, someone wanted to kill me. There was nothing I could do but stay alert every moment. If I relaxed I would die.

Why had the spike board been abandoned? Had he found another weapon? I started toward the deadly piece of wood only to stop in the nick of time, realizing it was within range of the concrete blocks. That must be it. It had been left there to draw me under the window.

I turned away in frustration. The distress signals had to be constructed as fast as I possibly could. At first consideration, it seemed a simple job, but most rocks of adequate size were scattered along the shoreline toward the point. I thought briefly about having breakfast first, but the thought of missing a passing plane stopped me.

It was a simple, four-letter sign, H E L P. Still, the job of lugging thirty- and forty-pound rocks into position soon became an arduous, back-breaking agony. When the last small boulder was finally rolled into place, it was midafternoon, and I was hungry for the first time in several days.

I couldn't fool myself about why I had neglected eating breakfast. I was afraid to open the kitchen door.

Lack of nourishment, coupled with exhaustion from sleeping so little, was sapping my remaining resources at an alarming rate. I had to have food.

Revolver in hand, I reentered the house. The interior was dark, cool, and hostile. The ambience of the house drained my resolution, and I found myself tiptoeing quietly toward the kitchen.

I stood at the door for a short while, listening to the stillness beyond, postponing the possible confrontation. It had to be opened. Rigid with anticipation of the worst, I braced my weight against the wood to absorb any sudden push from the other side and eased it open.

The anticipated assault didn't materialize. The door swung wide to reveal the shadowed kitchen and, beyond it, the light-filled sunporch. The rear of the house was vacant.

I scanned the room, looking for something out of place and finding it. The doors to the freezers and the refrigerator were standing open, and their motors were running. Their white interiors were empty.

Out on the sunporch, nothing had changed since last night. The shower of glass on my unmade bed sparkled in the afternoon sun. I peeked under the bed. My specimen case was where I had left it.

Back in the kitchen, I opened a cupboard and stared in dismay, a cold knot swelling in my stomach. The shelves were empty! I clawed at the doors of the other cabinets, yanking them open. All the food had disappeared; only empty shelves greeted my frantic search.

Desperation overcame caution. Anger exploded in me, sending me storming toward the steps, determined to charge upstairs and settle the issue with my tormentor. I froze in midstride, my foot on the first tread, my gaze riveted on the head of the staircase.

Crouched there, its front casters barely on the topmost tread, sat the three-hundred-and-fifty-pound steel safe. With the slightest push, it would crash down that narrow stairway, crushing the life out of anyone caught in its narrow confines.

I backed away, watching it. It loomed above me, massive, gray, and deadly. There would be no going up the steps.

It was a stroke of luck that the intruder had not been in position to launch that steel juggernaut when my defenses were down, coming through the door from the living room. There could be no further question about the intruder's intentions. Everything he had done—even what seemed like mere harassment, cutting down the flag, ruining the pump—was intended to confuse me and make me vulnerable to his attack.

Where was the chain saw?

I didn't want to think any more. Grabbing a galvanized bucket from beneath the sink, I leaped past the menacing staircase into the living room, slamming the door behind me. The sound of the lock's bolt sliding home was an odd, metallic click in the quiet of the building. From now on, there would be no going upstairs or even into the kitchen. Except during the daylight hours, my only refuge would be the front room. Even with the sun up, I dared not leave the vicinity of the house.

It was clear that the revolver was the only thing keeping me alive. My life depended on retaining possession of it and staying alert. At least I had quit thinking of zombies. My tormentor was human and afraid of bullets.

I left the house, determined to stay outside as long as possible. The generator's steady throb, rebounding off the walls of the two buildings, served as a reminder that it hadn't been shut down for the day. I headed toward the shed, detouring around the far side of Mayfield's to keep its bulk between me and the dead. Fatigue and hunger had left me too befuddled to appreciate that the generator's only use anymore was to provide light for corpses. Cautiously, I stepped into the shed and flipped the switch off, unaware that it was for the final time. The resultant hush was startling.

The inside of the generator shed was in shambles. I sat down on a wooden box to survey the mess. My gaze wandered about the cluttered shed, fitfully examining its contents. I stared thoughtlessly at the rectangle of sunlight coming through the doorway, alive with dust motes dancing above the hard rock floor, and idly pondered how I would react if a sudden black shadow fell on that patch of sunlight.

Terrified by the thought, I looked up and saw the rotting corpse of Pete Delvecchio filling the doorway.

With a shriek I lunged through the empty doorway. Nausea swept over me, leaving me on all fours, dry-heaving, my heart racing wildly.

Shaken by the hallucination, I staggered across the open slope, soaked with perspiration, and slumped down next to the massive supports of the water tank. I stared hopelessly across the lake. I was so tired and so screwed up with not eating right that my imagination was playing tricks on me. I needed to think clearly if I was going to stay alive.

Only when the sun hovered low above the horizon, staining the island with its lurid bloodiness, did I finally arise. The wind was quickening, forcing the damp, chilly air across the stony pitch. The evening mist was thickening against the surface, screening the dark, ever troubled waters of Stone Warrior Lake from the scrutiny of worldly eyes.

I shivered in the chill of the late Thursday afternoon and decided to bring enough wood down the hill to have a fire. Its crackling warmth would bring some life into the hated room that would be my prison during the long hours while the madman that stalked me waited nearby for my one mistake.

Desperately weary, I brought two armfuls of wood around to the front of the house, detouring around the far side of Mayfield's each time. By the time I had gathered a third load of small wood scraps to kindle the fire, the sun was settling into the nest of distant trees, spotlighting the two homes with a last lone ray of fiery iridescence before night wrapped them in gloom.

Too exhausted to follow the circuitous route a third time, I started between the two buildings, hurrying to finish before

darkness drove me inside. My eyes were fixed on the ground
ahead of me, refusing to glance toward that house with its
disintegrating bodies. In my peripheral vision, my elongated
black shadow twisted and cavorted against the garish, sun-
stained crimson of the log walls. I was almost through the gap
when I spotted, from the corner of my eye, some change at
Bengston's. I wanted to ignore it, yet could not halt my slow
pivot, overwhelmed by the need to know what was different.

The wood crashed painfully down on my insteps as the
"Oh, my God!" burst from my throat.

Each of the three windows displayed the face of a dead
Delvecchio. The corpses appeared to be sitting in straight
chairs, their bodies sagging forward, supported by their faces
pushing against the glass. Terry was at the front window.
Strands of pale blonde hair failed to mask the hideous snarl set
into her ruined and darkening face. Dolores, the mother, sat at
the middle window. Her face, bearing part of her weight, was
distorted against the transparent pane, with the open, bulging
eyes flat against the glass, smeared at its contact point by
them. At the back window the grossly swollen, grinning face
of Pete Delvecchio, his blackened tongue protruding between
white teeth, was beginning to show the first pronounced signs
of decay.

I was unable to look away from those open, dead eyes that
met mine in locked gazes, protruding from faces that smiled
forever in macabre invitation. The turgid countenances were
stained by the setting sun.

To a sobbing litany of "Oh, God!" I clawed at the revolver
in my waistband. Even in the throes of hysteria, I couldn't
bring myself to shoot directly at the bodies, but I did shoot.
The gun roared again and again, four times altogether. The
bullets, smacking into the wood above the windows, sent
showers of splinters leaping into the air.

With the gunshots like drumbeats, I shouted in cadence at
my impassive tormentors. "Damn you! Leave me alone!
Damn you! Leave me alone!"

The echoes of the gunfire faded across the broad sweep of
water. The shots purged me of the need to shout. Silence
returned, save for the ever-present funereal music of Stone
Warrior's timber stands.

I backed away from the sickening sight, tripping over my feet. Whirling, I ran for the porch steps, searching frantically in my pockets for the key.

My composure did not return until full night was at hand, and bringing in firewood was out of the question. The chill edging into the room was not helping my bruised toes or alleviating the throbbing of my tender ankle. The need to get a bucket of water from the lake had slipped my mind in the shock of my discovery. In its absence my hands felt stiff and gritty with dirt, and my finger was stinging where the splinter had sliced under my nail.

The full impact of my stupidity with the gun hit me. I hadn't bothered to buy any cartridges and had only the six that had been in the gun when it was purchased. After losing my head and blazing away, two rounds were left. The madman who stalked me obviously had no firearms. If he had, he could have ambushed me a dozen times over in the past three days.

The pistol represented the balance of power between us, and most of that advantage had been squandered in one idiotic act. Could my tormentor be smart enough to have predicted that I would waste my bullets like that?—or that I only had the six shells? Not unless he had searched my room—but when?

Huddled there in the dark, I thought of how often my lack of self-control had betrayed me. Wasting the bullets was only the latest example. The man from Seattle had not understood that.

Maybe the world believes what that poor gas station owner said about me being a coward. I'm the only one who knows that the blow to my head so stunned me that I didn't think of Laurie, much less realize that I had left her behind on that hillside until it was too late.

The Delvecchios might be alive even now if I hadn't reacted to having my feelings hurt by stomping out of their place. I would not have been sitting down by the tip of the island sulking while they were being murdered. Maybe it would have simply added one more victim to the killer's toll, but that might be better than what was happening now.

Somewhere in the midst of this line of reasoning, sleep

overtook me, and I started to slide from the sofa, awakening with a start. I was approaching the point of being physically unable to maintain consciousness.

I pushed the heavy chair over to where it was wedged against the kitchen door so that I would have ample warning if the killer found another key that would unlock it. With the room as secure as I could make it, I tottered back to the sofa and was instantly asleep.

The Delvecchios were landing on the island again—but not the family as they had been on that first day. These Delvecchios, with bluish, puffy faces, dead eyes, and hideous grins, moved in stiff gaits, like Frankensteinian monsters, back and forth between the dock and their abode.

I shot into an upright position, terrified, sweating profusely despite the chill. Another nightmare! I couldn't allow that to happen. It had been a nightmare that had caused me to attempt suicide two years ago.

God, I had been frightened—no, terrified—that night in Laurie's and my apartment. I still wonder if my sleeping mind, off guard, had been caught up in some sort of psychic teleportation. Was I destined to witness a never-ending series of violent deaths on that godforsaken hill?

I had fled into the bedroom. Laurie seemed so near—as though she might step into the room any moment. The idea leaped into my mind. I could escape a world filled with murderous thugs and ugly dreams. I could be with Laurie, forever.

The medicine cabinet held the solution. On the shelf was an untouched bottle of thirty-six sleeping pills, a medication prescribed for me but never used. I reached for a glass of water and methodically set about my task.

Returning to the bedroom, I gathered an armful of Laurie's clothes from the closet and, holding them in a tight embrace, lay down to die.

An hour later, just as I was slipping into a coma, the police, summoned by her parents, broke into the apartment.

On the day I was released from confinement to enter a suicide prevention program, I packed my bags and, in the middle of the night, sneaked out of Seattle.

I spent the next year bumming around the West, going from

one menial job to another. Finally, Rod, who had never stopped searching, located me at Grand Teton National Park. A few days later I returned with him to Sequim to live.

My unpleasant memories vanished with the sudden appreciation that something must have happened to snap me out of the nightmare about the Delvecchios.

I gripped the welcome heaviness of the revolver and listened, scarcely breathing. The minutes went by, and still all was quiet. Something had awakened me—but what? There was no light coming in at the window except from the slice of star-speckled sky.

Then I heard it—the faint rattling against the house, followed quickly by the sound of a squeaking board overhead. The intruder was inside again.

I tried to concentrate on the menace upstairs, but thirst and growing weakness demanded my attention. The physical ability to defend myself was all but gone. Overhead, the night prowler moved slowly down the hall, growing strong as I became weaker.

Tiptoeing to the door, I pushed my ear against the cool wood. A faint rumbling puzzled me, but only for a second. The safe on the landing had been moved. I understood why. The progression of protests from weight-laden wood began moving down the sides of the living room wall where the stair treads abutted against its surface. The walking nightmare was coming down the stairs after me.

The insane impulse to fling open the door and spring out into the kitchen for a final confrontation swept over me. As quickly, I felt a revulsion toward even touching the wood surface.

I jumped.

There was a soft brushing against the door. The stroking crept slowly around its frame, stopping, then moving on, like ghostly fingers seeking a passage through its cracks.

I backed away from the door, my hand on the gun, gasping for air, aware that I could be heard. I fought the urge to shoot through the wood. It was what my tormentor wanted—for me to use up the last of the ammunition.

Trembling violently, I forced my hand away from the butt of the weapon.

The soft brushing went on for two or three minutes, then ceased abruptly. Soon the stair treads renewed their progressive protest as the night visitor retreated to the second floor. The footsteps retraced their way along the passage overhead. I listened for the rattling sound that would tell me the ladder was being used again, but it didn't come. The sounds simply ceased.

A delicious feeling of relief swept over me. I returned to the sofa with an insouciant disregard for my circumstances. How odd it was that the tension slipped away so quickly—almost as if one built up an immunity to terror. It didn't seem to matter that a murderous presence still might be lurking only a few feet above my head.

I was asleep within thirty seconds, and this time my dreams centered around a full-of-life, happy Laurie, whose lovely green eyes sparkled in the light of a crisp Seattle morning.

The dream fell apart, and I was awake with the feeling that something was terribly wrong.

Chapter
TWENTY-SIX

From somewhere outside came an odd rushing sound that I could not identify. Still half-asleep, I took a deep breath. There was a strange smell in the air. Recognition exploded in my mind. Smoke!

My eyes flew open, seeking the window. The sidewall of Bengston's was illuminated by a shifting pattern of yellow light. Fire! The back of one of the houses was on fire!

I grabbed the revolver and flashlight and raced out the front door, oblivious of the pain in my ankle, forgetting about the madman who might be lying in wait. I ran up the slab between the buildings, past the dead onlookers, more bizarre than ever in the strange light, and rounded the corner.

The flames were mostly at ground level, burning at the base of the Mayfield house beneath the windows of the sunporch. Some parts of the log facing were beginning to catch fire. A small stream of lively yellow and pale blue flames danced back up the grade into the shed. The glare illuminated the blue-and-orange gasoline drum, which had been connected to the generator. The fuel line had been loosened, and a small jet of gasoline spurted out of the barrel into the pool of fire below it.

I leaped across the burning stream and plunged into the small structure, expecting the drum to explode into a fireball at any moment, taking me with it. I located a shovel among the stack of tools in the corner and careened back down the pitch. Pockets of soil, caught in small basins in the slab, provided dirt to smother the fire. The flowing gasoline, dammed by the back wall, was being shunted to the corner of the building and was draining down the far side of Mayfield's in a thin tracing of flames. I ran to the corner and, working feverishly, built a dirt dike. It diverted the flaming liquid away from the sidewall to where it spilled harmlessly down the slope into the lake. I turned back to the source of the fire. The stream coming out of the generator shed had become a mere trickle, but flaring curls of flame were visible now at several spots on the siding under the windows.

Racing back into the shed, I grabbed a bucket and sprinted for the lake. I lumbered back up the hill, conscious of how much I was spilling, and splashed the icy water against a burning patch. I started shuttling water from the lake, more aware of my increasing exhaustion than of the effect it was having on the conflagration. A dozen trips later, I was soaked from the waist down and ready to fall on my face, but the last of the burning spots had been quenched. The gasoline had drained away or soaked into the ground.

It was pitch black around the sheds, with only the odor of the fuel and the charred wood as evidence of the fire. With the excitement gone, an awareness of my vulnerability returned. Every shadow seemed filled with movement, and a chill ran down my back. The sickening thought hit me that I had left the front door unlocked.

I fled down the rocky face. Stopping at the foot of the steps, I stared upward. The door stood wide open, revealing a dense, impenetrable blackness in which a maniac might be awaiting me.

Turning away, I sought the openness of the dock. I began to pace its surface, knowing that to sit down even for the shortest time would be to fall into a deep sleep. An hour and a half later, with my eyes burning and my legs aching, I watched the sky gradually change from blue-black to gray to opal. It was Friday! I had been on this miserable island eight days.

When the first rays of sun spilled across the low crest of the island, I returned to the generator shed; there was one remaining task to be done before I slept. It was unsafe to stay indoors unless all the gasoline was dumped.

The barrels rested on a bed of steel scaffolding. The first drum—the one that had fueled the fire—was almost empty and easily handled. I tilted it forward and watched the last half-gallon of gasoline drain out onto the ground.

A simple chain hoist served to lift fresh barrels onto the metal bed. It would be necessary to swing the full one off on to the ground and roll it out of the shed. Once clear of the house, it could be safely drained down the slope into the lake. Lifting one of the barrels would have been a demanding job anytime because I was unfamiliar with the hoist. Now, after thirty hours without food and with only naps for the last seventy-two hours, the task was almost impossible.

I struggled painfully to secure the chains around the heavy drum. Despite my tugging at the steel links, they seemed at least two inches too short. But at last, with my fingers bleeding and pain slashing through my back, I was able to secure the hoist cables. I started to winch the drum free of its bed but was so weak I had to rest after each couple of turns of the winch handle.

With stubborn slowness, the heavy steel container came free of the framing, swaying ponderously in midair. I didn't have strength enough, standing below, to pull the hoist bar around to where the drum could be lowered to the ground. It would have to be done by climbing on top of the metal scaffolding.

Fatigue caused me to lose my balance, and my leg skidded against the rail, gouging a bloody groove along my calf. I sprawled in the dirt beside the hoist for several minutes, gasping for breath, seeking the strength in myself to try again. My second painful try was successful, and the hoist bar with its dangerous load hung clear.

The struggle to unhook the chains was no easier than the grim endeavor to secure them had been. Finally, the drum was on the ground and free to maneuver through the shed door. Bracing myself in front of the greasy cylinder, I started it rolling. Moving backward, my foot slipped, and I almost went down under the steel barrel. It wouldn't have run over me, but it could have trapped my arms under its four hundred and fifty pounds, leaving me unable to free myself. Straining against its curved surface, I regained my feet, trying to ignore the stinging of my torn calf under the ripped jeans. Turning the drum on its axis, I rolled it out across the granite until it cleared the Mayfield residence.

It took quite a search to locate the wrench for loosening the drain cap. My first futile attempts at opening it were enough to show me why there were crossbars to lock the barrels in position on the steel rack. Every time the wrench applied pressure, the steel cylinder started rolling. In desperation, I removed several rocks from my HELP sign and wedged them around the drum.

With the barrel immobilized, the plug finally yielded. Pungent, golden gasoline poured out, stinging my torn hands, and drew a wet, wavering line down to the water's edge. When the drum was empty, I turned it sideways and sent it bouncing into the lake, disposing of a potential bomb, which the vapor-filled cylinder was. Soon the other drum was out of the shed and following its mate into the lake.

Back in my living quarters, I slumped into the heavy chair and stared across at the unspeakable caricature of a human face that was Teresa Delvecchio's. Then I remembered—she wanted to be called Terry. Her death, to me, seemed more tragic than that of the others, even that of her little brother. She had been so full of life. I remembered how she had flirted

with me in her childish way. She would never know love—
the kind of happiness Laurie and I shared. I wished there had
been time to tell her about my Laurie. I think Terry would
have liked that.

After I had recovered, Dr. Molloy persuaded my father to
pay my way through the University of Washington, where I
majored in forest entomology. Father agreed only on the condition that he never had to lay eyes on me again.

I met Laurie Satterfield one fall afternoon when Rod and
Evie, on a visit, couldn't locate my apartment. Laurie, a
"townie," guided them to my place. When they arrived, I ran
out to greet them, giving Laurie, whom I didn't know, no
more than a curt thanks.

Laurie, also a student at UW, used to sit out on her front
steps doing her homework. Anxious to apologize for being so
ungracious, I memorized a stilted little apology. The next time
I saw her, I tried to make amends. Without any preliminaries,
Linc Wilhite, the original smoothie, started babbling before a
visibly startled Laurie. I stammered my way to a lame conclusion and quit looking at my feet long enough to see that she
was gazing up at me, a slightly quizzical, even mocking smile
on her face, her green eyes twinkling.

She laughed and patted the porch step beside her. "Bravo, a
wonderful speech! Now why don't you sit down and let's start
over?"

I spent two hours with her that afternoon. It was the first
time in my life I had talked—really talked—with a girl without wondering if I was screwing up.

After that, I stopped by to chat whenever she was outside.
As the weeks went by, my shyness disappeared. Finally, there
came an afternoon when Linc Wilhite finally did something
right. Dismayed because she had not been on her porch for
several days, I blurted out that I wanted to take her out. To my
amazement she accepted.

Over the next few months I came alive. I learned to love
life, and Laurie changed, too, growing more serious, more
subdued. I finally summoned the courage to ask her to go
steady.

The next year was one of overwhelming joy. There was but
one shadow. I struggled all year long with the fear that I

would lose her if she knew my background—having the nervous breakdown and all.

One chilly spring morning I told her everything as we stood on a point of land overlooking Puget Sound. I couldn't stop, afraid she would flee even as I talked. When it was all said, I kept my head down, unable to meet her eyes.

Her arms were amazingly strong as she tugged me around to face her. Her face had a glow, a radiance, that I had never seen before in a person.

"Linc, I'm in love with you. Don't you understand that, you idiot? The past doesn't matter. It's the present that counts. I've never met anyone like you. Please let me love you... forever."

I became aware that my focus had narrowed to where I was staring straight into those dreadful eyes of Terry Delvecchio's, and I hastily averted my own, suddenly afraid. Terry had been so young and full of life when she leaned out the upstairs window that first morning. I wanted desperately to be fourteen again at that moment—not that it had done her any good. I remember repeating the word fourteen a couple of times, and the next I knew, my chin was on my chest. For that long moment the front door stood open and unlocked.

Terrified that I could lapse into unconsciousness so easily, I rushed outside, forgetting the key to the kitchen as well as the revolver.

It was no wonder that I forgot the gun. While I was fooling with the gasoline drums I had gotten gunk on the pistol. I had been sitting wiping it with an old T-shirt when I noticed Terry. Without thinking, I had shoved the revolver, wrapped in the shirt, under the easy chair.

Desperate to do something that would keep me moving, I thought of the rocks that needed replacing—the two I had removed to help hold the barrel steady. I had paid little attention to the sign when I grabbed the hunks of granite, but now, looking more closely, I saw that something was amiss. The change was easily noticed from below. Most of the branches wedged in around the rocks to give them more substance had been stripped away, and some of the small boulders had been rearranged. The HELP sign had been destroyed. Just enough alteration had been done to render it useless. Studying the rock outlines one by one, I saw that the word HELP now formed a rough, 1181F—utter nonsense.

It would be hopeless to reconstruct it. The letters would last only as long as the sign was guarded. My energies could better be spent gathering wood for a signal fire. Even if piles were scattered, it was far less backbreaking to replace them than to continually rearrange the boulders.

Walking awkwardly on painful feet and legs, I worked my way along the beach, piling driftwood into stacks. By early afternoon, six caches of wood were heaped along the shore, and a sizable mound rested on the shingle above the dock.

As I was dumping the last armful on the pile, I heard glass breaking somewhere ahead of me. Flinging the wood aside, I ran awkwardly toward Mayfield's.

From out front, no damage was apparent. A few steps more brought me to where I could see between the buildings. The upper pane in the rear window of the Mayfield living room had been broken. There was very little glass on the ground—nothing but a piece of firewood from the stack by the porch.

I opened the front door and looked inside. The floor beneath the window was thick with shattered glass. My initial feeling was one of relief that so little damage had been done, but the more I thought of it the more puzzled I became. The broken pane would be of no help in sneaking in. It was about seven feet above ground level, and besides, anyone trying to climb through that jagged gap would slice himself to pieces. So why had it been broken? Just to harass me further?

I returned to the site of my emergency beacon and gathered the wood I had flung aside. Still unsettled by the strange episode, I wandered on down to the tip of the island and perched on one of the boulders, still trying to ferret out why the window had been broken.

It was no use. I was incapable of thinking. Even the icy lake water, splashed onto my flushed face, proved an ephemeral remedy for my exhaustion. I was reaching the point, light-headed and sweating, that I could no longer tolerate staying on my feet. It was time to either retreat to the house or pass out.

Absently, I reached to pat the reassuring bulk of the gun and felt nothing but the flatness of my waistband. Of course, that's when I remembered I had left it in the house under the easy chair. A cold chill swept my spine. A look at the sun told me I had been outside and defenseless for over two hours.

I forced myself to walk slowly back to the dock without undue haste. A sigh of relief escaped me when I reached the ramp leading to the float. Maintaining my insouciant air, I stopped and gazed across the lake. The unmarred water moved in glassy swells now with the afternoon doldrums approaching.

Pivoting, I eyed the shoreline past Bengston's and then studied the facade of the structure. In the yellowing sunlight of afternoon, nothing seemed changed about it. The windows remained shut, and the door, which had slammed with such awesome force in the night, was still tightly closed.

Turning away, I started toward the Mayfield house and froze in midstride. Dear God! The front door was standing wide open—not closed, as I had left it!

Chapter
TWENTY-SEVEN

I stared, transfixed, at the shadowed interior, trying to remember if I had closed the door firmly. Was it possible that I had not pulled it shut hard enough for the latch to catch, allowing the wind to reopen it?

The faint movement within the room probably would have gone unnoticed if I had not paused when I noticed the open door.

There are no words to describe the intensity of emotion that gripped me at that moment. My sanctuary had been despoiled, and my gun was in the hands of whoever was inside.

Deliberately, I glanced toward the woods to my left, trying to disavow any awareness of danger that I might have revealed. I tried to assess my situation, but my exhaustion was such that the most simple decisions were becoming impossible to make. While gathering driftwood earlier, I had paused once, for perhaps as much as a minute, trying to decide whether I should add one more stick to the bundle of wood I was carrying.

I could not resist the urge to glance again toward the ominous unguarded entry.

Despite the bright sun, it was possible to see into the interior of my quarters, thanks to the faint illumination from the side windows. The longer I looked, the surer I was that the full length of the room was visible. It appeared vacant. Could the vague sense of motion have been no more than another display of my overwrought imagination? I was about to start for the porch when the intensity of light within somehow altered, and I knew that someone out of my field of vision had crossed before the windows.

On legs so rubbery they would barely support me, I turned, not knowing what else to do, and walked slowly away. Crossing in front of Bengston's, I passed the long-abandoned basketball backboard, noting with a curiously detached air the Canadian flag wedged into the angle of the bracing behind the backboard. I pushed through the barrier of brush into the thick woods beyond. The tables were turned now, with me weaponless, shelterless, and chased to the part of the island I had sworn not to visit again.

My flight carried me into the midst of the twilight world of stunted, gray tree trunks and dank soil, dimly lit by the eerie green light filtering down through the sunlit crowns far overhead.

I crept along as quietly as possible, pausing from time to time to listen for indications of pursuit. I continued walking until half the island's length was between me and the two residences. Spotting an unusual little clearing, formed by a pod of trees growing so close together as to look like a stockade, I squirmed through a miniscule gap and hunkered down in the middle to rest and to listen.

The woods were quiet. Again I was overwhelmed by the lifelessness of this miserable island. What was there about the place that apparently made it impossible for animal life to survive? Probably, that moment marked the point when I began to accept that there was some truth to the legends about Stone Warrior Island. Only by accepting that some foul and unholy presence existed here could one account for the extinction of life. I really believed that now.

For the next hour I huddled in the tiny living stockade, finding solace in the protection it offered. The feeling of comfort disappeared when a persistent if distant rustling caught my attention, coming from somewhere beyond my hiding place and downslope toward the lake. The disturbances were short-lived but repetitive, followed by lengthy periods of silence. Gradually they grew louder, moving in my direction. The chase was under way; my nemesis was closing in on me.

I dared not rest any longer in my refuge. Rising, I found my legs so stiff as to be painful. I had to make a decision. If the killer had my gun, it was imperative to stay out of sight. If, by some miracle, it remained undiscovered I had to find a way to get back to Mayfield's first.

Although the ground was steep and slippery with needles from the spruces and pines, it was easier to travel high on the sidehill where the brush was scattered, so I headed uphill, climbing slowly, carefully eyeing the ground. I tried to avoid as much of the noisy ground litter as I could. Still, enough unseen twigs snapped beneath my feet to make me cringe. Ahead of me, the grove was thinning out and growing brighter as I drew near the island's summit. With the wide-spaced trees on the crest, there was less cover, and I would be more easily spotted. But I could put more distance between me and my pursuer, who must still contend with the more difficult footing in the dense growth lower on the hillside.

When I reached the ridge top, I turned back toward Mayfield's. Traveling more quickly through the scattered brush and widely spaced trees, I soon burst out into a large clearing. The area was bathed in sunlight, yet it felt alien. Somehow, it seemed a place in which gloomy twilight would have been more appropriate than the bright reality of the sun.

Massive timbers were strewn about, incompletely covered by the brush growing thick among them. Up close, the giant beams showed signs of charring. They looked as if they had lain there, undisturbed, for many years. Scattered among the heaps of ancient timbers was a rubble of quarried stone. On the far side of the ruins there was a jagged, crested column of stone, reaching fifteen feet into the air. A heavy coating of vines clasped its sides in a leafy embrace. The vines so distorted the towering structure's shape that it took a moment to understand what it was. The strange monolith before me was the remains of a massive chimney.

I knew then where I was. Around me were strewn the bones of the Brobham chalet. For the first time, I sensed presences, just as that crazed man at Two Mile Lake had said, but there was sorrow, not menace, in these shades.

The sharp crack of a branch breaking somewhere on the hillside below me brought a sudden end to my reverie. My pursuer had closed the gap between us.

As I hurried in the direction of the old chimney, I could make out the square opening of the fireplace, intact and well camouflaged under a curtain of vines. Afraid of being spotted before I could escape the clearing, I wormed my way through the tangled covering of vines and into the niche created by the fireplace. Hastily rearranging the vines to conceal the opening, I tucked myself into the shallow cavity, trying hard to control my heavy breathing.

Within a half a minute, my pursuer was barging through the underbrush at the edge of the ruins. The intruder circled the site but did not approach my refuge. For a minute I could hear nothing, and then, abruptly, the sounds of pursuit moved rapidly away from the clearing.

It was impossible to determine in which direction the tracker had gone.

The small stone grotto soon grew quite warm. Reveling in my comparative safety, I became extremely sleepy. I knew I should leave but yielded to the demands of my fatigued body. My eyes closed and I slept.

I awoke in a surge of panic, unsure of where I was. The masonry that enclosed me was hard and unyielding, and for one dreadful moment, I thought I was entombed. Only when my thrashing arms encountered the screen of vines did I remember.

Aware that my flailing about had caused the drapery of leaves to stir, I huddled there a bit longer, afraid of hearing returning footsteps. After a while, I quietly worked the natural screen apart and stared out.

It was like a frontispiece of a Gothic novel. The last of the twilight bathed the scene, but it was not that which so distorted the lonely clearing with its melancholy memento of a broken dream. The treetops were motionless in the absence of any wind. Stone Warrior was without its requiem. The absence of a breeze had allowed a mist, rising off the lake, to pile up over the island, topping the crest, creating a dense fog.

I struggled out of my rocky haven, wincing at the protest from my cramped muscles.

Never had I seen such a fantastic scene in all my years of outdoor living. It was like a work of an outré surrealist. The fog was as dense as pea soup and of a thickness that allowed it barely to overlap the ridge. It was impossible to make out the ground more than a yard or so away, and yet the taller bushes were quite discernible, standing out above the vaporous ground covering. The trunks of the trees around the clearing were unobscured except for the bottom foot or so where they entered the thick mist.

I felt a sense of urgency. The fog would be around the Mayfield place. If I were ever to have a chance to regain the house and look for the revolver, it would have to be before the night wind dispersed the thick mist. Of course, the minute I left the crest and plunged into the cloying drifts of vapor, I would be lost, but the slant of the hillside would keep me going in the right direction. Even if I didn't encounter the log pile, my trek would eventually bring me to the low tip of the island. From there it would be a simple matter to grope my way around to the dock and home.

Standing there trying to decide on a course of action, I again had a sense of presence. Although the sunlight was no longer around me to bolster my courage, I was still without fear. Whatever the presence was, it engendered a spirit of sadness, of infinite longing. I felt I was being watched—but not as the madman watched me.

I could delay no longer. When the wind returned, the fog would be shredded in a matter of minutes and carried away. It was with some feeling—how can I say it?—of regret that

I left the clearing. I was sure that on some future day I would come again to the eerie quiet of the ruins.

Moving carefully, I started to descend the far slope. But as I reached the beginning of the thicker, spindlier growth that extended down to the shoreline, I felt an irresistible impulse to turn around. What I saw I will never forget.

There, above me in the clearing, stood a large, two-story chalet, reaching like some dark sentinel through the low-lying, milky fog. There was no way, at least on this earth, that it could be there. Yet I was awake and sane, and it towered over me. I could even see the pale reflections of the night sky from its dark windows.

Unable to stop myself, I started back up the hill. It must have been to try to verify what my senses perceived. Maybe those tormented souls I had sensed were trying to show me their place in time.

I had not gone five paces before the house started to disintegrate before my eyes, dissolving into vague dark masses that coalesced and became groups of shadowy trees. The glinting from the windows was no more than the gaps between tree-tops that allowed a glimpse of the night sky.

I stopped at the edge of the cleared area. There was no need to go farther. All that remained were the ruins of a dream home savaged by whatever evil possessed this wretched island. Even now, I cannot describe the depth of my feelings. Was it an apparition—a product of my fear and my fatigue? I will never believe that—not with the emotions that stirred in me or with what happened next.

In the act of turning away, I fell. Did I slip? I don't think so. It was as if the ground suddenly slid from beneath me. I sprawled out flat, and in the same split second, agonizing pain lanced through my hands and feet. For a moment I writhed on the ground, gasping at the intensity of it.

I struggled to get up, but—I swear to God—it felt as if I was being held to the ground! Then it was over, and I scrambled to my feet, stumbling down the ridge away from the clearing.

Pausing where the thicker timber began, I rubbed my hands across each other. They were unmarked—without the slightest residual of pain. Still more hallucinating?

That was probably as near as I came to wanting to give up the struggle. It was terrifying enough that a lunatic stalked me. If I were going to become a victim to my own delusions as well, I could not resist much longer. I still refused to admit there might be more to the world than natural laws could explain. Maybe I kept going only because it's the nature of man to strive to the end.

The eeriness of the stifling mist about me was accentuated by the patter of condensed vapor falling from the trees. On the lower ground, the fog was so thick it slowed me to a snail's pace. The countless blighted tree trunks were impossible to see and ready to punish the face of the unwary walker. For the next hour I struggled along the hillside, lost, without the vaguest idea how far it was to the house. The one thing I was sure of was that I was still laboring along the island's far slope.

Uncertainty was stirring again within me even though common sense told me there was no way I could become lost. I should have long since reached the tip of the island.

Pausing, I leaned against a fog-dampened spruce, trying to decide whether to cross the ridge and come down somewhere on the front slope where I would be sure to encounter the granite slab.

My concern about the noise of moving blindly through the woods had evaporated long ago. The fog effectively muffled sounds. Standing there, expecting to hear nothing because of it, I became aware that I was hearing . . . people.

I listened intently, but the distant voices grew softer until they faded out. I waited another moment but heard nothing more. Too nervous to remain in one spot, I started forward again.

I took about ten steps and paused again. This time there was no need to strain to hear voices. They were close. It was impossible to make out the words, and yet there was a cadence and a repetition of sounds. It had the rhythm of conversation, rising and falling in volume with the shifting of the fog banks. The longer I listened, the more certain I was that the voices were those of women—not just two, but three or more.

I tried to tell myself it was foolish—that it was some sort

of aural illusion, a companion piece to the bizarre visual illusion that had unfolded in the ruins of the Brobham chalet—yet it seemed so unlikely. The voices were not fading away, as the phantom building had done.

Moving with great caution, I stalked the spot from which they emanated. In the dense swirls of vapor it was difficult to know how far away they were, but they were definitely downslope from me. When next I paused I was much lower on the hillside. My descent had been quiet enough that I was certain they were not alarmed. It was still impossible to see anything through the banks of fog, which was even thicker this close to the water's edge. Still, I knew—I just knew—the owners of the voices were not more than twenty or thirty feet away.

At that moment I distinctly heard words in English. I heard the word "God"—I know I heard the word "God"—several times, and also the word "prayer." I was so close that I could detect strong emotion in the speakers—even, perhaps, a tremor of fear.

I suppose I was beyond rational thought. An explanation flashed into my mind, and I accepted it without reservation. Mayfield and his friends had landed during my nap in the ruins. It was Friday and I thought he'd said something about probably arriving on a weekend. I did have sense enough to question why they were blundering about in the mists, apparently frightened. I found an answer for that, too. Perhaps they had gone into Bengston's, discovered the corpses, and understood the desperate situation they had blundered into. We had to make contact at once.

I started forward again, not wanting to frighten them. But as I neared the shore, the sound of the waves lapping against the shore grew louder—so loud that it was drowning out their voices.

I stopped, listening, afraid of losing the direction. When last I checked, they had been immediately in front of me. They had to be within arm's reach.

Throwing caution to the wind, I plunged forward, grabbing a sapling just in time to prevent myself from sliding down the wave-polished rock rim into the lake.

There was nothing there!—nothing but the unusually loud

slap of wavelets, caught in a sharp little niche in the rock. There never had been anything. I had been so anxious to find someone that my mind had shaped the sounds of splashing water into human voices.

The thought of the Brobham ruins flashed into my mind. Could I—could I actually have been hearing the voices of those English women captured by the Métis?

I shook my head, angry with myself. God, I had to rid myself of those stupid superstitions!

I turned away, wanting to flee from the site of my ignoble investigation. A few more strides, and I knew where I was. I almost walked, face first, into a jutting tree trunk—the one from which the chain saw had disappeared.

Ducking beneath it, I turned upslope, feeling my way through the untidy heaps of cut timber. If I had been moving slowly before, I was no more than inching my way now. The blinding drifts of fog were as dense as ever, yet the dwellings were close at hand, just across the crest. It was probable that, with the visibility reduced to zero, my nemesis would be lurking around the houses, awaiting my return.

My hands, already battered, were sore from the hundreds of trees they had gripped as I groped through that impenetrable gloom. The tips of my fingers were hurting from the countless painful encounters they had endured with unyielding spruces and pines. Still, when I left the last fringes of that dismal glade and felt the solid rock of the ridge under my feet, I dropped down on all fours, inching ahead, until I reached the crest. I must have stayed there fifteen minutes, postponing the moment I would have to walk down that naked slab to find sanctuary or death.

The fear of the fog abruptly lifting finally prodded me into action. Terrified, I remember very little about how I reached the house. I can't even recall if I walked between the buildings or circled around the Mayfield place. When I stepped through the doorway into the living room, the first thing I saw was that the kitchen door was open. I felt calm—maybe resigned is a better word—crossing the room to close the door. The key was still in the lock. Slowly, deliberately, I locked the door. Only then did I slide my hand under the easy chair and encounter the cold steel of the gun. Pulling off my shoes, I lay down on the sofa. I remember thinking how much I wanted to be back in Sequim—how much I wanted none of this to be happening. The next minute I was asleep.

Thank God I had no idea what awaited me when I awoke Saturday morning.

Chapter
TWENTY-EIGHT

I came awake feeling unusually warm. Usually our Seattle apartment stayed cooler than this, even in the heat of the summer . . . and it was so light, too. I rolled over to face Laurie, feeling her cool flesh against me. I didn't know how she did it. She never perspired, even on the warmest days, and now her skin felt marvelously cool.

I called softly, "Laurie—"

She was playing coy again. Laurie always awoke before I did and then would pretend to be asleep when I tried to get her up.

"Laurie . . . I know you're awake. Laurie—"

I snuggled my head against the coolness of her shoulder, feeling her hair against the side of my face, wondering what she had done to it. It seemed much longer and coarser than usual. Even my nuzzling against her neck failed to produce any reaction.

I came up on my elbow. "Laurie, if you don't wake up, I'm going to give you the nerdiest, wettest kiss you've ever had."

The threat evoked no response. I had married a stubborn woman.

I leaned forward and pressed my lips against hers. She was still clowning around . . . kissing with her mouth open like that.

"Darn you, Laurie. You kiss me right, or I'm going to send you packing home to—" The odor struck me—an over-

whelming, nauseating, disgusting odor that swept everything
out of my mind.

I gagged, "My God, Laurie, that smell! Wake up, for God's
sake! Something is—"

My lips were brushing hers when I awoke, my eyes coming
open the length of an eyelash away from the dead, bulging
eyes of Terry Delvecchio. Oh, sweet Jesus, I had been kissing
the decaying corpse of that girl!

I know that I shrieked as I spun away from her and dived
out through the door, crashing onto the floor in the middle of
the sunporch. My throat was convulsing so violently I
couldn't breath, and a hot gush of bitter bile spilled from my
mouth. I rolled onto all fours, and then I could think of nothing but the agonizing spasms racking my stomach and my
throat. I could hear nothing but the roaring in my ears.

And then I remembered. I looked back through the doorway of what had been my sleeping quarters. That . . . thing
was lying on the bed in my cubbyhole, and I had . . . God help
me . . . I had held it in my—oh, God! I had kissed it.

My stomach heaved at the smell of her dead flesh on me.
Moaning, I lurched to my feet and raced through the kitchen,
careening off the butcher-block table and slamming heavily into
the wall. I staggered off-balance through the doorway and fell.
Clawing at the sofa, I got my feet under me again and plunged
out the front door, clearing the steps in one tremendous leap.

I bounded down to the water's edge and threw myself flat,
grabbing handfuls of silt, grinding it against my lips, tainted
with rotten flesh. I was unconscious of the pain I was inflict-
ing on myself until I saw the smear of blood on the back of
my hand. The gut-wrenching odor of putrifaction permeated
my clothing. I tore them off, ripping the T-shirt away and
jerking off the jeans, and threw the vile-smelling garments as
far as I could out into the water.

The force of the wild, off-balance heave sent my feet flying
out from under me and I crashed backward into the lake. The
icy shock of Stone Warrior closing over my head brought me
back to reality, and I splashed my way back ashore. I began to
curse—every obscenity I could think of—and it was something I had never done in my life. Why? Anger, frustration,
terror of dying a horrible death . . . I don't know why.

I huddled in my shorts and gripped the gun, which had fallen, luckily, on the slab as I yanked off the jeans.

My hysteria subsided, and I started to think not of myself but of how the corpse of that poor girl had been abused, lugged around to terrify me with no regard for her dignity as a human being. The more I thought of it, the angrier I became. I found myself on my feet, shouting, using language I never used before. "Goddamn you! You son of a bitch, you won't get the best of me."

My voice rang over the clearing.

Still furious, I stormed back up the granite face and into the front room. For those few moments I would have welcomed a face-to-face meeting with the maniac that haunted Stone Warrior Island.

But the living room was empty. I think I would have marched all over the house, demanding a showdown, if the vileness of decay hadn't slammed into me as I started into the kitchen. It swept me backward into the living room like a great hand, and the anger was gone and the fear was back, and I slammed the kitchen door and locked it.

I slunk back out onto the porch and sat down in the morning sunlight, whose warmth made little headway against the coldness that had invaded my body. A good hour passed before I came to my feet, resolved to go on with the task of trying to stay alive until help arrived.

It was well along into the afternoon. What sleep I had gotten had been of little use. I had tossed and turned, tormented by feverish dreams. And then to awake in bed with . . . her. My God, how had I gotten onto the sunporch? Then I remembered.

Have you ever had something pop into your mind that you haven't thought about for years? It was like that. Suddenly, I remembered the sleepwalking. I had been maybe ten or eleven at the time. Some of it was kinda funny—except to my father. Once my best buddy's mother had offered to take me along with them for a day in Portland. Mother had gotten up during the night and found me missing from bed. She found me sitting out by the curb in my pajamas at 4:00 A.M. waiting for them. Something similar happened when my Uncle Jim was going to take me fishing. Later on, after Dad and I started having so much trouble, Mom found me several times wandering about the house. I remember now talking with Dr. Molly about it. He agreed with what our family doctor had told my family way back then. It was the way some people acted when they were under great stress.

I began to relax but the feeling of well-being was of short duration. I had thought I was safe, locked in for the night, but—my God, if I was leaving the room, wandering around absolutely defenseless, I was as good as dead.

I thought again of poor Terry. How could anyone, even the most maniacal creature, stand to carry that decomposing body around? My next thought was even more frightening. How in Heaven's name could he have known I would go to the sleeping porch? Suddenly, that horrible moment of awakening entangled with that gruesome corpse was vivid in my mind again. My stomach began to heave. Grabbing a towel, I headed out the door, anxious to wash my sweaty face in the icy lake water before I began to dry-heave again.

The shock of the frigid water pouring over me steadied me, and I climbed onto the dock to pull on the clean shirt and jeans. There was little wind—the normal early afternoon pattern. Stone Warrior's surface was hazy despite the bright sun. Draping the towel over my shoulders, I seated myself on the edge of the dock, letting my feet dangle just above the water.

The distant scream was cut short by a huge splash.

Chapter
TWENTY-NINE

I forgot everything—the danger I was in, the horrid encounter with Terry, even my exhaustion. I dashed across the granite slab in front of the Bengston house and plunged into the woods. I could hear someone thrashing about in the water maybe thirty yards beyond me. Reaching a spot directly uphill

from the source of the noise, I plunged down the slope, barely
stopping myself from stepping on the slick steep rock rim that
would have carried me into the lake.

Directly below me a girl, a long-haired blonde in her late
teens, was half out of the water, clawing futilely at the smooth
granite. When she saw me she screamed and threw herself back
into the water, sinking out of sight. I caught myself in the
moment of diving in. I no longer had the strength to swim up to
the shallows by Bengston's, much less to tow someone else to
safety. I spotted a sizable tree branch some twenty feet behind
me. I burst back through the screen of brush just as the girl's
head broke the surface again. I thrust the long branch toward
her, and she screamed again. She dodged away from the branch
and cried, "Oh, God, please don't kill me. Don't kill me!" A
wavelet washed over her face while she was still yelling at me,
and she started to cough, clutching at her throat.

When she broke the surface again, I shouted, "For God's
sake, I'm not trying to hurt you. Grab the branch. I don't have
strength to come in after you."

She clutched at the branch, gagging and coughing too much
to talk. Then she seemed to realize that she had hold of it and
released it as though it was red hot.

"Grab it, damn you! You're going to drown if you don't."

She closed her hand on it again and this time held on.

I tried to talk more calmly, to get her to listen to me. "Listen, I'm not going to hurt you. Hang on and I'll try to pull up.
Do you understand?"

She said nothing, still having a hard time clearing her lungs
of water.

It was a horrendous job, with the condition I was in, but
when she was free of the water, she managed to get her knees
under her and help.

Once she was off the rock, I unceremoniously pulled her
back through the brush where she sprawled on the ground,
still coughing and retching. I slumped down by her for a moment, too exhausted to help further until I rested.

The gap in the brush and the small bush in the water where she
fell gave mute evidence of what had happened. She had been
moving along the shore and had chosen to try to work her way
around the clump of brush rather than detouring up the hill. She

had lost her balance and tried to save herself on the glassy granite. If I hadn't been there, she would have had to have the ability to swim to Bengston's or she would have drowned.

But who was she? Where had she come from? I was still so stunned by her sudden appearance that it hadn't really registered with me.

As I rose she pulled herself up onto her hands and knees, her body heaving as she struggled for air. She began to sob. "I'm going to die. No, don't. Oh, please don't. I don't want to die."

I didn't know what was wrong with her—why she was talking that way—but I wanted to get her out of those woods. Putting my arms around her chilled, compliant body, I pulled her to her feet, half-carrying and half-walking her toward the open ground. She was shivering uncontrollably, her teeth chattering, but she was breathing more easily now. Pulling off my T-shirt, I ran it over her arms, shoulders, and legs to dry them.

Her brown eyes, vacant and unfocused, narrowed as she realized I was there. They dimmed again, and she muttered, "Where am I? What is this place?"

I grabbed her by the shoulders, not sure I was getting through to her. Her eyes skidded away in panic, looking anywhere except at me. There was the odor of fear about her.

"Listen, it's okay," I said. "I'm not going to hurt you. You're on Stone Warrior Island. Where did you come from? Where are your friends—the party you are with? You don't know how glad I am to see you."

She twisted free of my hands and laughed—a shrill staccato, near hysteria. "My friends, my party? You want to know about my party? My party's over. They're dead . . . all dead."

I reached for her, as much to stop the words that were shattering my hopes as to comfort her. She backed away on rubbery legs, breathing hard again. When she finally spoke her voice trembled and was barely audible. "Oh, my God! It was awful! We were in a plane—my mom, my dad, my boyfriend, and the pilot. We crashed. I've been wandering through that damned forest for days. I had about given up . . . then I stumbled out of the woods across from this island. I thought I saw houses."

I looked at her, puzzled. She was a big girl and looked

strong, but it seemed impossible that anyone except a trained
distance swimmer could have swum across that two miles of
icy water.

"How did you get over here to the island? I mean . . . you
didn't swim, did you?"

She shook her head, her eyes intent on my face. "No, of
course not. I found a canoe over there. There was a hole in its
side, but I knew I couldn't last much longer unless I found
help. I was hoping to keep its side tilted so that the gash
would be above water, but it was too exhausting to keep pad-
dling in an awkward position like that. After a while the boat
started to take in water with every stroke. After that, I paddled
as hard as I could, trying to get as close as possible to the
island before it sank. I had to swim about two hundred yards.

"It was almost dark and the most god-awful fog came in. I
knew I could never find the houses in that, so I stayed down at
the end of the island all night. It was so cold. I finally
dropped off to sleep about dawn. When I woke up I started
for the houses, and then I slipped and fell in the water."

"The canoe—what kind was it? Where did you find it?"

"It was just an ordinary canoe, a red one. I found the canoe
pulled up on the bank of a small stream that empties into the
lake. When I saw it, I started yelling, hoping somebody
would hear me, but there was no answer. I just knew that
there had to be someone around here because of the canoe.
Thank God, I was right! You must call for help."

My last hope that this girl's sudden appearance might prove
to be my salvation vanished. I shook my head. "I'm sorry, but
I'm no better off than you are. I'm marooned here. There
have been some problems . . . and the food is gone. But if we
can hold out a while longer, a supply plane is due. Anyway,
you're safe for now."

She looked up sharply at me, a frown on her face. She must
have found my statement odd. At least she didn't know how
ambiguous my use of the word "safe" had been. I remember
thinking that she would have been a heck of a lot safer, the
way things stood, if she had stayed on the far shore, but I
remained silent. The time would come all too soon when she
would have to be told. For the moment I wanted companionship—a companionship untainted by terror.

She was not a pretty girl, but despite her size, she was quite feminine and had a strong, attractive woman's body. Her restless brown eyes, constantly moving in quick, darting glances, followed every move I made. Her arms and legs, the skin strangely pale beneath the flush of a sunburn, were badly scratched, and her hair, despite the time in the water, still had bits of twigs and bark caught in it.

My visitor struggled with some inner turmoil before she asked, almost shyly, "Do you have anything at all that I can eat? All I can think about is food. God, what I wouldn't give for a cheeseburger, or maybe some ham and fresh eggs and a hot cup of coffee. I could eat a horse!"

Her graphic descriptions sent so much saliva surging into my mouth that I could scarcely answer without drooling. "I'm sorry, but all the food is gone. We'll have to tighten our belts until the plane comes. We're going to become awfully hungry, but at least we won't starve to death that soon."

Her eyes bright and quizzical, she asked, "How long since you've eaten?"

"It's been about two days now, and I wasn't eating very much before then." I tried to grin. "It sure is a hard way to join Weight Watchers."

She was watching me closely. "Hey—you're laying a real guilt trip on me. I ate just before I started across the lake yesterday. It seemed a good idea to store up some energy before trying to paddle that far. I had a half-full knapsack of food with me—emergency rations from the plane—chocolate and soup, stuff like that—but when the canoe swamped, I had to let the knapsack go. I shouldn't complain, though. At least I'm alive."

I wondered how she could keep talking so much about food after stuffing herself like that. Well, she would be subsisting on memories of food just like me after a couple of days.

Abruptly her face changed, and she was fighting to control herself. "Oh, God . . . they're dead . . . all dead."

"Gee, I know it's terrible, but you should thank your stars for how lucky you were. You don't look as though you were hurt at all."

She broke eye contact with me and, shaking her head, stared down at her shadow on the granite. "I was real lucky. When I saw that we were going to hit, I dived behind the front seats of the plane. It came in low and smashed through the treetops. The plane slid out into the middle of a swampy spot. It didn't feel as if we hit very hard. For a few seconds I thought everything was going to be all right—until I crawled out from beneath the seats and saw the others.

"Oh, Christ, it was ghastly! They're all dead . . . my family is dead and I'm alone."

She raised her face upward to the sky, her eyes tightly shut and her fists clenched. She stood like that for a moment before relaxing abruptly. She looked toward the house. "Can't we go inside and find something warm for me to put on? I need to get out of these wet clothes."

As much as I wanted to ignore her request and revel in the company of another human being, it was time to tell her. "Listen, I don't know how to tell you this after what you've been through, but you made a bad mistake when you came over here thinking you would find help."

She looked startled, and fear stained her features.

I told her everything that had happened, talking faster and faster, unable to stop. I told it all—about the timers the Delvecchios had used on their lights, the killings, the realization that there was a maniac stalking me. Yet that isn't true. I didn't tell everything. I forgot completely about those forlorn corpses buried on the other side of the ridge. My thoughts were of the staring cadavers next door and of the creature that roamed the second floor in the nighttime. It would have meant little to me, at that point, if a flotilla of bodies had floated past the dock. I wonder if it would have made any difference if I had remembered to tell her about the murdered Texans.

Her reaction to my macabre story bewildered me. At first she seemed incredulous, shaking her head as if in disbelief. But as I continued, her features grew set, revealing nothing. Only her eyes were alive. She watched me closely, scanning my face feverishly as I talked. She appeared more interested in my emotional reaction than in the details of my story.

Then I understood. In my joy at seeing a fellow human being, I hadn't thought of the mental shock that would follow a traumatic experience like a plane crash. Even so, there was no way to avoid telling her what awaited her at Stone Warrior. When I finished my tale, she shifted her gaze to the two log structures that loomed above us like sentries, guarding Stone Warrior's bloody killing ground. Her face suddenly contorted, and she was close to hysteria. "God help me! Maybe I would have been better off if I had died with my folks."

I looked at her with pity. She had lived through her own personal nightmare, and now she had to face mine, too.

"Don't be afraid." I said. "If you help me, then we both will have a far better chance of surviving. I'm so exhausted I'm almost asleep on my feet. You can spell me on watch, and I can get enough rest to keep going. You don't know how tired I am. That madman is waiting for me to fall asleep. He doesn't dare attack as long as I'm awake and armed.

"If you can survive a plane crash and stay alive this long in the wilderness, nothing is going to happen to you this close to being saved. And your luck hasn't been bad since you landed. You could have run into that monster. All we have to do is hold on until the plane arrives. Do you understand? Just survive until it lands."

I reached for her shoulder to give it a reassuring squeeze.

Her head came up, her eyes widening. She jerked herself free of me, almost falling. "No! Don't!"

I stared at her, bewildered. Her arms were rigid at her sides, her fists clenched, her eyes mere slits. Abruptly, she relaxed. "I'm sorry. I didn't mean to act that way. It's just that I'm so wound up. Please forgive me."

Maybe I'm too sensitive, but her rejection hurt my feelings. After all, I had saved her life not fifteen minutes before. My intention had been to comfort her, and she acted as though the thought of being touched by me was disgusting.

Hesitantly, she touched my arm and managed a strained smile. "Forgive me?"

I was being too thin-skinned. She was as frightened and lonely as I. "Sure, I forgive you. You forgive me. I guess I'd act the same way after wandering for days, lost in that forest.

"Hey, don't you think we'd better get on a first-name basis? I'm Linc Wilhite."

She appeared to turn the matter over in her mind a moment, then nodded gravely. She looked down as if abashed at having to introduce herself. "You're right. I'm Michelle Black."

"Hey, I like that. Michelle—that's a pretty name. Well, with that blonde hair, I bet you aren't nicknamed Blackie."

I was talking nonsense, acting as ridiculous as always around females, but she didn't seem to notice. She looked at me solemnly. "No, no one called me Blackie. My dad always thought us kids should use the names we were given."

"Good. Now I won't have to call you Friday."

"Friday?"

"Yeah, that's in Robinson . . . oh, forget it. It was a stupid joke."

Although my new companion had stopped shivering, her clothes and hair were still wet. I knew she must be uncomfortable, but I dreaded taking her to the house and exposing her to the reality of the situation sooner than I had to. Besides, with two more hands to help, I could do more before nightfall to prepare our defenses. The afternoon hours were hurrying by, and the driftwood cached along the shoreline needed to be placed on the brush heap for the beacon fire. It must be ready to light in case a plane flew over after dark. There was a good chance that the aircraft searching for the site of the plane crash would extend their sweeps as far as Stone Warrior Lake.

I was less than truthful with her. "Michelle, I know you want to get inside and let your clothes dry. If you'll help me gather some wood, I'll build a big fire in the fireplace."

"More firewood," she said. "I don't understand what—" She broke off in midword and shrugged.

"I hope your hands aren't too tender for a little hard work."

She turned them, palms up. They were swollen and bruised and had skinned places on them. She made a face. "They have had quite a workout in the last few days. I don't think carrying a little wood is going to hurt them any more. Besides, moving around will keep me warm. Let's go and get it done."

Although she walked with mincing steps, she soon outdistanced me as we headed down the shore to the nearest cache of wood. She was far fresher than I, despite her near drowning and the night in the open. I didn't appreciate until then what the lack of food and sleep had done to me.

Once we started to work, it was a different story, though. Although large and strong, she paused often to catch her breath, flexing her arms and shoulders before returning to the job. She was obviously not a girl who was into exercise. Her untanned skin and flabby muscle tone convinced me that she was more a party girl than an outdoor girl.

We carried four stacks of driftwood to the bonfire site and were gathering a fifth when I stopped her. "We have enough driftwood now to build a fire visible for fifty miles. Besides, if I carry another stick of wood, I'll have to crawl all the way back to the house. What we need to do now is cut a few armfuls of green branches to produce black smoke in case a plane flies over during the day. Duck back into that patch of seedlings and start cutting branches while I keep watch. Here's my knife."

I pulled my hunting knife out of its scabbard and thrust it toward her. With a squeal she leaped away from me, reaching down in the same motion to grab a heavy chunk of driftwood from the ground. Her eyes were wild and unfocused as she crouched, facing me, looking like a trapped and fear-crazed animal.

I was appalled. "For the love of heaven, Michelle, I'm not going to hurt you. If I wanted to, I've had a dozen opportunities already. Don't you understand? We're in the same boat. We have to trust each other. Please."

As I watched, afraid to move for fear of spooking her, she slowly relaxed, and the driftwood dropped from her hand. "I'm sorry, Linc. We're both on edge. I didn't mean to act that way. I know you're my friend, and I trust you . . . honest."

She moved toward me, her hand extended for the knife, but seeing the odd stiff way she walked, I knew she still harbored a residual of fear. Trying to smile, I laid it on one of the larger boulders for her to pick up. "Just remember, kid. You and I play on the same team."

She moved ahead of me into the grove of saplings and began to strip branches from the young spruces and jack pines struggling to survive in the granite sands. I worked slowly along the rocky beach, gathering additional driftwood into small heaps, but never straying far enough away to lose sight of her. She was holding together well, despite the trauma of the aircraft accident and the new fears my strange story must have brought to her.

Michelle worked steadily, head down, apparently unconcerned about the maniac that was probably watching us at that very moment. By the time I stacked the wood I had collected, she had cut and piled two big armfuls of boughs and sat on a boulder, watching me approach.

We filled our arms with the freshly cut conifer branches, smelling of pitch, and carried the bundles back to the head-high mound of wood below Mayfield's. After I finished working the fragrant boughs into the pile, we walked down to the water's edge to wash the sticky resin from our hands.

I grinned at the solemn-faced Michelle. "Hey, it's not too bad, having somebody around to work with. I'll take my knife."

Her eyes narrowed. "Your knife? Oh, hell, what did I do with it?"

Chapter
THIRTY

I was furious with Michelle, both for her carelessness and for her indifference to it. We couldn't afford to lose that knife —not when our lives depended on having it and the revolver.

"Do you realize what you have done? Come on! We have to go back and find it before it's too late."

My angry outburst snapped her head up, and she watched me, eyes wary, muscles tense, motionless. Again, I was puzzled by her response.

But I was far too concerned about the knife for subtleties, so I grabbed her wrist and started running awkwardly down the beach, pulling her after me. She fought me to a stop.

I whirled on her. "Don't you understand? I have to find it. You had no right to be so careless. It's the only weapon I have except for the gun. Now come on."

She broke free, but loped along the rocky flat ahead of me, running gingerly as she threaded her way through the drifts of pebbles lying atop the rocky surface. When we reached the island's tip, I dashed back into the grove of young trees to where she had been cutting. In my desperation to find the knife, I forgot my earlier caution. While I searched among the saplings, marked by wounds from the freshly cut branches, she remained near the water, staring idly into the woods. Her obstinacy was infuriating.

"Quit standing there doing nothing. Help me look for that knife."

Relief flooded through me when I finally spotted it. She had apparently place it on a stump from which it had fallen. It was lying with only a glint of the blade marking it under a small cut branch in the shadow of the stump. With a sigh, I wiped the blade against my leg and resheathed it.

Embarrassed at the anger I had directed at her, I walked over to where she stood, poking at the ground with her foot. She had the look of a small girl caught doing something wrong. I squeezed her hand, which was still sticky with resin.

"Hey, why wouldn't you help me look for it? After all, you lost it. You really had me worried there for a minute."

Michelle looked up, but refused to meet my gaze. "I'm sorry, but I don't have any shoes. All I had were sandals, and I lost them when I fell in the water. These rocks hurt my feet."

I blushed with embarrassment. Any idiot would have noticed that her feet were bare. I had been too preoccupied to notice her discomfort when I bullied her into carrying loads of wood across the slab strewn with sprays of fine pebbles and windblown needles from the trees. She was not the type of girl who would have done much barefoot walking.

I issued another of my endless apologies. "I'm sorry. I didn't think about your feet. I'm not the smoothest guy around girls, and being on Stone Warrior Island sure hasn't helped. I'll try to do better—okay? It's just that it's been sheer hell the past few days—sheer hell."

She weighed my words for a moment and then nodded. "I'm glad to hear you say that, Linc. It's okay. Forget it for now."

We walked slowly along the water's edge toward the house. I took her cold hand in mine. It fluttered, struggling against my grip for a moment, and then relaxed. The time had arrived for Michelle to face the horrors of Stone Warrior Island.

"Let's go inside. It's getting late. I'll build a fire so you can warm up and dry your things. I have blankets you can use."

She made an effort to lighten the atmosphere but, weighed against the lengthening shadows of late afternoon and my dread of another grim, unending night, her attempted coyness sounded hollow. "Well, I like that. You kept your guest out here feeling lousy while all the comforts of home were waiting inside."

I stopped dead in my tracks. A peculiar sense of déjà vu swept over me. With the sun behind her, making her features indistinct, Michelle reminded me eerily of a larger Laurie. With that odd tilt to her head and her arms akimbo, she had adopted the same pose as Laurie when she was kidding me.

Looking away, I said gruffly, "I'm sorry. I wasn't thinking."

I had first postponed and then forgotten to warn her about the unholy spectacle at the windows next door. With the memory of her own dead family still fresh in her mind, I thought it enough for her to know that death had visited the island without talking about the hideous display visible in the living room.

As we approached the steps, she was glancing about, examining her surroundings. Too late, I tried to warn her not to look toward the Bengston house. Her gaze fastened on the ghastly duo at the windows.

It appeared to be happening in slow motion. Her eyes glazed over, and her mouth opened. An unearthly scream cleaved the quiet afternoon. She slapped her hands over her eyes and staggered backward.

I reached out to steady her. She lashed out viciously at my face, so hard that she almost fell from the momentum of her swing. Her hands flew back to her own face, the short nails gripping the sun-roughened skin of her cheeks.

"God help me! I don't want to see them displayed like that!" she sobbed. "It's horrible!"

Michelle looked away from the gruesome spectacle, shaking her head as though the gesture could erase the reality of what she had seen. I waited, letting her get over the shock.

She remained still for what seemed a long time, her eyes closed. Then she looked at me calmly, her brown eyes meeting mine. "How did they get in that position? It looks as if they are sitting there watching you . . . just waiting for you, Linc."

My self-control vanished in an instant, and I shouted at her. "That's what I've been trying to tell you! Those people are dead. My God! Did you think I was kidding? Some maniac has propped them up in the windows. There's something—somebody—an insane person on this island. He'll kill us, too, unless you help me."

I fought to control myself. We had to help each other. We weren't going to last this way—with me losing my head and screaming, and with her unnatural periods of paranoia. I needed a companion with whom I could share the fight for survival, not the strange unpredictable creature before me.

I held out my hand to her. Her eyes wavered for a moment, and it appeared she was going to reject me. But then she gripped my hand and gasped, "Oh, Linc, it's terrible. It's like a horror movie—with us trapped in it. I . . . I didn't dream that it was going to be like this. Please take me inside. I can't stand this. I . . . I thought I could. I thought I was strong enough to take anything, but . . . please."

I hustled her up the steps, shielding her view of the corpses with my body. Inside the room she stopped, surveying my refuge with its musty atmosphere. Her gaze lingered on the broken glass. She glanced at the heavy chair pushed against the kitchen door, then back at me.

"Why are you using only the one room?"

"I thought I told you. He's been prowling around upstairs at night. There's a booby-trap on the stairs, so it's impossible for me to check the upper floor. I can't even use the kitchen. I . . . I don't know how to tell you this. There's a . . . oh, God, I don't want to tell you this. There's a body in the house with us—a young girl. She was one of the family next door . . . and I . . . heaven help me, I—"

She never took her gaze off me, watching me intently.

"I can't talk about it. Besides, there is no point in going in the kitchen. The food supplies have been stolen. There was an attempt to burn the place last night. The only safe spot anywhere on the island, especially after dark, is this one room."

She moved close, as if what she had to say was best whispered. "I don't understand. Aren't you afraid to go out in the daytime? Couldn't you be attacked then?"

I patted the revolver wedged under my belt. "This is the only reason I'm still alive, but I just have two cartridges left."

Michelle's face was close to mine, her eyes gentle. "Two? You only have two bullets altogether? Don't you have a box full of them?"

"No. I didn't think to buy any extra ammunition before I left Seattle. In fact, I almost didn't bring the gun. Yesterday, I lost my head and wasted four bullets. I guess I'm pretty stupid, but I'm still alive."

She leaned against the wall, her head tilted back and her eyes closed. "What a screwup! If I hadn't been so damned clumsy, I—"

She looked at me, suddenly thoughtful. "I almost gave up when I fell off the bank. It seemed like fate didn't want me to do what—to survive. God, I was terrified when you found me, but—but seeing you up close, trying to get me out of the water, I found the strength to hang on to that branch until you got me up. I just had to stay alive—to keep going.

"But how about you, Linc? What happens when the last two bullets are gone? Do you have any other plan for saving yourself?"

"My only other weapon is the hunting knife you almost lost out there. If I waste the bullets, there'll be nothing we can do but lock ourselves in here, try to keep him out, and wait."

"You're counting on that, aren't you? A plane coming to save you?"

She brushed past me and sat down on the sofa, shivering and hugging herself. When she spoke it was to herself, softly at first and then with her voice rising, "I want my family. They have always taken care of me when I got into trouble. Oh, God, I need them so much, and I want all this to end."

Her voice wavered on the edge of hysteria. "Don't you understand? This has to end. I can't go on."

I clamped my hand atop her shoulder. The wild outburst ceased instantly, and she was absolutely motionless, her muscles rigid beneath my fingers, the only sound from her a noisy gulping of air. I tried to turn her to face me, but she resisted.

"Be quiet, Michelle . . . please. We are safe now with you

here to help. I promise you it will be okay. Please believe me.
I can protect you. Trust me."

Her shoulder muscles tensed still more, and I thought she
was going to swing at me again. Instead, she jerked free of
my grasp and, in a terrible voice—one that held overtones of
long fingernails being drawn over a chalkboard—cried, "Me
trust you? I'll never trust anybody again."

I didn't know what to say. I couldn't beg anymore. I guess
if she had known how I failed Laurie, she would have laughed
in my face when I asked for her trust.

The silence lengthened, and when she spoke again it was in
a near-whisper. "Please forgive me. I do believe in you. And,
Linc, I want you to trust me. It's just that I keep remembering
everything that has happened. I'll be okay."

She was shivering, and I felt guilty. I had forgotten to build
the fire that I promised her.

Soon a good blaze was crackling in the fireplace. When I
suggested that she strip and lay her clothes on the hearth to
dry, she failed to react, save for a tightening of her lips. I
blushed again, aware I was acting as awkward around girls as
I had before my marriage to Laurie.

"Hey, what I meant to say is put one of the blankets around
you while your clothes are drying. I'll keep my back turned
while you're undressing."

She nodded gravely. "Okay, Linc."

Turning away, I stared at the barricaded door. From behind
me came rustling sounds as she undressed. The truth of the
matter was that fear and fatigue had so eroded my masculinity
that I could have watched her without reaction.

"Okay, you can turn around. I'm decent."

"Listen, I don't want you to think I have any ideas about
you. After all, this place isn't very conducive to—"

"Let's not talk about it. I know you're not thinking about
fun and games."

She seated herself on the rug before the fire, facing me,
hunched over so that her elbows rested on her crossed legs,
with the blanket drawn tightly about her. I slumped into the
chair by the kitchen door, hoping she would start talking. I
have never been much good at small talk, and she wasn't

helping. As the minutes dragged by, our eyes avoided each other like blips on a video game screen.

The long silence was too much for me. I blurted out, "Well, tell me about yourself."

She jerked her head up, her eyes wide.

I tried to adopt a bantering tone. "After all, I think I should know something about the woman I'm sharing my quarters with, shouldn't I?"

Chapter
THIRTY-ONE

No smile rewarded my attempt at levity, yet my request turned the spigot on a stream of words. Once Michelle started, she talked in short, staccato bursts, as though she was reciting. As abruptly, she would seem to lose the thread of what she was saying and pause in midsentence. I wondered whether she might be showing the effects of a mild concussion from the crash.

"Hey, maybe you'd better not talk so much. You've had a hard time."

"No, I want to talk. It keeps my mind off things. I'm okay."

I smiled at her. "I don't know about that if you can't even remember the name of the company your father owned."

"I told you it was some chemical company. I remember now—it's Chicagoland Chemicals, Incorporated."

"That shouldn't be so hard to remember."

She lowered her eyes. "Don't cross-examine me, Linc. I'm so mixed up I don't know what I'm saying. I keep thinking about them."

Her voice broke for a moment. "Dead. All dead. I still can't believe it. Even now, I can't believe it."

She took a deep breath before resuming the strange monotonic recitation of her life. "I was an only child. When I was growing up, all I had to do was start fussing, and my parents would give me anything I wanted. That's the trouble with when you're grown. All the rules change. People expect you to be perfect—no mistakes. If you do screw up, they start trying to run your life.

"I guess my father was successful in his business. He never talked much about it. We had a really nice house and there were servants, so Mother didn't have to work. It wasn't all fun, though. I had to go to a private high school while most of my friends went to public school. They made me take piano and ballet lessons and all that stuff."

"You took ballet lessons?"

She frowned. "Yes . . . why?"

"Oh, no reason. It just surprised me."

"You think I'm too big and awkward for ballet, don't you? You don't think I had a boyfriend, do you? Well, someone loved me very much. It wasn't his fault that—"

She stopped talking, clamping her hand to her mouth in the involuntary, childish gesture of hushing herself. "I'm talking nonsense—sitting here, a thousand miles from nowhere, rapping about boyfriends. I like talking to a working guy like you. I went to college. Those guys were all so phony."

I raised my arms in mock surrender. "Oh, no, I'm in trouble. I'm afraid I'm one of those phony college graduates posing as a handyman. Where did you go to school?"

Her gaze snapped up to meet mine, and I could see a hardness creeping in around her mouth. I thought for a moment that she was going to say it was none of my business. Her voice was low. "Ohio State."

It surprised me. I couldn't see a rich girl like her enrolling in a land grant university. "You went to Ohio State? How on earth did you end up at a school like that?"

Her brown eyes were riveted on me, and there was a strangeness in them. Anger? Fear? Her voice held a hint of pleading. "What's wrong with going to Ohio State? They have a good football team."

That was so unexpected that I laughed—the first chuckle I'd had since setting foot on this terrible island. "Well, excuse

me, Miss Black. I didn't think you had the size to be on the
football team. What position did you play?"

Her expression remained guarded, unreadable. Had I insulted her? After all, she was larger than the average girl.

She smiled, a tight little smile that appeared forced. "Oh,
hell! I keep getting confused, trying to talk to you. What I
mean is I've always enjoyed football. You can't grow up in
the Chicago area without being crazy about it. Since I
couldn't have cared less where I went to school, I thought I
might as well go to a college that was big time in sports. My
friends used to say football weekends are something else at
the big schools, and Ohio State sounded like fun."

Such criteria for choosing a college were alien to the Wilhite household, but I nodded as though I understood perfectly.
"It sounds as if you didn't let a little thing like education stand
in your way. Maybe my family should have been more like
that. I haven't met many people like you, Michelle. What was
your major?"

She tilted her head back and laughed, but it was hollow—
more a series of repetitious yelps than anything. "You're certainly trying to give me the third degree, aren't you? Before
long, you'll want to know the names of all the guys I dated in
school. Where did you go to school?"

I started to ignore the question, but I knew that to do so
would have ended our conversation right there, and I wanted
to talk. She heard the same story that Chambord had—about
attending Oregon State and later the Univeristy of Washington. For one perilous moment I came close to telling her about
my troubles with my dad and about my marriage to Laurie. I
wanted to. I experienced the strangest desire to tell her everything. At that moment I felt that it would be a catharsis to
confess all my heartbreaks and disappointments to this strange
girl. But it was too soon. Too much intimacy so quickly
would have frightened her and, maybe, me.

When I finished my little tale, she said, "Well, as long as
we're being so nosy, why did you transfer from Oregon State
to Washington?"

"Oh, I had a few bad grades at OSU, goofing around too
much. I transferred to get a fresh start."

It wasn't a very sensible explanation, but Michelle appeared perfectly satisfied with it.

"That's certainly nothing to be ashamed of. Most of my friends had their share of low grades."

"No wonder Ohio State has a tremendous football team. It sounds as if the student body consists of jocks and airheads. I thought rich, good-looking blondes and their friends always made nothing but *A*'s. What kind of crowd have you been hanging out with? By the way, you didn't tell me what you majored in."

She was getting restless. She stuck out her lower lip, directing a stream of air against the rapidly drying strands of blonde hair on her forehead.

"I guess I've been running around with a more interesting crowd than you have. I really didn't major in anything. I just took a general course. Why don't we just drop the subject?"

"A general course?"

An edge crept into her voice. "That's what I said. The only reason I went to school was because there was nothing else to do. I never did find anything I really liked, so I took whatever I felt like. Didn't you ever hear of anybody doing that before? Can't you do that out West?"

I shook my head. I was rapidly coming to the conclusion that Michelle and I had very little in common. "Not that I know of, but don't ask me. If they gave you a degree, I guess it was legit.

"I always thought students had to file a plan and have it approved . . . whatever their program. Maybe things are different in the East, but I sure didn't know that any college issued degrees without majors or approved programs."

Again she laughed—the same repetitious yelping as before—but louder now, again on the brink of hysteria. She stopped in midlaugh, appeared to be listening intently, and turned to stare out the unshuttered windows toward the charnel house next door. She shuddered, and her face turned gaunt with the ravages of some inner turmoil.

I started chattering aimlessly, trying to divert her mind from the creature that lurked outside with an unsated appetite for death. My anecdotes about life in the national park drew no response and were soon exhausted. She seemed equally uninterested in hearing about Rod and Evie and their life in Sequim. For a moment she did become more animated when I told her about the ad in the Seattle newspaper that resulted in my coming to Stone Warrior Island. But the flow of conversation soon subsided to a trickle before the dam of her indifference.

She took advantage of the developing silence to say, "I think my clothes must be dry by now."

The blanket drawn tightly about her, she rose and gathered her clothes from the hearth. Miffed by her indifference to my conversational efforts, I was determined not to turn around until she asked. Our will clashed for a moment, and then she murmured, "If you'll look the other way, I'll get dressed. Then we can do whatever we need to before it gets dark."

She paid me back in kind. There were the sounds of her dressing, and then all was quiet. I grew anxious, wondering what was wrong, but she didn't speak. Not until I finally asked did she acknowledge that she was dressed. Upset with her pettiness, I walked past her without speaking and opened the front door to find the sun low above the distant forest. Saturday was coming to a close. Not much over an hour of daylight remained. With the approach of night, the sense of urgency was growing in me. I couldn't afford to act as childish as my guest.

"Michelle, I think we ought to keep a fire going all night. It will seem more cheerful, and besides, it's the only light we have. My flashlight is about shot. I'd feel better if we had a bit more wood. I'm going up to the woodpile on the ridge and bring down a few more loads. If you want to come, you can. Otherwise, you can lock yourself in until I get back."

"How . . . how far away will you be? Will you be too far for me to yell if I need you?"

I shook my head. "Hey, don't get scared. I wouldn't go if I thought it would jeopardize your safety. It's not over fifty yards away. If you call for help, I can reach you in ten seconds."

She considered for a moment and then shrugged. "Okay, I'll wait here until you get back."

Making sure that the revolver was securely wedged in my waistband, I fished the key from my pocket and handed it to her. "Lock the door behind me. When I get back, I'll call to you to let you know it's me at the door."

As I was going out the door, she stopped me. "Linc, why don't you let me have your knife?"

Sensing my rejection, she added, "You know, in case he got in someway. I want a fighting chance. Please Linc. Besides, it means you wouldn't lose both weapons. Or, if something happened to you I wouldn't be defenseless."

"No, Michelle, I can't do that. It's me that he'll come after."

She followed me out onto the porch and called softly as I went down the steps. "Be very, very careful. Remember, one mistake and you'll be dead—just as dead as they are."

I started to protest, but she turned her back to me and vanished inside. I wanted to remonstrate with her about talking so negatively, but it would have strained our uneasy truce even more.

Frightened by her remark, I chose to go the long way around to avoid walking past the abominations that watched my every step.

I had just started downhill, with the second load when I heard glass breaking somewhere below me. A moment later I heard Michelle's shrill, urgent cry. "Linc! Come here! Quick!"

Flinging the wood aside, I charged down the slope, running awkwardly on the steep pitch. As I raced around the corner of the house, I pulled the revolver from my waistband.

Michelle was standing on the porch, huddled against the wall. Even as I called to her, I was overwhelmed by an awesomely vile odor. It was also affecting her. The pale-faced girl's hand was over her mouth, and she was coughing—a hard, gagging hack. She pointed toward the Bengston place.

The upper pane of the window displaying the grotesque cadaver of Dolores Delvecchio was smashed, and the heated air was rushing through the break, carrying with it the putrid smell of rotting meat. My stomach churned, and I started dry-heaving.

Turning, I stumbled up the porch steps and grabbed Michelle, shoving her ahead of me into the house. She was racked with uncontrollable sobs. I choked off the desire to shout at her to shut up so I could listen for anyone moving outside.

Gradually she quieted, sitting with her head in her hands.

She looked up at me. "Oh, God! It's ghastly—like a nightmare. How much more can you stand?"

"For heaven's sake, what happened?"

"I don't know. I was sitting here when I heard the glass break. I thought it must be something you had done. Without thinking, I ran outside to see what was going on. I knew the sound came from nearby, and I thought you would be out front. I was startled to find nobody there, and then that terrible odor hit me. I knew it must have something to do with them. I saw the broken glass right away, and then I saw . . . her." Her voice was breaking badly.

Only vaguely aware of what I was doing, I grabbed at Michelle, clutching a handful of her blonde hair, and pulled her head up to where I could see her face in the firelight. "Shut up! Please shut up. What good is it going to do to keep talking about them?"

Instantly I was sorry, embarrassed at manhandling her that way. I patted her shoulder, not knowing what to say. How could I admit to her that I was terrified? Guys are supposed to remain cool.

As before, she shrank from my touch but caught herself and stood, rigid and unyielding. Gently I pushed her backward onto the sofa and sat down beside her.

My nostrils flared as the sickening miasma of decay filtered into the room. I understood now why the windows, one in each house, had been broken. The insane intelligence stalking us was as cunning as it was deadly.

It was important to me that she knew that I felt terrible about treating her so roughly. "It's okay. You're going to be fine. I'm sorry I yanked your hair. I was upset—no, I'll be honest. I was scared half out of my wits."

As we sat side by side, staring blankly out the windows, the setting sun went through its daily color display against the log wall across the way. The horrid stench slowly, almost imperceptibly, grew stronger in the room. I wondered if the decaying thing on the sunporch was contributing to the smell. I fought to control myself—to think. We had to find some way to flee the horrors of this island.

Michelle sniffed the air. Her voice was dreamy. "I can smell death. I can smell it coming into this room. Are . . . are we going to smell like that when they find our bodies? Are we?"

The last vestiges of control slipped from me, and I exploded off the sofa, screaming at her. "Shut up, damn you! My God, why are you talking like this? Just shut up, please. What are you trying to do to me? Don't you care whether you live or die?"

The fear faded from her face as quickly as it flared, and she grinned—a real grin this time—a horribly sardonic grin. "What's wrong, Linc? Maybe you're not really sure yourself . . . you know . . . that we're going to be okay."

Her grin faded into a pensive look, her eyes squinting as she studied the dancing flames in the fireplace. "Listen— maybe this is hell. Maybe I died with my folks and went to hell. Do you think so?"

For some reason I remembered Marvin Klugg's words that night in the chalet cellar. It was as if she was crazy with her talk—like Klugg. For a moment I wanted to slap her—do anything to shut her up. I was close to fleeing from the safety of that locked haven into the arms of the fiend who patiently awaited my fatal mistake. She was tearing at the very fabric of my dream of having someone—her—believe in me, knowing I could save her—of giving me back the confidence my father had taken from me. Frustrated, I pushed my forehead against the wall's cool surface and pounded the wood surface with my fist in a steady, painful tattoo.

I tried a last time to get through to her, and I'm afraid that I was begging. "Listen, I'm just an ordinary guy, but just give me a chance . . . please."

She spoke no more, maintaining a careful truce.

While we struggled to understand each other—if that was possible—the reflected sunset had lost its brilliance. There was no more time to waste. "Michelle, I have to bring some firewood in if we are going to keep the fire all night. I have to do it now; it will be too dark in a few more minutes. Give me the key."

"No."

"I want the key. I'm not sure you won't panic and lock me out."

Our tension-filled impasse seemed to last forever before she yielded. I don't know what I could have done if she hadn't.

I was aghast at the savage splendor of the western sky. A massive but shredded cloud bank had rolled in over the horizon, stretching a gaudy veil across the sinking sun. The sky in that direction was a crazy quilt of oranges, vivid pinks, and dark purples. Long golden strands of sunlight streamed across the sky where they found rents in the clouds. Never in my life had I experienced such a bizarre—even sinister—close to a day.

A sudden wind had come up since the broken window chased us inside—much stronger than I had yet experienced. The waves were washing heavily onto the shore, throwing spray far up the water-darkened granite. Stone Warrior was singing its dirge so loudly in the tumultuous wind that it would have been impossible to speak without shouting. I wanted to flee from that strange scene. One load of firewood would have to suffice.

I dashed down the steps, grabbed as large an armful as I could manage, and retreated into the living room. The warmth and firelight would be as much a comfort against the wild night descending on Stone Warrior as against the maniac haunting the island.

Dumping the load on the hearth, I paused for a last look at the spectacular sunset before sealing us in for the night. I was conscious of her standing behind me, her voice a bare whisper.

"We'd better take a good look at it. It may be the last time we'll ever see a sunset. Such a wild night! I remember reading a book when I was a kid. Every time the wind blew like this, the dead would come out of their graves to avenge themselves. It makes you wonder about us—and them—doesn't it?"

Chapter
THIRTY-TWO

I was too exhausted to protest Michelle's morbid rejoinders. She had become an albatross about my neck. It may have been a cruel twist of fate for both of us that she stumbled onto Stone Warrior in her wanderings. She acted as if she wanted to die. Perhaps it would have been best if she had drowned in the lake. The heroic fantasies she inspired in me upon her arrival had long since vanished, routed by the corrosive torrent of words with which she had eroded my confidence. I sure had picked the wrong lady to give me an ego boost.

"I have to figure out a way to hang blankets over the windows," I said. "With it dark next door and the firelight in here, we will be exposed before the windows."

After a search through the few drawers in the room yielded neither nails nor tacks, I sat dejectedly, eyeing the amateurish paintings on the long wall—probably a hobby of Mayfield's wife. An idea hit me. There would be hanging hardware for the frames. Removing the canvases, I used my knife to pry out the picture hooks and hammered them into the window moldings with the heel of my shoe. The wire sagged ominously under the weight of the blanket, but it held. Maybe someone on the second floor of Bengston's could see part of the room, but we were safe from an observer on the ground.

As I was hanging the second blanket across its wire, Michelle called softly to me. "I'm sorry, Linc."

I said nothing until I was through and flopped down on the couch again. "Sorry?"

"I mean—I'm sorry about acting like such a bitch. I keep thinking about my family lying there dead . . . with me still alive. Somehow, it doesn't seem right that I should have survived, but I know I was spared for a reason. Everything that happens is for a purpose. It's going to work out okay, Linc . . . all okay."

Her words struck me like a lightning bolt. Everything happens for a purpose? My God, what a brainless, silly platitude. I felt like shouting at her. If there was purpose to life, then she should explain to me about Laurie. Why had it happened to Laurie—to my poor, wonderful wife?

We married and lived and loved together for four short months.

On a warm early October night, Laurie lost her life.

One weekend, young, happy, and foolish, we drove up a narrow rural road into a field above a solitary gasoline station on the far outskirts of Seattle. Our car was new, and we wanted to make love in the back seat—something that we had never done before. It was stupid, but our friends talked about "making out" in their cars before they were married. So, feeling a little wicked, we pulled off into the lonely spot.

We were surprised by three punks, intent first on robbery and then rape when they found us making love. Laurie's piteous pleas triggered in me the same mindless explosion of violence that had battered my father years before. I have a vague memory of smashing one of them to the ground with no regard for his weapon. But then a gun butt bounced off my head, and I blacked out.

I found myself racing down the lane toward the lighted service station, confused, remembering nothing but that something was wrong and I needed help. Only as I was running the last few yards along the shoulder toward the brilliant glare of fluorescent lights did I remember, with sickening clarity, what had happened.

"Help me!" I shouted. "For heaven's sake, help me! They have my wife up on the hill, and they're hurting her!"

A hard-faced, muscular man in his early forties, his bright red hair in an old-fashioned flattop, charged out of the lube bay. "What in the hell's wrong, kid?"

Trembling violently, I managed to stammer out a half-intelligible story. Without a word, he ran heavily into the station and grabbed the phone. It seemed as though he talked for hours, but then he was sprinting toward me, his big-boned hand clutching a .357 magnum.

"Come on, fellow. Let's get the hell up there. The cops are on their way."

His words meant nothing to me. The station was spinning crazily and the concrete kept tilting up. I grabbed at a pump to steady myself, wondering where Laurie was.

The attendant took a couple of steps before he realized I wasn't following him. He whirled toward me. "Snap out of it, man! It will take the fugging cops ten minutes to get here. We're gonna have to keep those bastards busy."

Still I stood there, trying to sort out what he was saying— something about the cops. Again, I wondered where Laurie was. I was getting queasy and wanted to go home.

He seized me by the arm and yanked me forward. "What's wrong with you, you son of a bitch? That's your wife they're raping! Come on! It's up to us to stop them bastards."

He ran awkwardly toward the lane, pulling me along. Before we had gone thirty yards, a crystalline scream split the night, followed by the heavy detonations of two gunshots. Ahead of us we could hear running footsteps and the slamming of doors. A motor roared to life.

The station manager stopped, and the world seemed to explode as the heavy revolver discharged.

"Christ, I'd better not shoot," he gasped. "We might hit your wife. God knows where she is."

Ahead of us a van leaped over the crest of the hill and disappeared. The cool breeze sliding down the slope brought the smell of dust to us. The hillside was suddenly quiet. Deadly quiet.

When we reached the car, we found Laurie sprawled on the grass, her skirt tucked up around her waist and her undergarments torn away. She lay, unmoving, her eyes wide open, sightless under the night sky, with dark blotches spreading on her blouse. I felt myself falling through space.

"Linc, are you all right? What's wrong?"

The nightmarish daydream fell to pieces, and I opened my eyes to find Michelle peering intently at me. She was sitting cross-legged before the fire, looking very young and vulnerable. I felt ashamed of how near I had been to cursing her for her innocuous remark. At that moment my only thought was to protect the strange, mercurial girl with my life.

"That's the way to talk, kid. You're darned right we're going to be okay. I won't let anything happen to you."

My spirits were buoyed by that slight note of optimism from her. Beyond her shoulders the yellow flame played along the logs. My lids grew heavy. Summoning my ebbing energy, I climbed to my feet, momentarily light-headed. I couldn't go to sleep until Michelle had satisfied me that she would stay alert and call me if she noticed anything out of the ordinary.

I leaned against the rough rock front of the fireplace, watching her as she plucked at the nap of the rug with her broken fingernails. Her attention was concentrated on her restless hands. For a moment I didn't appreciate that she was addressing me in a barely audible voice.

"It's so funny, but somehow I'm beginning to understand you—at least in a way. That seemed beyond the realm of possibility when I first saw you.

"You've had a lot of bad things happen to you—far more than the things you told me about. You have a lot of scars that you can't hide. It's in your eyes. Maybe we're more alike than I thought. I don't guess either one of us could avoid what life has done to us. We can't help what we have become. Still, we have to do what we have to do. One has to pay, Linc."

"I . . . I don't understand what you mean. What brought this on?"

She patted the floor next to her in invitation, her face strained in the flickering firelight. "Sit beside me. I'm not afraid of you anymore. You're so very tired, but I won't let you go to sleep until it's time."

I sank down in the floodplain of firelight beside her, puzzled by my ever-changing companion's cryptic words.

She leaned toward me, her warm breath tickling my neck. "Tell me the truth about yourself. You'll feel better if you let it all hang out. I want to know how you were hurt so badly. Don't deny it. It's written on your face—there for anyone who knows how to recognize it to see. Please, Linc, it will be so much easier if I understand. Think of it as judgment day. We all have to be judged—family, lovers, you . . . and me."

I resisted her entreaties. God knows, there was a desire to

talk, to catalog the years of heartache, but my naked soul had been hidden far too long for me to reveal it without an emotional struggle. But in the end, with overwhelming fatigue eroding the last of my defenses, I yielded to her persistence and poured out my tale, the real, unvarnished record of my life. The one thing I could not bring myself to confess was the year I spent away from home. At the end of an hour, with my voice hoarse, she knew the history of my misadventures.

But the murky reservoirs of pain, accumulated with each of those traumas, remained undrained within me. As I slumped back, silent now, watching the ebb and flow of light against the far wall, I knew I had not helped myself at all. If I couldn't discharge the pain now, even after stripping away every pretense behind which I had ever hidden, my suffering was going to remain with me to the grave. I could only hope that Michelle had found what she sought from me.

I don't think I heard her first few words, so deeply was I into my own thoughts. Sounding puzzled, hesitant, she was asking, "That's all you really know about yourself, isn't it? It's honest to God all you know! Linc, did you ever hear of a Greek named Euripides?"

She surprised me with the question, coming out of the blue. It was even more of a surprise to me that someone like her would know a name out of classic literature. "Yeah . . . sure. He was an ancient Greek poet, I think. Why?"

"He wrote one of the memory passages we had in high school. I still remember it—about the only thing I remember from that class. I guess it stuck with me because I realized even then that what he said was true. This guy said, 'Good and bad may not be discovered. There is, as there should be, a commingling.' You see, everybody has both good and evil in them. Sometimes the evil grows so strong in people that there's very little room for goodness left. People can't help it. It's like a disease. Now—"

"What are you talking about, Michelle? What are you saying?" Her preoccupation with the morbid was getting to me again.

She pulled me forward, her face as stricken as if she were in intense pain. "Forgive me. I didn't mean to start rambling —there's a point in talking about it now. Oh, Linc, you don't know how much I wanted to be happy. I yearned for a normal life—a husband and kids—but it wasn't to be. Sometimes, when I can think rationally about things, I know that it was all my fault—that what Euripides would call my evil nature was too strong for the good."

She leaned forward, resting her chin on her knees, tears welling in her eyes, watching the fire.

Whenever she allowed me to see the turmoil welling within her, I would feel a surge of tenderness for this strange, tortured girl—not a romantic tenderness, but the appeal that comes with the recognition of a kindred spirit. I slid my hand onto the back of her neck and caressed her tense muscles.

She caught her breath, holding it long seconds before releasing it in a lengthy sigh. Whispering, she begged, "Don't . . . don't do that. Please."

I let my hand rest quietly on her shoulder. "Hey, relax. I'm not going to hit on you. My God, that's the last thing I can think of right now. Don't be so hard on yourself, talking about evil and all that heavy stuff. Keep fighting, Michelle. We're never licked unless we quit. Listen, if anybody's screwed up, it's me. I didn't have the guts to tell you this, but I've . . . well, darn it, I've been in a mental institution."

I was so groggy I didn't understand what was happening. She was on her feet, slamming backward against the front door, making the whole house rattle.

The firelight accentuated the ugly contortions of her face as she screamed at me. "Shut up, goddamn you, shut up! I don't want to hear about it. You don't think I know about nut houses? Oh, God, do I know! I've seen how people sidle away when they find out someone's been in one of those places. I've watched the embarrassment families endure when they have to admit where you've been. Don't you think I know it all—about the nights—the moaning and the crying in those godawful, long nights?

"And call me Mickie, you son of a bitch. I hate the name Michelle. That's all I've heard all my life—Michelle, Michelle, Michelle. I'm Mickie, you bastard."

It was so unexpected that it took me a minute to sort out what she was saying. It was as if I walked in on the middle of her conversation.

I had terrified her. She was babbling nonsense. She probably thought that she was trapped on a deserted island with a homicidal maniac. Afraid to move toward her, I turned my hands, palms up, in a placating gesture.

"Please, don't be frightened. It's not like you think—like you see in the movies. Not everybody there acts like they are nuts. Nothing was wrong with me but a nervous breakdown—honest. I was working too hard, and there was too much pressure from my father. I'm okay now. I won't hurt you. I've never hurt anybody in my life. I wasn't thinking. I shouldn't have sprung it on you that way. Let's be friends—okay?"

Like a spring winding down, her agitation diminished, and she finally nodded. "It's okay. You don't have to say anything else. I understand now. Lie down and go to sleep. I'll keep watch. It's the best way."

She cut off my protest. "Hush, Linc. I said there's nothing else to say."

"Listen, I don't understand this Mickie—Michelle business. What do you really want me to call you?"

She was glaring at me, and I was afraid that she was going to start yelling again, but then she relaxed. "There's nothing to understand. I want to be called Mickie, that's all. My name is Michelle, but I hate it. I thought maybe you had—never mind. Let's drop it."

She walked the length of the room and dropped into the easy chair. Folding her arms across her chest, she stared moodily at the diminishing fire. My efforts to renew the conversation were futile. At first she acted as if she didn't hear me, then she grimly shook her head.

The silence in the firelit room vibrated with a hostility that I didn't understand. It was something more than the unseen menace that lurked outside in the dark. It had to do with my unexpected guest—with an anger that raged deep within her. I began to wonder if there was more to the circumstances that had left her stranded in the wilderness than she had told me.

I settled down, listening to the tempest outside, trying to find comfort in the warmth of our quarters. My ears strained to filter away the wind's howl, to hear the dreadful rattling of the ladder and the shuffle of footfalls overhead. I heard nothing but the squall.

My grim struggle to remain alert was floundering. To lose concentration for a moment was to find my chin resting against my chest. The fire was consuming wood far faster than I thought it would. The last chunks of pine were on the grate, which hosted few flames now among its glowing red coals. The room's brightness had diminished to where the night sky was visible again. I tried counting stars, but my eyes, blurring with fatigue, made it impossible. I returned to the contemplation of the fire, only to find myself, almost immediately, sagging sideways, ready to sprawl on to the rug.

Clambering to my feet, I scooped handfuls of cold water from the bucket and wet my face and my T-shirt. The clammy, unpleasant sensation of damp fabric pushed back the cobwebs of unconsciousness. I paced slowly before the dying fire, turning frequently to the bucket for more water.

She stirred behind me. "Linc, do you ever go to church?"

"What?"

"I said do you ever go to church?"

"No—at least not since I was a little boy. I remember we used to go, but the minister gave a sermon about family responsibilities one Sunday. My father had a bitter argument with him about it outside the church after the services. We never went back."

"Do you really know how to pray? Do you know any prayers?"

"Not really. Why do you want to know?"

"I want you to pray now."

She had caught me off-stride again. "If you want to pray, go ahead. It's okay with me."

She shook her head. "No, all I know are church prayers, not really personal ones. Please, say a prayer for us—aloud."

"I can't. The only prayer I remember is one my mother taught me when I was a little boy. It's silly—just kid's stuff."

"Did it help when you said it?"

"What?"

"You heard me. Did it help when you said it?"

"Well, yeah, sure, I guess it did."

"Guess?"

I was remembering how my mother used to come into my room when I was five or six and sit by me, stroking my hair, while I knelt by the bed saying the little prayer aloud. It's funny how I had forgotten until Michelle—Mickie—asked.

Later, through those miserable years of growing up in Astoria, when my mother no longer came in at bedtime to comfort me, I still said the childish verse. Many a lonely night, hurt and crying after being rebuffed by my father, I would get down on my knees and, to the accompaniment of heavy trucks moving along the distant highway, say those childish words. They helped, too. God, did they help!

I kicked the grate to conceal the emotion of my memories from my companion's sharp gaze. "Yes, it did make me feel good at times."

She rose and walked to the window, peering over the top of the blanket toward the dark windows screening those poor bodies. "Say it aloud, Linc."

"I don't know if I remember it all."

"Please, say your prayer for all of us."

Then it was clear in my mind, and I recited it, involuntarily. "Now I lay me down to sleep. I pray the Lord my soul to keep. If I should die before I wake, I pray the Lord my soul to take."

Chapter
THIRTY-THREE

Mickie stood at the window looking out as I prayed, and after I finished, she stayed there several seconds more. Turning back to face me, she nodded as if she were satisfied and took my hand. It was the first spontaneous gesture she had made toward me. She pulled me down beside her on the rug before the remains of the fire. "You're just not going to give up and go to sleep, are you? How much longer can you last— two hours?—eight hours?—all day tomorrow?"

In a hoarse voice I scarcely recognized, I mumbled, "I don't know. I can't give up—not after toughing it out this long. I want to trust you to keep watch, but I'm afraid you'll be tricked. I just can't be sure how you will respond. It's okay. I can stay awake. I can make it—honest to God, I can. I told you I'd take care of you."

She slumped forward, saying nothing, resting her chin against her folded legs. The dying coals yielded enough light to make her face a faint scarlet mask, floating disembodied in a dark emptiness. We remained that way for several minutes until she abruptly rose on to her knees and pulled me closer.

"I have a plan. We can't sit here hiding like animals in a cave. Maybe we can trap this lunatic of yours. If we catch him, we'll be safe. We can hold on until help comes. We can surely find something to eat in the woods. Maybe we can even find where he hid the food he stole from you."

Her words brought me new found hope, thinning the mists of mental fatigue. My resistance had diminished to the point that I was willing for her to take charge. "Okay, Michelle, I'm—"

"Mickie."

"Okay, Mickie, I'm game to try anything. What's your plan?" I remembered the broken window. "Better keep your voice down. He could be by the window, listening."

She shifted around until I could see her as a vague shape between me and the dying embers. She was silent for a moment, and then I felt her warm breath against my ear again. "It's kill or be killed. The time has come. I say we set an ambush. We've got to get him before he gets us. We can't survive if we sit around like a couple of wimps."

I tried to follow what she was saying. The idea of seizing the initiative was too sudden for me to think out. "Ambush? How on earth can we set up an ambush?"

"According to what you said, there's only the one guy, and there are two of us. He can't watch us both if we split up."

"Split up! We can't—"

She hushed me vehemently. "Keep your voice down. You may be right about him being right outside. What I have in mind is for you to sneak out and work your way up the slope behind the house to where you can watch the backs of both places. When you are in position, I'll take the bucket and go down to the lake. I'll pretend to be getting some water—take my time about it, rinse the bucket out several times, maybe take something to wash. He has to be watching the front because he knows that you don't dare go through the kitchen."

I struggled to grasp the details of the plan, trying to force my exhausted mind into some orderly thought process. "But if he's watching the front, wouldn't he see me come out before you?"

"We'll go outside at the same time, and I'll make a lot of noise going down the steps. While he's watching me, you can slip over the side rail without his noticing. Even if it doesn't work, it's better than sitting here doing nothing. He will still have the gun to worry about."

I couldn't get straight in my mind how the scheme was supposed to work. "But what then? What's the point of all this?"

"I'll make sure I keep an eye out behind me all the time. If he breaks cover and comes for me, I'll wait until he's close and then scream. You come running when you hear me. You should have a clear shot at him before he can get away.

"Look—I know it's not perfect, but it's the only idea we have. I'd rather do this than wait here for this killer of yours to come for us when he's ready. Even if we don't catch him, he'll be more cautious. It will buy us some time. He'll find out what it's like to be the one being hunted. He will have to think out every move he makes, knowing that we might spring another trap on him."

"But why should I go up the hill?"

"Damn it, Linc, you're not thinking—because that's the only way he can approach me that might cause us trouble. I figure he must be on the far side of the other house so that he can watch the front. If we let him sneak in from behind the building, he'll cut off my escape route. This way, you'll be safe out in the open and yet near enough to get down to the dock quickly and trap him."

I didn't see why it wouldn't be even more effective if I waited just inside the living room. That way, if he went after her or if he tried to sneak up on the porch to surprise her, I'd have him. I wanted to suggest it, but was sure there must be a flaw in my thinking that escaped me in my fatigue. I offered no further resistance.

"Okay, we'll try it. I guess it's better than cowering in here waiting for his next move."

She picked up the bucket, and I slid the revolver from my waistband. As I unlocked the door, she gripped my arm.

"I know you're worn out, but don't make a mistake. It's my life on the line out there. I'm going to stay down at the dock as long as I dare. I want to tempt him to come after me. Give me one of your dirty T-shirts, so I can pretend to be rinsing it out. Linc, listen to me. You must be very patient and not move until you hear me yell. Remember—my life depends on you. Whatever you may think, don't make a move until I call to you. Promise me?"

"Don't worry, Mickie, you can count on me. I won't let anything happen to you."

I tried to slip my arm around her to let her know that I admired her bravery. She didn't resist, but her muscles tightened in protest. We stood that way for several seconds, then she pushed my arm away and slipped out the door. I sneaked out behind her.

The wind was still gusting fitfully, but it had weakened from the near-gale of dusk. The cloud bank in the west had disappeared, and the sky was perfectly clear. The sliver of new moon cast the faintest gleam of silvery light on the smooth rock surface in front of us. With the wind as strong as it was, we would have to depend on our eyes and not on our hearing. The wailing in the trees rose, again and again, to a shrill pitch before descending to a low hum as sudden swirls of air whipped across the island. The floating dock rocked amid the waves splashing noisily about it. The sharp spires of the trees were clawing at the deep blue velvet of the night sky as the stronger blasts struck them.

Mickie descended the steps, feeling for the treads in the darkness, letting the bucket bang against the steps. She glanced back to where I waited, watching her, and then headed toward the dock.

I lowered myself over the porch rail, keeping my eyes on the ladder, which was wobbling in the swirls of wind. Crouching low, I scuttled up the grade, giving the ladder a wide berth. The upstairs windows were black rectangles, concealing God knows what. Clutching the revolver in my hand, I paused every few strides to scan the woods stretching in front of me.

Several yards beyond the rear of Mayfield's, I hunkered down behind a low bush, conscious of the brush behind me moving in the wind. Crouching there, remembering that it was Saturday, I thought about the Delvecchios, whose last night on earth had been last Saturday night, a week ago. Gradually, the moonlight became noticeable. At first it appeared too dim to provide any illumination, but as my eyes dilated, faint shadows became visible, nesting under the small shrubs scattered across the pitch.

I waited impatiently, spooked by the plaintive howling of the gale and the rustle of the brush. Once I thought I heard the clanging of the bucket in the distance, but it was not repeated.

The minutes dragged by, making me increasingly nervous. What we were doing was stupid. There was no way I could hear Mickie's shout above the noise of the storm. For all I knew, she might be lying dead by the dock or, worse yet, dragged into that crypt to become a ghoulish new display at the windows.

Fear surrounded me like a tightening shroud. Unable to stay there any longer, I started for the dock, ready to call the whole thing off. I took several steps and stopped, trying to blink away the tears the wind was bringing to my eyes. A figure had stepped into view beyond the front corner of the building.

The revolver was wavering in my outstretched hand. The dimly seen shape was beckoning to me with a sweeping motion. I couldn't tell whether it was Mickie or not!

I moved slowly, not knowing what to do, trying to hold the gun steady. If it was the killer, he had gone insane, exposing himself like that. I was no more than thirty feet away when I recognized it to be Mickie.

She shouted, her voice slicing through the uproar of the squall. "Come here—quick! Something is wrong! I think the house next door may be on fire!"

I broke into a trot, running awkwardly in my haste to reach her. Just as I came abreast of her, I saw a flickering yellowish glow stretching across the granite from Bengston's.

I caught her by the arm. "Quick! Where's the fire?"

She shook her head. "I don't know what's happening. It

started only a few seconds ago while I was trying to get your attention. Hurry!"

She grabbed my free hand, and we raced toward the burning structure.

Her scream ripped through my nerves like a sonic saber, echoing off the hard rock and mingling with the hellish wailing in the woods. I heard another voice—my own voice—shouting, "No!" over and over again. My forehead was sopping with perspiration, and I felt deadly sick. For a moment, I was close to fainting. We were looking at a sight straight out of hell.

Chapter
THIRTY-FOUR

A spill of soft yellow light illuminated the bare slab beneath the living-room windows. Candles had been set on the sills below the faces of the sagging corpses. The ballooning, rotting faces bore stark patterns of black shadows and saffron highlights. They appeared to be moving as the fingers of flame writhed in the air currents of their windowed tomb. The direct light from the wicks shone off white teeth, framed within shrunken lips, and the reflected glare from the window glass illuminated the glittering, milky pop eyes that looked as if they were about to explode out of their heads. This close to the house, the vile, gut-wrenching stench of putrefaction was strong, spilling out into the night air. I believe, even now, that I hovered on the brink of complete disassociation from reality as I stared, unable to move.

Suddenly Mickie slammed into me, the wet T-shirt slapping me hard in the face, wrapping around my head, her hand wrenching at the revolver in my hand. She almost had it away from me before I realized what she was doing. Then I had both hands clamped to it, and we were locked in a grim struggle, grunting and gasping for breath.

She was sobbing, "Die! Goddamn it, die!"

Even as we slipped and skidded across the granite in a fray grown savage and desperate, the shirt fell away from my face, and my eyes locked again on the horrors highlighted in the Bengston living room. Mickie was stronger than I because of my lack of food and sleep, but she had been able to get only one hand on the weapon. Her foot slid out from under her, sending her sprawling heavily on to the rock. She lost her grip on the gun as she fell.

I ran up the steps onto the porch. Scrambling to her feet, she started after me, her voice raised in repetitious supplication. "The gun—give me the gun. Just give me the damned gun."

I managed to unlock the door and lunged into the dark interior, Mickie right behind me. I found the flashlight in the corner of the sofa and turned its beam on her, afraid of a second attack.

She was crouched in front of me, one hand bleeding, her face frightening in its intensity. "You bastard! Why didn't you let me have it? It would have all been over. If only you had given me the gun."

I slapped her, harder than I intended. "Come on, snap out of it! Please! You're hysterical. You don't know what you're saying."

Grabbing her, I pulled her out of the doorway so that I could lock the door. She tumbled onto the sofa, sobbing. Once again, for a few precious seconds, we had been defenseless before the madman.

Mickie cried, her body racked with the intensity of her emotions. She was biting her lip, her eyes clenched tightly, her head moving back and forth mechanically. There was nothing I could say until she had it out of her system. Leaning warily against the wall, I kept her framed in the fading illumination of the electric torch.

Five minutes later, she looked up and giggled. "Well, at least I gave it the old college try."

As much as she had terrified me only minutes before, I was filled with admiration now for the way she was pulling herself back together. I tried to find the words to apologize for slapping her.

"I knew how you felt, but I couldn't let you be as stupid as I was and waste the last two shots. That's what he wants—don't you understand that? He probably figured out that we were trying to trap him and decided to turn the tables on us by tricking us into blowing our last advantage."

I stopped, aware that I was babbling nonsense. How could anyone know that Mickie would react that way, trying to seize the revolver and blast away at the horrors in front of us? With the excitement gone, fatigue was rapidly taking possession of me again. I tried to think of something I could do to get through the night without losing consciousness.

"Mickie."

She had undergone another of her mercurial mood changes. Her voice was sullen. "What is it?"

"Maybe we should move outside to the dock. The wind is calming down. We could light the brush pile and keep it burning all night. There must be planes looking for you by now. They surely checked the route indicated in the flight plan first, but they would broaden the search area when they reached the crash site and found that there was a survivor. We might get lucky. A search plane—even one too far away for us to hear—may spot the fire."

In the dim glow of the flashlight, her eyes lost their dullness, and she observed me with interest. She paused a moment in thought, then shook her head. "No, I'm sure the pilot didn't file one."

"Didn't file a flight plan? Everyone flying in this country would have to file one at his point of origin if he was carrying passengers."

She grew annoyed. "Well, I happen to know he didn't."

"But . . . but why, Mickie? Why wouldn't he? Wasn't it a regular bush pilot who flew your plane?"

"No, I told you it wasn't, so please don't hassle me about it. Don't you understand? It was some fellow Daddy hired. He got the guy a lot cheaper. It wasn't a regular bush pilot, and I'm sure he didn't have any flight plan because they were talking about it. They were saying that no one would know where we were if we had trouble."

I couldn't understand why she was so angry, and I surely couldn't believe what she was saying. Suspicion was growing in my mind that maybe Mickie was someone other than Daddy's little girl on a vacation. Could she be involved in some sort of illicit smuggling? God knows, there are enough illegal drug operations using small aircraft. Though she was young, plenty of girls her age had become part of dope smuggling networks.

If she was in the drug business, I certainly couldn't expect her to be eager to meet the police. She wasn't going to admit anything to me or tell me the truth about the downed plane. As long as she thought there was a chance of escaping, Mickie would be playing her cards close to the vest. I wondered just how naive I had been about her.

To preserve the fading power of the batteries, I switched off the flash and tried to stir a little life into the darkened coals, wishing that we had brought in more wood before dark. The crystal face of my watch had become so badly scratched during our struggle that it was difficult to read, but as well as I could make out, there was about an hour and a half of darkness remaining. I had no choice but to pace the dark living room, warding off the lurking disaster of sleep until the new day broke.

Mickie slipped off the sofa and seated herself on the rug before the moribund embers of the fire. She called softly to me, "Linc, come and sit down. There's no need to be afraid."

I tried to ignore her request, but my legs ached, so I gave in. She stirred in the darkness, and I could sense that she had turned to face me.

"I want you to understand. You know how it is with families and how you don't like to admit things about them. There won't be anyone searching for the plane. The pilot Daddy hired didn't have a license to fly in Canada, so he couldn't file a flight plan. When I told you how much money we had, it was a lie. Daddy has always had to scrounge around to provide things for me and my brother and sister. The only way that we could afford to make a trip to Canada was for him to cut corners everywhere he could. I should have told you the truth before. I'm sorry, but I hate to always have to admit how poor we are. Let's not talk about it anymore."

I tried to sort out what she was saying. Not a word of it

made sense. "But I thought you said you were an only child.
What's this about a brother and sister?"

She stirred, and for a moment I thought she was going to rise.
Her voice was shrill. "Well, I didn't know you were taking notes
on every word I said. What I meant was both my brother and
sister are a lot older than I am, and they left home years ago. My
parents and I are the only ones living there. That's what I meant.
I haven't seen either of them in ages. I don't even know if they'll
be able to come home for the funeral. But you're picking on
me . . . judging every word that I say . . . being hateful. Why
can't you understand me—how hard it is on me?"

I wanted to ask her why people couldn't understand Linc
Wilhite. God knows, I could have used some understanding
that night on the hillside above the gas station with my Laurie
lying dead at my feet. I have memories of that awful night,
but none of words of sympathy, none of efforts to console me
in my loss. My reminiscences are of disconnected fragments;
of flashlights and noises; of light bars flashing atop squad cars
that housed squawking radios; of beefy unsmiling men shouting; and of a night pierced by the plaintive howling of an
ambulance siren. I tried to answer the overlapping choruses of
shouted queries, but I couldn't explain why I had left Laurie
—that I was so stunned by the blow to my head I had no idea
what was happening. I sensed the reservations slowly forming
in those cold-eyed men who questioned me.

One of the burly cops shook his head. "Hell, what a mess!
This guy's gonna need to see a neurologist before we question
him. Maybe he has a concussion."

The station attendant, his hard face mottled with anger,
pushed his way into the circle of cops and glared at me.
"Concussion, hell! This punk's a goddamned yellow-belly!
You shoulda seen the bastard at the station. I had to drag his
ass up here to try to save his own wife!"

I was only vaguely aware of the yelling and of thrashing
against the strong arms that had me pinned to the ground. In
the distance, someone shouted, "Let the skinny bastard up!
I'll clean his clock for him."

That is the last thing I remembered until I awoke the next
morning in a hospital ward.

Yes, I could have told the girl Mickie that there were a lot of misunderstandings in a lifetime. I tried to relax — to keep the hurt inside. What good would another argument between us do?

"Mickie, get off my case. I was going by the story you told me. All I know is what you said. Okay?"

There was an interval of silence, and when she spoke again, it was not in answer to my question. Her mood had changed once more, and her voice had a dreamy, ethereal quality. She was like a different person.

"I can still smell the odor, can't you? Why do their poor bodies have to smell so bad? They're sitting there . . . dead . . . and not a mark on them. It's impossible to think of them now as living people. They don't even seem like a mother, a father, a couple of kids. They're like strangers made up for Halloween, vile and horrible to look at. No, not a family . . . just discarded, unmarked shells that sit there and rot. Why did they die? Because they took a human life? And how did they die, Linc?"

Her fingers were at my waist, plucking at my belt. My mind swirled in a vortex that mixed sensations and fragments of thought. Fatigue and hunger had driven me beyond controlled memory and orderly mental processes. I was close to hallucination. What was it she said? I had just heard something important, stared into the core of a squirming, living evil, but I couldn't remember what it was. I was struggling to recall what the thing was she had said when a faint droning from somewhere outside found its way into the room — the distant but unmistakable sound of an airplane.

I staggered to my feet, almost tumbling forward into the fireplace in my vertigo.

"It's a plane! I've got to get out there and light the signal fire. I have to hurry!"

She caught at my belt and tried to drag me toward her. Her protest bore an edge of hysteria. "No! You're crazy! I don't hear anything. There's no plane. You're having hallucinations. Listen to me, Linc. If you go out there, you'll be killed!"

Clinging to me, she pulled herself to her feet and clasped me about the waist with her tenacious arms. I struggled against her, trying to break her grip around my midsection. She seemed incapable of understanding that I was sure I had heard something.

"Let go of me! That's the sound of an aircraft engine. I

have to light that fire. Surely you can hear it now—it's louder. It will be coming right over us."

Screaming "No!" over and over, Mickie drove me backward into the wall, her hands hooked into my waistband, trying with all her strength to pin me there. Then abruptly, the arms about my waist dropped away, and I was free.

I dashed out the door and cleared the porch steps in a frantic leap. I raced past the dock, searching the sky. Far overhead, a tiny blinking red light was moving across the dark void.

I crashed into the brush pile before I could stop, dug out my matches with awkward haste, and lit the dry pine needles at the base of the pile. They caught with a crackle and wavered in a sudden puff of the dying breeze before the whole resinous branch exploded into flames. Within seconds the entire mound of driftwood was burning furiously, sending a blinding pillar of flame twenty to thirty feet into the air. There was a moment of utter exhilaration at the sight of the flaming beacon and, as quickly, a deadly chill when I realized how exposed I was.

I looked behind me at the impenetrable wall of blackness outside the circle of light. Alarmed at my vulnerability, I reached for the gun at my waist.

There was nothing there! I had made my mistake! The revolver was still in the house!

Chapter
THIRTY-FIVE

I was a defenseless target, silhouetted as I was against the fire. I trotted toward the house, trying to appear casual. Once away from the brightness of the fire, I could see Mayfield's dwelling ahead of me, bathed in the reflected light of the blazing pyre.

Mickie was waiting in the open doorway. She looked

stunned at the sight of the pillar of flames that lit the granite face before the house, and I had to shove her aside to enter the living room.

"Mickie, I made an awful mistake. I don't have the gun. I could have sworn it was in my waistband. We have to find it . . . right now! It has to be somewhere in here."

Without answering, she slammed the door shut behind me and locked it.

It was pitch black inside. I felt my way to the sofa, pawing at the cushions until I encountered the cool metal of the flashlight. The beam was quite feeble, the bulb no more than a dying ember itself.

If the revolver had fallen from my waistband onto the wood floor, we surely would have heard the thud. Nevertheless, using the failing torch, I scanned the floor, but it wasn't there. The weapon must have slipped out as I fled the wrestling match with Mickie, or else it had fallen out of my waistband as I raced out to light the fire.

The faint light revealed Mickie standing with her back pressed against the door, a tight smile plastered on her face.

Frustrated, I yelled at her, "Blast you, don't you understand what I'm telling you? I've lost the revolver. We must find it! Our lives depend on it."

Her voice was flat, devoid of emotion. "Why bother to shout at me? It's gone. It was only a matter of time until you made your mistake. I tried to keep you from making a fool of yourself with that bonfire. It really makes no difference at all. If I had known earlier, it might have, but not now."

I was stunned, amazed at her lack of comprehension. "It doesn't matter that I made a mistake? Can't you understand what I'm saying? The gun is gone, and we need to find it. We have to! Oh, Lord, could I have dropped it outside? I have to go back out there to look for it."

She didn't resist when I pushed my way past her and out the door. Every second was vital. Crouched low to better see the surface in the faint circle of the dying beam, I first circled the area where we had struggled before turning toward the burning beacon, moving as fast as possible, trying to follow the same route I had taken the first time, feeling the menace tightening around me in the night. All too soon I stepped into the bright circle of firelit rock. The gun was no longer mine.

With sickening certainty, I knew the killer already had it in his possession. I had to try to get back to the house.

Reversing direction, I raced up the slope, all pretense gone now. A loose pebble sent me sprawling on the granite, pain lancing through my knee as it skidded across the rough rock. The flashlight flew from my hand, rolled away, and was gone. I scrambled to my feet and dashed on up the slope, conscious of the bloody wetness of my knee.

The living room was pitch black in contrast to the brilliance of the blazing brush. I slammed the door and leaned back against its surface, sucking air into my lungs. I could neither see nor hear Mickie. Why didn't she say something? Was she already dead? Was the monster here in the darkness with me?

"Where are you, Mickie?" I was shouting in my terror. "Answer me. Are you all right?"

The silence was absolute. The seconds ticked by while I crouched against the door, expecting the final murderous assault at any second.

Something was moving quietly across the room toward me. I braced myself.

Her voice was a mere whisper. "Are you back for good, Linc? Have you given up? It was useless all along, you know."

Relief surged through my spent body. "Thank God, you're safe. Quick! Help me push the sofa in front of the door. He has my pistol now. We must make a last stand when he tries to break in."

Her hand found me, flitting against my arm, then closed about my elbow. I let her lead me into the room, pacified by her strong, sure grip and compelling voice. "Don't worry. It's all right. It's all going to be okay. I knew things would finally work out. Come and sit down. There's nothing to be afraid of."

I wanted to protest, to cry out again that we needed to barricade the doors with furniture, but I felt too tired, so utterly defeated. You know, her voice was like I had wanted my mother's to be during those terrible years of growing up, strong but soothing, assuring me that everything would be all right.

I let her lead me to the rug and pull me down on it. She sat down next to me, her strong body pressing against mine. We faced the fireplace and the dead, stinking ashes that had once been bright, living flames.

Her words, so slow and breathy, wafted dreamily through the darkness about us. "Linc, I had a boyfriend named Tommy. I loved him. God, I worshiped the very ground he walked on. I thought he loved me the same way—that he would do anything for me. Maybe he would have . . . before they started on him, nagging at him, poisoning his mind with lies that masked mortal sin."

Her voice became more assertive. "Eventually we found that we were going to have a baby, and we were so happy. We thought our parents would have to let us marry when they found out. Both my folks and his had been against our dating all along. They raised hell when we started going steady. They were upset because our religions were different. We were so childish and naive that we thought a baby would make them accept our marriage. Tommy and I both wanted that child—I know he did. I didn't believe being pregnant could make families hate each other so much.

"We were underage and needed parental permission to get a marriage license. His family wanted me to have an abortion. Mine were Catholic, and they were sure we had committed a mortal sin. They started looking around for an older man to marry me . . . as if I were some girl born two hundred years ago in Italy. They didn't think Tommy was mature enough to handle the responsibility. Finally his folks and mine became so mad at each other that they refused to let Tommy and me see each other. I became more frightened with each passing week. It was so hard to sneak out to see him—even for a few minutes.

"When I realized that they would never let us marry, I sent word to Tommy that I couldn't stand it there anymore—that we had to run off and I would do anything he wanted. Two days later I managed to sneak out of the house and meet him. I was so thrilled that day, thinking we would elope. But my happiness quickly turned to misery. It was horrible—a nightmare that wouldn't stop."

I didn't want to hear what Mickie was saying. I wanted her assurances that we were safe from our own nightmare lurking outside. I tried to interrupt, but she wouldn't stop talking.

"After Tommy showed up, we started driving—just cruis-

ing around without really going any place . . . trying to talk it
out. But we hadn't been together fifteen minutes before I
knew that he had become a stranger, brainwashed by his family. All he could talk about was me having an abortion, saying
I had promised I would do anything he wanted.

"Late that evening, we were back in the suburbs of Syracuse trying to decide what to say to my folks. He looked at me
with a smirk on his face and said, 'We're going to be a lot
better off, honey, without a little bastard to worry about.'

"Something exploded in me, and there was blood all over
everything. I remember sitting in the car, waiting for the ambulance and the police. We were both drenched in blood, and
it was all over the car seat."

I didn't need this girl to explain to me what it was like to be
a victim of treacherous slander. I knew what it was to expect
compassion and receive public vituperation.

The day after Laurie's death I was released from the hospital
at midmorning and spent the rest of the day at the Satterfields,
listening to the endless repetitive consolations of their relatives.
By late afternoon I was desperate for privacy in which to vent
my grief. Around seven o'clock I escaped to the only sanctuary I
had, the apartment Laurie and I had shared so briefly. I promised
to return to spend the night with my in-laws.

I stopped at a newsstand and bought an evening paper. Once
back in the memory-laden apartment, I broke down and
sobbed until I was so exhausted that I dozed off. Awaking
about nine, I prowled restlessly through rooms that cried out
for her presence. Finally I sat down to read the paper.

The news item about Laurie and me was on the front page.
The story was so painful to see in print that I almost put the
paper down without reading the quotation, but as my glance
slid down the column past her picture, the last paragraph
jumped off the page at me.

> "Mr. George Wenchamp, forty-one, owner of the
> Quik-Save Service Station, declined to accept credit
> for his role in attempting to avert the tragedy. Ac-
> cording to Wenchamp, 'I might have had a chance to
> save that poor girl if I hadn't wasted my time trying to
> get her husband to go up there with me. I couldn't

believe it when he refused to accompany me back to the scene. Maybe the poor guy was hysterical or something, but my God, she deserved better than that.' Chief Scott declined to speculate on whether Wenchamp's efforts to thwart the rape-murder would be enough to gain him a nomination for the citizens' heroism program of the police department."

My hands trembling, I read the paragraph a second time, trying to find some other implication. I was stunned. Wenchamp had heard the detective say I probably had a concussion. The newspaper could have checked with the doctor that examined me. There was but one way to interpret the write-up. There would be no charity in Seattle toward my grief.

I cried aloud, "My God, he's saying that I'm a coward—that I cost Laurie her life. I didn't fail her! Please, Laurie, believe me. I was so confused. I'm not a failure! You taught me not to be."

I didn't want to think anymore. My hands seemed endowed with a will of their own, beyond my control, methodically tearing the paper to shreds. My mind stopped.

I shook myself free of the grim memories, aware that Mickie was still talking.

"Two weeks later, I almost killed my mother. She had come to see me during visiting hours. I didn't feel like talking, so she was having to make all the conversation. I know she didn't intend to, but she forgot and said something about the baby. I couldn't control myself. I leaped from the bed and ran for the door, trying to escape her words . . . the memories . . . I don't know what. She grabbed for me and shouted for the attendant. In the struggle, we knocked a water carafe onto the floor, and as we wrestled around the room, she slipped and fell. Her head struck the corner of the bedframe. I saw her lying there, looking as if she were dead, and something snapped. It was six months before I was well enough to understand that she had suffered nothing more than a concussion. But I understood more than that, Linc. I had become a child of Satan with a touch that brought death."

Mickie scrambled to her feet and moved toward the covered windows. I heard the ripping of the wood as the hangers came down. She tore first one and then the other blanket-laden wire free. Her sturdy figure was outlined against the sickly yellow glow illuminating the gruesome display across the way.

An involuntary exclamation of protest escaped my lips.

"What's the matter, Linc? Are you too terrified to look at them now? They can't hurt you. They wouldn't if they could. They're nothing but the poor, decaying hulks of a family that thought they were coming to Stone Warrior Island to help an errant daughter find herself. Instead, they found a child of Satan."

I knew then that she was mad. At that moment I remembered about the Texans and told her, hoping to divert her attention. "Mickie, listen. They aren't the only ones dead. I found two other bodies. They have been here several months."

"You mean someone—? No, you're lying. You would have told me before."

"I forgot. I—"

"Hush. Talking does no good."

She had turned sideways to look back toward me as she spoke, and I could see that her hand wasn't empty. Hopelessly, I clutched the scabbard on my belt. It was empty! She had my knife. My panic was shortlived, receding before a floodtide of resignation. Had she taken it, realizing that I could no longer protect us, or had she taken it to kill me?

She floated back to me, standing behind me. Panic flared in me once more, but it disappeared in a twinkling. I remained seated—passive, worn out, and defenseless.

"I was so happy with them that afternoon after the first day had been so miserable. I wanted to show my appreciation, but then I heard you downstairs, and I realized that Mom had planned the whole thing as a chance for me to meet a new man—one they could keep an eye on. I was wild with rage. Earlier, in my closet, I had found a trap door leading to the attic. I climbed up there and hid when Rick came up to call me for dinner. They were so nervous about me that I knew it would frighten them to find me gone. I wanted to punish them because they had invited you.

"They were crazy with anxiety and rushed out to search the island. I heard you when you finally quit stomping around downstairs and left the house for good, leaving me alone inside with the dinner. They never did think to come upstairs and search it thoroughly. I guess they thought I was hiding in the woods and would come back when I got cold and hungry.

"After a while they gave up looking for me and returned to eat. I had climbed down out of the attic and was sitting in my room upstairs, staring at the rafts of geese out on the lake, when they gave that silly little toast Dad always insisted on. Then they died.

"Later, I set the timers—Mom brought a box of them by mistake."

She began to cry, crying and talking at the same time. "I brought the four of them into the living room, carrying them —dragging Mom and Dad . . . treating them like dummies, goddamn you! I hoped that it would confuse you and give me more time to get away.

"All the time I was afraid you would pop back in and catch me. But once I spotted you sitting down at the point, I waited until dark and then sank all the canoes but one. I intended to escape through the woods, but after I reached the mainland, I knew I couldn't survive—couldn't ever find my way out of that forest—so I came back to the island the next evening."

She was very close to me now. "I intended to stay away from you—camp out at the far end of the island and wait until someone came—try to convince them that you killed my family. But then, that afternoon, you wandered down the island and I saw how frightened you were when you almost spotted me. I realized then that I was stronger—tougher—than you. I knew I could kill you myself. Despite your gun and knife, I could kill you. But I wanted you to suffer—to be scared to death . . . and you were. But then I slipped and fell in the lake like a klutz, but it doesn't matter now."

She dropped down behind me on her knees, placed a hand on my shoulder, and rested her cool, soft cheek against the side of my head.

Her voice was no more than a whisper. "Now, it's not so bad, is it? All the anger, all the hatred is gone now. I understand, but still, it must be done. I told you all along it would be okay."

I asked the question I already knew the answer to. "Are you

crazy? I'm Linc Wilhite. You just met me. I just wanted to help you, protect you. Please, Mickie."

I felt her stir slightly behind me, and then her arm came in over my shoulder, and the cold, thin kiss of steel was against my throat.

"Why did they have to die, Linc? Was it because of being involved in taking a human life? Maybe. God knows. But you and I . . . I know all about us . . . we're full of evil."

I managed to croak against the terrifying menace of the razor-sharp blade. "Listen . . . for God's sake, listen, Mickie. Maybe you just imagined the whole thing. You're not well. Maybe they died of carbon monoxide poisoning or something."

Her voice was deep, resonant, and sure. "No, Linc, it was the wine. You see . . . I filled the carafe. Goodbye—"

Terrified beyond conscious thought, I found my hand on her wrist, holding the knife clear of my throat. Our arms trembled in their confrontation. Strength ebbing, I clutched at her head with my other hand and found her hair. I pulled her forward over my shoulder as I sagged sideways. With her arm trapped under my neck there was nothing she could do to stop her fall. She crashed down on top of our arms and the knife.

She uttered an agonized shriek. There was silence and then she moaned, her voice eerie, trailing away to nothing. "Oh, God! . . . no . . . oh, no."

Chapter
THIRTY-SIX

We remained frozen in that position for long seconds with my arm pinned under Mickie's body. Her mouth was still near my ear, but I no longer felt the caress of her breath. I pulled my arm free of her weight. It had a warm wetness to it, and I knew it was soaked with her blood.

I scrambled to my feet and looked down at the dead girl. It was possible to make out her form, huddled on the floor. Her body had turned as I dragged my arm free, and now she lay on her side as if she had curled up and drifted into a deep sleep.

I glanced toward the window and understood why I could see her so clearly. The early dawn of the northern latitudes was breaking over Stone Warrior Island.

Gingerly, I brushed the fingers of my other hand against my stinging neck. They came away bearing a light tracing of blood. The knife had done nothing more than nick my skin.

I stepped around her and went outside onto the porch. I had no sensation of stepping out into danger, only of fleeing a last distasteful scene.

A quick glance toward the other house revealed the swollen faces of Pete and Dolores Delvecchio maintaining their eternal vigil, but even as I watched, the last flickering candle flared explosively two or three times and then went out. There remained within me only the normal aversion to the dead displayed so flagrantly.

I walked down the dark gray incline to the dock, inhaling the chilly morning air. The lake had drawn a low, swirling mist over itself, awaiting the sun before throwing off its night clothes of fog. I stooped at the water's edge to wash away Mickie's blood.

Climbing onto the dock, I lay down and was asleep in an instant.

The thunder of low-flying planes, circling overhead in the morning sun, awakened me. It was one Sunday morning when prayers were answered. As I watched, one of the two circling aircraft swooped in over the forested edge of the lake, dropping toward the water. White water flared from the pontoons as it touched the surface and made its way across the lake toward the float. As it slowed to a crawl and turned in toward the landing, the second plane, a Canadian government aircraft, settled onto the water.

Painfully, with every joint in my body aching from lying against the hard boards of the dock, I came to my feet and watched the smaller craft working its way in. While it was still fifty or sixty feet away, through the spinning arc of the propeller,

I recognized Mustard Chambord and the surly countenance of Earl Higgins. Behind them, in a rear seat, was another man.

I look around at the ring of silent men in the den. "That's everything I can remember. I don't think I've left anything out."

A tall, heavy-framed man, his face hard and weather-roughened beneath his gray thatch, nods at me. "Okay, Mr. Wilhite, your story checks out, as well as we can determine so far. Higgins, here, is going to fly you back to Saskatoon. The doc feels you should spend a couple of days in the hospital. You'll not be allowed to leave Saskatoon until we complete our investigation and the inquest is held, but I want you to understand that, as far as we're concerned now, your detention is a mere formality."

He looks around him at his associates. "I think we can accept as fact that the bodies Mr. Wilhite discovered on the east side of the island are those of two of the men reported missing last summer. We located that finger, incidentally. It appears to have been severed by a bullet. These deaths will be treated as a separate crime and handled as an independent investigation."

He glances at the others as if challenging someone to dispute the statement. He motions toward the doctor, the man who had flown in with Chambord and Higgins. "Okay, John, do you have anything else to add at this point?"

The middle-aged man clears his throat nervously and riffles through a small leather notebook in his hands without really glancing at the pages. "As I told Inspector Mathieson here, I'm not prepared to make an official statement until after the autopsies. Even then, it will be extremely difficult to document the time of death within forty-eight hours.

"Off the record, I'll bet you a hundred to one they died of cyanide poisoning. It's probably in that fettucini—smells like it—but they never had a chance to eat. There is a carafe of wine on the table. It must be loaded with cyanide. All the wine glasses are upset, lying on the floor or table, with spills of wine from them. I think they started their meal with the wine—probably a toast of some kind. I've heard that proposing a toast to begin dinner is a custom with some traditional Italian families. If that wine is as strongly laced as I think, they would have died within seconds of ingesting it.

"I can believe the girl's story about moving their bodies to positions before the TV shortly after their deaths, before rigor mortis set in—scuff marks and all that. The younger girl was moved the second time after rigor left the body. My God, I can't imagine anyone carrying a cadaver around in their arms with it in that condition."

The tough-looking inspector nods and turns toward one of the uniformed Mounties. "Corporal, any luck in finding cyanide in the Bengston house?"

The young Mountie shakes his head, his excited voice betraying his French-Canadian origins. "No, sir. We've searched from top to bottom—even the attic. We found the keys to the man's pharmaceutical cases in his pocket and examined them, but they contained nothing like that. Each case has a documented inventory sheet, and everything listed seems to be intact."

Inspector Mathieson bobs his head slowly, even regretfully, and turns toward the other suit-clad detective. "Jeff, what did you find out from Syracuse?"

The younger detective rises to his feet. He reminds me of a professor I knew at Washington who could never answer a question without standing. "I think we'll have to assume that the girl brought the poison to Canada. It will be a hell of a lot cleaner if Syracuse can tie her to it or, at least, the opportunity to acquire it. It would establish premeditation. Even without it, we have physical evidence placing her in both houses after their deaths. Her prints are all over the upstairs here in the Mayfield residence. There are some real beauties on that safe she rigged as a booby-trap for Wilhite. We really got lucky with the gun and knife—usable prints on both. I would say there is sufficient circumstantial evidence to support Wilhite's accusation of attempted murder. Couple the evidence with his statement, and I believe we could have filed a murder complaint against her in the deaths of her family . . . even without the cyanide. Of course, she would never have gone to trial—a classic insanity plea.

"The girl's real name was Michelle Maria Delvecchio, incidentally. She wanted her friends to call her Mickie. Apparently the family—the father and mother anyway—would forget and call her Michelle every once in a while and there would be a row. She had a reputation for being hard to get along with—not mean, just stubborn and very independent. She must have figured they would use Mickie in talking to Wilhite, so she started using Michelle with him. She had no way of knowing that there hadn't been any occasion between the father and Wilhite to use her name at all."

He looks directly at me. "You misinterpreted her remarks about her boyfriend, though. She didn't kill Thomas Wollencopp. What happened was that he took her to a quack for an abortion. As they were returning to Syracuse, she started hemorrhaging and almost died.

"The Syracuse police have done a hell of a job coming up with this much information so quickly. They lucked out—made contact with her psychiatrist on the first try and had a report for us within two hours. She was overwhelmed by guilt after the abortion. During the early stage of her mental collapse, she accused her boyfriend and both families of being murderers, a term she also applied to herself. The psychiatrist was concerned about the attack that led to Mrs. Delvecchio's serious head injury, but the mother steadfastly denied that the injury was intentional.

"In the light of what has happened here, he should have been more concerned, shouldn't he? In my opinion, the evidence is sufficiently developed, Inspector, to satisfy an inquest of her guilt. In the absence of contradictory information, we can support the position that the girl was emotionally incompetent and that she slaughtered her family while mentally deranged."

The detective turns back to me with an apologetic smile and continues. "This afternoon, we checked Mr. Wilhite's background, especially after his disclosure that he had been in a mental-health facility. Barring the single episode that involved his father and which traumatized him to the degree that he was committed to a mental institution, there is no record of violence in his background. The tragedies involving his wife and Wenchamp were certainly not of his making. As a matter of fact— and I apologize—I know this is painful—Mr. Wilhite was publicly castigated by an eyewitness for inaction during the tragic assault that led to his wife's death. As for the fight with his father—I daresay more than one of us sitting here have sooner or later tried to find out whether the old man was as tough as he acted.

"By the way, Mr. Wilhite, Dr. Molloy confirms that you have an extensive history of sleepwalking, especially in your preteen years. He thinks it not unlikely you reverted to the habit under the extreme stress you endured here. So the episodes with the burning candles and even the unpleasant encounter with the younger Delvecchio girl are not quite as macabre as they first seemed. I would say you were most fortunate you didn't run into Michelle Delvecchio during your last somnambulistic adventure. I hope that puts your mind at ease about those episodes."

The detective pauses, glancing around to invite questions. When there are none, he seats himself.

The detective is right. There has been but one episode of violence in my life, the attack on my father, and I can remember nothing of that. But that dream—that horrible, so vivid dream in the aftermath of the death of Laurie—it still terrifies me—especially knowing that it really happened!

It was the evening I read the libelous story in the Seattle newspaper. What happened that night when my mind short-circuited was so frightening that I tried to kill myself. I had a psychic nightmare—what parapsychologists call a clairvoyant dream.

I could see the filling station again, tucked in at the bottom of the hill. The building was sheathed in flames, and burning rivers of gasoline poured from the pump hoses that lay twisted on the concrete. The place was an inferno. Somehow I could see George Wenchamp sprawled in the lube bay, outlined in the flaming material of his coveralls. The back of his head was a mass of blood and brain, with a darkly glistening wrench lying beside him.

I had fought my way out of the nightmare to a loud, persistent ringing in my head and opened my eyes. I found myself still slumped in the chair, the floor around me cluttered with shreds of torn newspaper. The telephone on the table repeated its shrill demand.

"Mr. Wilhite? This is detective Coughlin of the homicide

detail of the Seattle Police. I hate to bother you, but have you had any unusual calls today? Has anyone tried to enter your apartment, or have you seen any strangers loitering nearby?"

His questions were not helping me shake the cobwebs from my mind. "I'm sorry, I just awoke. What's wrong? Why are you asking me these questions?"

"The owner of the gas station where you sought help last night, George Wenchamp, was discovered dead about an hour ago. It's definitely a homicide."

My frightening dream was vivid in my memory. Dreading the answer, I asked, "What happened?"

"He was found beaten to death. The station was torched. Gasoline was poured over everything, and the pump nozzles were tied open. Luckily, the gas flowed away from the building, or we probably wouldn't have found a recognizable body.

"It could have been a robbery, of course, but the attack may be related to last night's assault on you and your wife. Your assailants may believe that Wenchamp could identify them by their vehicle. Perhaps he worked on it. In your case, you saw their faces. If you see anything out of the ordinary, I want you to call us immediately."

I mumbled an acknowledgement and hung up.

I become aware of a silence in the den and wondered whether I have been asked a question, but the inspector is glancing at a large, redheaded Mountie wearing sergeant's stripes. The sergeant feels the need to remove his hat before he replies.

"The crime site search appears to confirm our speculations. We found one red canoe sunk at the far end of the island. A bit more diving will probably turn up the rest of them. We also found her camping spot at the far end of the island. The missing food supplies were discarded there.

"If I may say so, sir, I wish she had told Wilhite why she moved her sister's body. Personally, I think she brought the younger girl's body over here to make it look like sex was Wilhite's motivation. Of course, we will never know. I agree with Doctor John; she had a lot of guts to do what she did— handling those bodies and all that, even if she was crazy . . . ah . . . deranged. That covers everything, I think."

Abruptly the inspector stands, extends his hand, and shakes

mine. "You're free to leave, young man. You may have had some doubts in the past about your ability to endure, but my God, I'll tell you, son, it took quite a man to come through this."

Mustard Chambord sticks his head into the den, a smile creasing his weathered features. "Hey, Linc, I've got your stuff stowed in the plane. You and Earl had better get out of here before it gets dark."

Everyone in the room is trying to shake my hand. The inspector is right—I have endured. These men—tough cops—mean it. At last, I have fought my battle and won. I am free from my past, from my father.

I walk out of the den feeling ten feet tall.

Epilogue

...was discovered the morning after the crash. Constable Reger was diving along the sloping shelf off the point of the island, attempting to locate the last of the missing canoes, when he saw Wilhite's body in ten feet of water approximately twenty yards offshore. The body showed little evidence of trauma except for superficial burns on the exposed skin area. It is Dr. Coriglione's theory that Wilhite was not buckled in and was ejected forward an instant after impact. He was propelled through the exploding fireball into the lake. After the discovery of Wilhite's body, an immediate search was instituted for the remains of Higgins, causing a twenty-four-hour delay in the return of the investigation team to Saskatoon. After a close examination of the wreckage uncovered badly charred body fragments, the search was discontinued.

Forty-eight hours after Wilhite's death his cadaver, in the fetal position, remained in a severe rigor mortis. To discourage speculation, Inspector Jeffrey Poe, Dr. John Coriglione, and Inspector David Mathieson personally stowed the remains in a body bag and loaded the body into the aircraft. Upon arrival in Saskatoon, Inspector Poe and Dr. Coriglione placed the body in storage to await an autopsy. The cadaver remained in our custody for four days during which time the rigor did not abate. Dr. Coriglione filed an autopsy report indentifying cause of death as cardiac arrest resulting from force of impact. A private report from Dr. Coriglione, which accompanies this statement, documents the bizarre internal condition of the body, a state the doctor says is unparalleled in medical history. Dr. Coriglione concluded, based on an analysis of lung tissue, that the subject was not breathing at the moment of impact of the plane. That is to say, the subject was already dead at the time of the crash.

Faced with this evidence, the undersigned decided, in violation of law and through the forging of documents, to suppress these findings. Dr. Coriglione, in our presence, after numerous attempts to relieve rigor, made surgical alterations that allowed the body to fit in a sealed coffin for shipment to Mr. Wilhite's family. This document, plus all supporting analyses and forensic reports, will be placed in trust to be presented to the proper authority if our actions are brought to account.

We are aware of the magnitude of what we have done, but find we have no option if we are to accept the dictates of our consciences. Because of the aura of sensationalism surrounding the events at Stone Warrior Island, Mr. Wilhite's tragic life would become a media circus, bringing additional unwarranted suffering to his friends and family, if the facts of his death were made public. It is our view that Lincoln Wilhite was as much a victim as the Delvecchio family and deserves to rest in peace.

The publicity would result in Stone Warrior Island becoming a mecca for hundreds if not thousands of sensation seekers. The Bengston and Mayfield families have also suffered emotionally and financially. It is enough that we three be burdened with the awesome knowledge of the inexplicable events that occurred at Stone Warrior. We hope to persuade the Bengstons and Mayfields to relinquish ownership of this property, allowing it to return to its natural state. At the risk of being thought superstitious fools, it is our considered judgment that the island is not fit for human habitation!

Signed this 14th day of July, 1986
Inspector David Mathieson
Inspector Jeffrey Poe
Dr. John Coriglione

Nodding, Jeff Poe laid the stapled sheaf of typed sheets on the living room desk and signed the last page with a flourish. He flipped the pages back over and looked up to find Dave Mathieson's gaze switching back and forth between Lynn and him. He glanced toward where his wife was curled up on the sofa, barely visible in the room lit only by the single desk lamp.

Jeff tried to grin. "You don't have to worry, Dave. Lynn agrees that it's the only course we can follow in good conscience."

Dave Mathieson picked his hat up from the chair, almost dropped it in his sudden awkwardness, and looked earnestly at the floor. "I feel bad about this, Jeff . . . and Lynn. It's different for John and me. Neither of us have any family except for my two kids, and they're both grown. I wish to hell you hadn't been with us up there. Listen, maybe——"

Lynn Poe bounced off the sofa. "Dave, for God's sake, quit talking to your feet. You're damned right I wish Jeff had never heard of Stone Warrior Island, and I wish you hadn't . . . but it happened and we can't do anything about that."

She slipped her hand into her husband's. "I'm proud of my husband for caring about that poor young man and for not wanting to make a circus out of it for the ghouls. I'm proud of you, too, you old grizzly. You're nothing but a teddy bear under all that toughness. Now why don't you go home and get some sleep? You look as if you haven't closed your eyes since you got back."

When Jeff came back in from seeing the inspector off, Lynn rose from the sofa and slid her arms around his waist. "Darling, I'm glad it's over. I've been worried about you."

He brushed his lips against her forehead. "You get to bed, honey. Six o'clock will be here soon enough. I'll lock up."

She hesitated in the doorway. "Jeff, someday soon I hope you will feel like talking about what happened in those last few minutes as the Wilhite boy was leaving. You will never be completely through with it until you can."

He heard her climbing the stairs as he sank wearily onto the sofa, stretching out his aching legs before him.

He had seen the whole thing. He had been on the sunporch when they were putting Terry Delvecchio in a body bag, and it had been as gut-wrenching as anything he had ever been around. Desperate for a breath of fresh air, he had hurried through the house and out onto the porch. He remembered the scene with absolute clarity—even the scraps of conversation he had overheard.

Dave and one of the corporals—Manette it was—had stood on the great plate of stone above the dock, watching Chambord reach through the cockpit door for a last handshake with Lincoln Wilhite. Earl Higgins walked past the two Mounties, deliberately bumping the slight corporal as he passed. He took a couple of more strides and then turned to face the two men. He winked at them. "Poor Redcoats! Haven't got anybody to hassle this time, have you?"

He shambled on down to the dock, his loud laugh a taunt.

Manette hissed, "The bastard! You name it and he's done it—dope smuggling, gun running, the whole bit. God . . . if we could just get the goods on him."

The inspector had dropped his meaty hand atop the agitated corporal's shoulder. "Don't worry, Corporal. A couple of boys from headquarters will be waiting for Higgins when he lands in Saskatoon. I think they'll want to know about the sudden wealth Mr. Higgins was throwing around last fall and whether it had anything to do with those poor bastards from Texas planted over there in the trees. Yes, sir, I believe this may take care of our Mr. Higgins, at long last."

Of course, with what was to happen in the next few minutes, the case of the Dallas fishermen would never be officially resolved.

Higgins clambered into the plane without acknowledging Chambord, who waited to cast off the lines. The sullen pilot crawled over Wilhite without exchanging a word.

The propeller turned reluctantly and then exploded into a silvery arc. Soon the plane was clear of its moorings and, trailing blue smoke, working its way out into the lake between the two big RCMP aircraft, anchored offshore. Farther out, the small craft turned and taxied laboriously down the lake through the chop toward the south end.

Everyone outside, Dave and the corporal included, were squinting, half-blinded, into the last bright sliver of sun slicing across the tops of the distant trees. The big man dug in his pocket and pulled out a crumpled pack of cigarettes. All the men waited, listening to the diminishing sound of the aircraft's engine as it moved away from the island.

Dave was distracted by a shout behind him. He turned to see the doctor and one of the Mounties scrambling down the porch steps. The doctor was carrying a small wooden case. The inspector was about to inquire what the problem was when he jumped, startled by an incredibly loud scream, followed by another, and yet a third.

He whirled toward Manette. "God Almighty! What was that!"

The corporal was pointing toward the far shore. "Look over there, sir. It's a loon—the biggest damned loon I've ever seen!"

The ear-splitting cries continued to rend the air. They echoed and reechoed, caroming from the shore around the lake.

The doctor tugged at Dave's sleeve. Seeing the smaller man's agitated face, he shouted over the cacophony of cries. "What's wrong, John?"

"It's young Wilhite's specimen case. Chambord must have overlooked it. It was under the bunk on the sunporch."

The doctor was fishing in his pocket for something.

Dave, his eyes still on the physician, said something, but it was lost in the roar of the approaching plane.

The doctor pulled a small vial from his pocket. "That young fellow ought to thank his lucky stars. He had a vial of hydrogen cyanide in that case, but it's empty. Look."

For a moment Dave stared at him in openmouthed wonder. A stricken look flashed across his face, and then he shook his head violently. "Lucky? My God, no! Not very lucky at all."

"Inspector, you mean——?"

"Yes, damn it! Don't you remember? Wilhite said he had a lethal agent he had borrowed——a full vial when he arrived. That's it——the cyanide. The girl couldn't have gotten to it. When he returned to the house after the murders, he found the case open on the sunporch. He had to unlock the front door to get in. The only other keys to that house were in Seattle. When he checked the back door, it was bolted from the inside. Only Wilhite had access to the cyanide.

"Remember him saying the girl commented about what happened after her family ran out to search for her. She said he quit stomping around and *left for good*. She wouldn't have said that unless he left and came back, obviously going to get the cyanide."

Chambord, who had just joined them, cried, "Here comes Earl. He's taking off."

The inspector glanced at him and then back to the doctor. "Sweet Jesus, what that poor, confused girl was trying to do was avenge the slaughter of her family by a madman."

"Madman, Inspector?"

"Christ, yes! I see it all now. That boy doesn't have any idea what he is. He must have killed that station attendant in Washington as well. I think we will find he becomes an amnesiac when his violent episodes occur. He told us everything he knew. Didn't you see how proud he was of what he thought he had accomplished? Why——"

Suddenly Chambord shouted, his voice stark with disbelief. "My God, Earl! What are you doing?"

The Cessna thundered into view from behind the trees. It was maybe a hundred and fifty feet in the air and perilously near the shore, veering toward them. As the sunlight flashed through the cockpit, they could see Higgins and Linc Wilhite, upright, staring straight ahead, unmoving . . . like carved stone statues.

The plane abruptly dropped off on one wing and nosed

downward into a power stall. It smashed into the low, rocky tip of the island. There was the agonized screeching of rending metal and a moment of awesome silence. Then the shapeless wreckage exploded into a huge ball of orange flames and black smoke.

Doctor John's face was pale with shock. "My God, the legend about the loon—did you see the way they looked—like they were frozen?"

Mathieson brushed past him and touched the pale Chambord. "You," he said softly. "Say a prayer for him."

"A prayer? But—"

The burly policeman yanked him close. "You heard me."

"I . . . wait . . . I remember—a little boy I was flying north last summer—"

The loon abruptly ceased its shrill cries, and all the men—both on the slope and above on the porch—stood unmoving in a windless silence broken by the crackling of the burning wreckage. Chambord's voice rose above the sound of the flames in the prayer of childhood, of a time before the evils of the world came to possess and, ultimately, to destroy a boy named Linc.

"Now I lay me down to sleep. . . ."

LEAVE STONE WARRIOR ISLAND BEFORE IT LEAVES YOU STONE-COLD DEAD

Linc Wilhite has come here to escape a past of tragedy and fear, and to find the peace and happiness that have always been just beyond his reach.

What he finds instead is an eerie, whispering dead zone. Where all he has for company is a family of four—victims of a horrifying, silent slaughter, without a drop of blood or clue to their killer. Where someone, or something, is bent on driving him past the fragile borderline between earth and hell—through a diabolically slow, day-and-night siege of his body, his sanity, his soul.

The ancient legends say you can lose your life—and so much more—on Stone Warrior Island.

And legends never lie.

20672

ISBN 0-445-20672-1

0 18926 00395 1

POPULAR LIBRARY
COVER PRINTED IN U.S.A.
©1989 POPULAR LIBRARY